CHICAGO WARRIORS

Midnight Battles in the Windy City

John M. Wills

TotalRecall Publications, Inc.
1103 Middlecreek
Friendswood, TX 77546
281-992-3131
www.totalrecallpress.com

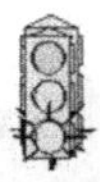 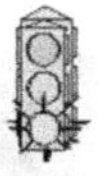

TotalRecallPress.com

This Book is Sponsored by TotalRecall Publications, Inc.
1103 Middlecreek
Friendswood, Texas 77546
281-992-3131 281-482-5390 Fax

Copyright © 2008 by: John M. Wills

Worldwide Book and eBook publication and distribution by: TotalRecall Publications.
Printed in United States of America, Europe and Canada

Paper Back
ISBN: 978-1-59095-841-4
UPC 6-43977-58414-4

eBook: Adobe Acrobat
ISBN 978-1-59095-842-1
UPC 6-43977-58421-2

The sponsoring editor is Bruce Moran and the production supervisor is Corby R. Tate.

This publication is not sponsored by, endorsed by, or affiliated with anyone

This book is dedicated to those who gave their lives so that we might all be safe. Their names are inscribed on the walls of the National Law Enforcement Memorial in Washington, D.C.

May God bless them and their families!

John M. Wills

About the Author

John was born and raised on the South Side of Chicago. After spending two years in the Army, he returned home to join the Chicago Police Department. During his 12 years on the force he received numerous awards and commendations, including the Award of Valor and The Blue Star Award.

John left the Department to become an FBI Special Agent, and was assigned to Chicago, Alexandria, Detroit, Houston, and the FBI Academy in Quantico, VA. He taught street survival to in-service and new agents, as well as internationally, to police in Budapest, Moscow, and Tashkent. He worked undercover for 2 ½ years in the Bureau's first ever steroid investigation entitled, "Operation Equine."

John has published dozens of articles on officer survival, training, and ethics, in print magazines and online with "Officer.com," "LawOfficer.com," and "New American Truth." He is a member of the Public Safety Writers Association, The International Law Enforcement Educators and Trainers, Association, The Virginia Writers Club, Riverside Writers, and the FBI National Academy Associates (175th Session).

John owns his own business, LivSafe, delivering presentations on "Situational Awareness" to schools, churches, and civic groups.

He is an authorized NCAA speaker on steroids and drugs, and can also be found working as a Personal Trainer at AnyTime Fitness.

John and his wife, Christine, have been married for 38 years and have three children and four grandchildren.

Introduction

This book is a result of the author finally listening and hearing His word. It's a story based on many personal experiences; any characters' names that bear a similarity to actual people is not meant to be a portrayal of them. This novel would not have been possible were it not for my wife. She encouraged me when I was without hope, and she kept me firmly rooted in family. She has been the light in my life through some of the darkest moments that I could ever have imagined. Without her as my moral compass, my ship would have surely run aground.

My children, John, Amy, and Tina have given me more joy that I could ever have expected. Now they have blessed me with four precious grandchildren, Colin, Courtney, Bella, and Aidan.

Tim Dees, Editor In Chief for the website, "Officer.com," was instrumental in developing my writing skills. His successor, Frank Borelli, continues to support and encourage my sometimes feeble attempts to make hundreds of words amount to an understandable essay.

The story, with an obvious Christian leaning, is helped by those people in my life that have been spiritual mentors. They are many in number and have no doubt been sent from above as markers to guide me along the path. Without them I would surely have been lost.

I didn't realize it at the time, but my parents' decision to send me to Catholic schools was fortuitous. That academic foundation has proven to be the foundation for my success.

Table of Contents

Prologue

"You got 'em covered Sal?" I was about to holster my weapon and move forward to cuff this guy when my whole world exploded! I heard the loud report of a weapon firing and felt a sledgehammer-like force strike me in the chest.

How could he have shot me? We had him triangulated, the bad guy at the apex, Sal and me at the base. After all, this guy had already dropped his weapon and was complying with my commands.

I'm hit, I thought..."Sal, Sal, I'm hit!"

But how? I saw this guy drop his gun. Did he pull another one that I missed?

Just then another shot, but I'm positive that it's not coming my way. *What's happening...?*

My vest saved me from serious injury; the kinetic energy of the round knocked the wind out of me and bruised my chest. But I'm alive....

Recovering some of my senses I see Sal standing over me.

"Help me up buddy."

Sal's not moving—something's wrong here. Sal has something in his hand--a gun, but it's not his police pistol.

"Sal, what's going on? Sal..."

Then the most intense pain that I have ever felt as I feel a bullet smash into my skull. The last thing that I remember is the smell of gunpowder, and then looking into Sal's eyes and feeling like I'm staring directly at Satan himself.

Praise for Chicago Warriors!

"I spent a lot of years with John Wills in the law enforcement trenches of Detroit, a place where Christian faith is rarely a survivor. Somehow John's flourished. In Chicago Warriors, he has created a unique narrative demonstrating how the worst of man can be defeated by the best in man. It is a parable of a morality that is vanishing from the American landscape."

--**Paul Lindsay,** author of The Fuhrer's Reserve and Traps: A Novel of the FBI

"Wills covers issues that are timely today, including date rape, violence associated with prostitutes, steroid use among body builders, young criminals and police corruption....By today's standards it is also acceptable for readers of most any age. There is no problem with language, sexual content or violence."

--**Marilyn Olsen,** President of Public Safety Writers Association

"Chicago Warriors" is the true voice of a battle tested street cop. A well written testimony of a Chicago Lawman. "A real cop's words, a real cop's experiences, John Wills knows how to tell a story!"

--**Randy Sutton,** is a 32 year Police Veteran and Author of "A COP'S LIFE", "TRUE BLUE, Police Stories by Those Who Have Lived Them" and "TRUE BLUE To Protect and Serve".

<u>1</u>
Chicago Lawn the 8th District

"Beth, I know that we've gone over this a hundred times, but explain it to me again. Why don't you want us to be tested? There's something wrong with one of us, otherwise we would have a couple of kids running around the house already."

"I know, I know," Beth said, "But Pete, I have resigned myself to the fact that I am not going to be blessed by Him in that manner."

That was always her answer, but it never rang true with me. And why does she never look me in the eye when she says it? There's something else going on here, but what? We've been married 15 years and we love each other dearly; deep inside I know that the Lord wants us to have children. We've been trying in earnest the past couple of years, but without success.

"We don't have time to talk about this right now," she said. "You've got to get to roll call. You know how Sgt. McNamara gets bent out of shape whenever someone strolls in late."

"Mac will get over it if I'm late." Mac does get upset with that kind of stuff I thought; I should go now and not risk the wrath of the good Sgt.

"Okay babe, but please, let's settle this soon. Neither one of us is getting any younger, and I know that we would make terrific parents."

"Pete, please...go. We'll get into this later."

I grabbed my gun belt and duty bag and made my way to the garage.

"What time do you start work in the morning babe? Want me to bring something for breakfast?"

"Pete, you're tired by the time you get home. Don't worry about me, I'll get something on the way and eat it at the office."

"Okay," I mumbled.

She was right; I am beat when I get home in the morning. I had been working the straight midnight shift for a couple of years now, trying to get through St. Xavier University during the day to get my degree. The Chicago Police Department was a great organization, plenty of chances to work your way up. Having a college degree was almost a necessity now; just about every cop that was making lieutenant and above had one. I still wasn't sure that I was ready to give up being a street cop though, I was having too much fun, but I had to plan for the future.

Anyway, I had gotten kind of used to being a "Midnight Warrior," as those of us that worked the shift on a permanent basis referred to ourselves. Being home during the day had its advantages too. Taking care of PB (personal business) was much easier. And my almost daily trips to "St. Xav's" gym meant that it was less crowded during the day than after dinner, plus our subdivision was right next door to the campus. So there were certain "bennies" involved with working permanent mids.

I hopped into my truck and backed out making sure that the garage door closed completely. I sure didn't want any scumbags getting into our house and causing problems for Beth. We lived in a great neighborhood, but you never know what kind of riffraff might be casing the houses.

The Southwest side of Chicago was loaded with city workers-- policemen, firemen, sanitation workers, teachers--the residency requirement meant that all of us had to live in the city where we worked. And while the area where we lived around 103rd and Pulaski was relatively safe, it was also somewhat affluent as well. That meant creeps were well aware that the homes in our subdivision contained lots and lots of electronic goodies—all way too easy to fence. My motto was, "better safe than sorry." I kept after Beth to make sure that all the doors were double locked and the alarm set, but I was constantly finding that she would forget.

The station was only 15 minutes from our house. Chicago Lawn, the 8th District, was once considered a plum assignment. Years ago it had one of the lowest crime rates in the city. Old timers used to burn all of their favors to get that gig. Once they got it they never left. Now much of the complexion of that piece of geography has changed for the worse. Lots of violent crime, thefts, pockets of immigrants, both legal and otherwise, were springing up all over the District. There were also lots of drug trafficking, prostitution, and muggings occurring in the once beautiful and serene Marquette Park area. The public golf course, once a haven for retirees who got their exercise and socializing in at the same time, had even seen a couple of shootings. Things were "going south" quick.

Midnights rocked. If you were a cop that enjoyed police work, mids was the shift to work. The radio never stopped, from the beginning of the shift till the end. Old timers who used to enjoy pulling behind a warehouse for a little nap during their shift, no longer had that option. Things were too busy and just too dangerous.

I pulled into the station parking lot and said a quick prayer. Being raised Catholic had taught me to develop a personal relationship with Christ very early on. All through St. Nick's grade school and then four years at St. Laurence High School, helped me to walk in my faith every day. In my mind, there was no better way to start each shift. I asked Him every night to partner me with St. Michael the Archangel. Michael had led the fight in Heaven against Satan; he was the Lord's principal warrior. Anyone that could defeat Satan and lead a band of Angels that could dispatch Satan and his ilk to Hell, was someone that I wanted backing me up.

Walking through the front doors of the station I spotted Mac seated behind the raised desk that ran from one end of the room to the other. In many ways it resembled the layout of most courtrooms, where the judge sits much higher than everyone else in the room. The "desk" was about five feet high, this design caused police personnel to tower over any citizen that came in to make a complaint or ask a question. It also served to give desk personnel not only a commanding view of anyone approaching them, but also to give them the high ground in case anyone was foolish enough to make trouble or display a weapon.

"Hi Mac," I yelled as I made my way to the locker room. "Anything big happening tonight?"

"So far so good Pete," he replied. "The afternoon shift had a couple of guys in a hot car that cracked up on 59th Street, the 'Tac Guys' got 'em."

The Tactical Team (Tac Team) were cops that worked in plain clothes and drove unmarked cars. Funny thing was that most of the guys that were working Tac were so glad to "get out of the bag," meaning getting out of uniform, that they went way overboard in their appearance. Freed from the fresh haircuts, shined shoes, clean shaven faces and pressed uniforms, many of them let their hair grow long, grew beards or mustaches, and some even wore earrings. The irony of this behavior was that most of the citizens stopped wearing long hair ages ago and mostly looked like all of us. Now the "undercover cops" were easy to spot just by their appearance.

The so-called undercover vehicles that the Tac guys drove were generally nothing more than full sized Fords and Chevys without the police markings or light bars on top, but most still had the spotlight on the driver's side. Bad guys could see these cars coming a mile away. Despite all the "give-a-ways," the Tac Team still made some great arrests.

"Pete, see me after roll call. I have a potential problem in your sector that I want to go over with you."

"Okay Mac."

I walked into the locker room, almost bumping into Sal as he was coming out. Sal was Sal "The Hammer" Rosato, a tough talking veteran cop known for his short fuse, and rugged interrogation techniques. Sal had been promoted to sergeant a couple of years ago, but after his involvement in a couple of questionable shootings and a "brutality beef" that almost got him fired, his sergeant stripes were quickly recalled and "The Hammer "was back pushing a patrol car on mids. I tried to avoid him as much as possible.

"Sal, what's up brother?"

"Shannon, how many times do I have to tell you--I'm not your brother?" He barked. "Call me 'The Hammer', or Sal, or don't talk to me at all."

"Easy boy, easy...you'll have plenty of folks to puff out your chest at once we hit the street. We're on the same team, remember?"

I kept on walking into the locker room, not giving him a chance for another comeback. Sal is the type of guy that always wants the last word. When he doesn't get it, he gets angry and takes it out on someone, somewhere.

I quickly changed out of my civies and into my uniform, threw my ballistic vest on, and checked my gun belt for all the weapons that cops use. My OC spray, collapsible baton, handcuffs, two flashlights, and my Glock .40 caliber semi-automatic pistol were all in place. I carried two spare magazines, 15 rounds each, knife, and radio. I also had a Remington 870 shotgun in a gun mount in the patrol car.

Wearing all of that equipment caused each of us to carry around an additional 15 pounds at least. If a cop had to jump out of his unit to chase someone on foot, they had better be in shape. Unfortunately, some of my colleagues were not, ergo the early deaths from heart attacks and strokes. The jokes that you always hear about cops and donuts isn't far off the mark. The donut and bagel shops in the 8th District always seemed to have a cop car parked in front.

Checking my appearance in the mirror, I was satisfied that I would pass muster at inspection. I strolled into the squad room for roll call. My partner, Joe O'Hara, was already there so I grabbed the seat next to him.

"How are you brother, God been good to you today?"

He looked up from the crime reports that he had been reviewing..."Hey Pete! Oh yeah, He's been good today and every day."

Joe and I had a long history together dating back to our high school days at St. Laurence. We played on the football team together—he was the quarterback and I was the fullback. We learned early on the importance of teamwork. After we graduated, we both enlisted together in the Army and spent two years in the same unit, the 2nd Infantry Division in South Korea. We had each other's backs—on duty and off.

"Joe, Mac wants to see me after roll call, said he's got something that he wants to go over with me...some kind of problem in our sector."

Joe nodded, "Yeah, he told me the same thing; could be a hot lead."

"We'll see."

Mac sometimes gave us some good info that he could have very well given to one of the other teams, but since our arrival here at The Lawn, we built up a very tight relationship with Mac. He knew that we were two guys that loved police work. We meant what we said, and said what we meant. Mac knew that he could depend on us, and we in turn were the two biggest supporters in the Sgt. McNamara fan club.

We came to know our good friend and mentor both on duty and off. He was a decent, kind, God-fearing man who had seen more than his fair share of hard times. He and his wife Shirley had been married 45 years; through all of those years Mac had treated her like a queen. For a cop to stay married to one woman for that length of time meant that Mac was walking with Jesus every day.

Mac's daughter, Joanne, was a stay at home Mom and had recently died unexpectedly from a brain aneurism. Their son in law, Tom, had to continue working his blue-collar job downtown as a maintenance supervisor. That left their kids on their own most times, so Mac and Shirley had the two children at their own house most days from dawn to dusk. That's why Mac was on permanent mids with us. Funny thing was that even though Mac would sometimes come in to work dragging his tail on the ground, you never heard a word about him feeling sorry for himself, or how unfair the world was. He was always cheerful and ready to give his all. He was truly a blessing to the men and women on the midnight shift. Most of us did not look forward to the day Mac would decide to retire.

"Fall in!" Mac came in the squad room and had everyone line up for inspection.   After a few comments to those whose uniforms or equipment needed some work, he got down to business announcing the assignments for the night.

Joe and I were in our usual sector car working a "power beat." That meant that while we would still be assigned the usual calls, we were also free to roam throughout the entire sector, giving special attention to known problems areas.

"Alright everybody listen up! There's some new activity around the area of 63rd and Western. The afternoon guys report that there is a new stable of hookers working out there whose pimps are ripping off the johns and seem to be enjoying it way too much. They've been taking their car dates over by the tracks, and as soon as they get their client all lathered up, the pimps show up and take their money, clothes, and usually cold-cock 'em with what's been described as a pistol. One john wound up in Holy Cross Hospital yesterday with a gash on his head that required 40 stitches to close."

Mac looked at us and said, "Pete and Joe give that area special attention. The Tac guys on mids are over in Morgan Park tonight helping those guys with a stakeout."

"Will do Mac, any description on either the hookers or the pimps?"

"Oh, you'll have no trouble spotting the ladies."

That brought out the laughs from our colleagues in the room.

"I've got a partial on one of the pimps' ride—looks like a black SUV, maybe a Cadillac Escalade or something similar," said Mac.

"Hey Shannon, want me to help you find the ladies tonight?" Sal had to chime in with something condescending. "Maybe you could give them a little Bible lecture when you see them on the stroll."

"Rosato, unless you want to be walking your beat tonight, you'd better keep your comments to yourself. Do I make myself clear?" Mac wasn't about to let his roll call get out of hand.

"Sure sarge, I was only trying to lighten the moment."

"I'll let you know when that need presents itself."

Mac gathered up his notes and said, "That's all I've got. Check your cars and hit the streets. God bless you and stay safe."

I gathered my stuff and said to Joe, "I'll go see what Mac's got for us, if you want to go and gas up the car."

"Ok Pete, I hope the afternoon shift took care of that rear tire that had the slow leak. I'm not driving around another eight hours on that, if we get in a chase we'll never hold the road."

"Good idea brother. See you in a few minutes in the lot." I made my way to the front desk where Mac had already assumed the position in the seat of authority.

<u>2</u>
The Business Trip

Driving south on Cicero Avenue, Beth hit a coffee shop for her morning jolt of caffeine. ***This should last me until I get on the train at airport,*** she thought. About 20 minutes later she pulled into the Park and Ride lot at Midway Airport, just in time to catch the 8 am train downtown. Once she got to work there was a coffee shop in the building where she could get another large cup to help her get through the rest of the morning.

Beth had been at Prudential Life for almost 10 years now, and had worked her way up to Executive Accounts Manager. Walking into Two Prudential Plaza gave Beth a sense of security and comfort. No one really got into her personal life here; it was mostly all business all the time. That was the front she was presenting to everyone now, but three years ago things were a little different....

It was at a conference in Boston where she met Bill Norris. He was a Human Resource manager for the Star Electric Company of Greater Boston. Star provided most of the installation and maintenance for a large percentage of the public buildings in the Boston area. His company was shopping around for a new insurance carrier, so he was attending a public forum put on by Beth's company to recruit new corporate accounts. Beth was presenting at the conference that was being held at "The Pru" in downtown Boston. Bill approached her after her presentation and asked if they might get together to crunch some numbers.

It was late in the afternoon by then so Beth said, "Bill, I don't know that I have the time right now. I have a flight back to Chicago tonight; I just came in for the conference."

"Miss Shannon, I was duly impressed with your presentation, and I am leaning towards Prudential Life as my company's new carrier. We have over 700 employees. If you can cancel that flight and meet with me tonight, I am confident that we can do business."

Beth quickly weighed the implications of landing a new account of this magnitude. She had been "this close" to being named Executive Accounts Manager last year, but she had not been able to land a "Platinum" account, one with over 500 employees. If she could close this deal with Star, she would almost certainly get that promotion.

"Let me make a couple of calls Bill, if you're serious about this then one more night here in Boston will be no problem."

"Ok Beth, I'll be down in the lounge. This is almost a done deal as far as I'm concerned. After your presentation, I'm almost sold on 'The Rock'."

"Give me 10 minutes Bill, then I'll see you down there."

He smiled and walked toward the elevators. Beth was feeling something inside. She didn't know if it was the excitement of the deal or something else. She cleared things with her boss in Chicago, and then contacted the airline to rebook her return flight. After a quick stop in the ladies room, Beth made her way to the lounge, prepared to make the biggest deal that she had ever made. If this didn't get her that executive position, then nothing would.

"Miss Shannon, did you cancel your flight home?"

Bill was seated at a table near the windows. He was sipping a glass of red wine and had removed his suit jacket. Beth couldn't help but notice that he had a lean, athletic build on his six foot frame. His tailored shirt fit snugly against his body; his five o'clock shadow was a striking contrast to his brilliant white shirt. He was stunningly handsome, with his sandy hair and blue eyes, almost to the point of looking like a male model straight out of one of the fashion magazines that she always read.

"Yes, it's all taken care of," she said; "we have the whole night to nail down the details on this matter."

"You sure you don't mind spending this much time with me," he replied, while looking directly into her eyes.

Beth felt that feeling inside again, this time she knew that it wasn't anything to do with the deal.

"I'm positive Bill, and please, call me Beth."

"Beth is a beautiful name."

"Actually my full name is Bethany. My folks chose it; they're big-time into the Bible."

"Well, I'm not much of a Bible guy," said Bill, "but that name suits you."

"Well, thank-you. I go by the name Beth most of the time... seems less formal."

Running his hand through his hair, Bill said, "Where are you staying while you're in town Beth? This place isn't exactly suitable for discussing the details that we need to get into."

"Actually I'm over at the Intercontinental."

"That's one of the best hotels in downtown Boston," he replied.

"Tell you what...they have a great restaurant there and it's getting close to dinner time. Let me buy you dinner, then afterward we can use one of their business rooms to iron out the details. How does seven o'clock sound?"

It sounded like a fantastic idea, Beth thought. After all, it was a business dinner and she did have to eat anyway....

"That sounds good Bill. I'll meet you in the lobby around seven. In the meantime I need to get back with my colleagues upstairs before I leave."

"Okay Beth, I'll stop by my office and get some figures on what we are paying with our old carrier. See you tonight; I'm looking forward to our dinner!"

He stood and pulled her chair back as Beth got up from the table. Taking her hand into both of his to shake it, Beth felt excitement at his touch and his closeness. She smelled his cologne as he turned and walked out of the lounge. She couldn't help but watch him leave, almost enchanted now by his persona.

She was feeling anxious now, a bit uncertain about what she had just felt towards him. She reminded herself that she was happily married to Pete, and that this was just another business meeting. But something deep inside told her that this night would be a test for her in many ways.

<u>3</u>
The Tactical Team

"What's up Mac?"

"Follow me," he said as he headed for the Watch Commander's (WC) office.

All three shifts were commanded by a WC; this officer generally holds the rank of lieutenant or captain. It is his responsibility to carry out the District Commander's (DC) policies and personnel assignments. His recommendations to the DC are almost always implemented. Our WC was Capt. Steele. Steele had risen through the ranks based mostly on his academic credentials; it seemed as though he was always attending schools and in-services. He had already earned his Master's Degree and was presently working on a law degree. He was most certainly a "rising star" in the department.

Mac pounded on the door.

"Come on in," Steele shouted.

"Captain, Pete Shannon's here per your request," Mac said.

"Where's O'Hara?"

"He's getting a tire looked at on our car out in the garage," I answered. "Want me to get him?"

"No, you can tell him what went on in here when we're through," Steele said.

Capt. Steele took off his glasses and stood behind his desk. He was a big man, probably 6'3", and still had all of his thick, dark hair, that he wore in a contemporary cut. Word was that when he was a young cop on the street, he was a tough-talking, rough and tumble kind of guy that loved mixing it up with the street thugs. After a few years when he started getting promoted he put on some pounds and gravitated toward the admin type assignments, probably to allow him to continue down the academic path. His waist line was now beginning to challenge the ability of the buttons on his uniform shirt to do their job.

"Shannon, we've got a potential problem on our hands here at The Lawn. There's a crew of home invaders operating next door in 22."

He was referring to the 22nd District, also known as Morgan Park. It bordered on our eastern side and had a great mix of affluent neighborhoods, one being my own, beautiful parks, and some great shopping. The dark side was that there were areas in 22 that were infested with the most ruthless ex-cons, dealers, junkies, and other criminal types that Chicago has ever known.

"They've already hit three homes in the Beverly neighborhood," the Captain said. "They're armed and dangerous. During their last robbery on Longwood Drive, they shot the homeowner because he wasn't responding fast enough for them."

Steele lifted a folder off of his desk. "Shannon you and your partner O'Hara are good cops; I know that you have been working that sector car for the last year, and you guys have made some great arrests."

"Thanks Captain,"

"I've got a personnel problem coming up, and I asked Mac for some recommendations on how to resolve them." Steele opened the folder, "You and Joe have been here at 'The Lawn' for almost five years—always working together. You know how each other work, you're mature and you're smart." Steele sat back down now, placing the open folder on his desk.

Mac spoke up, "Pete, we're losing two of our Tac guys—Smith and Baxter. Smith is being promoted to sergeant, and Baxter is being transferred to the Transit Unit downtown."

Mac shuffled over toward Steele's desk. "We think that this home invasion crew is going to be making its way into our area very soon, things are getting too hot for them in Morgan Park. We need to replace Smith and Baxter ASAP with two guys that can handle that type of action. The captain and I think that you and Joe are the guys."

"Great! Me and Joe in plain clothes...when would that happen?"

"End of period is next week, the 28th, that's when the promotion and transfer become effective," Steele said. "We need you guys right away. What do you think? Want to get out of uniform for a while and concentrate on the big cases?"

"I'm in Captain; I'm almost certain that Joe will agree as well."

"I know this is last minute, but until this home invasion thing came up I was going to take my time finding replacements. It probably still would have been you and O'Hara, but now we need to get you in place as soon as we can." Steele closed the folder. "I need an answer by the end of watch—let Mac know."

"Will do sir, and thanks for the confidence in both of us."

I meant it—to be considered for this type of assignment was huge for a street cop. It gave us the opportunity to make some important arrests and build our credibility within the department.

"No problem," Steele said. "But listen Shannon, I'm not lying when I say this pair of robbers is dangerous. They're bad actors that won't hesitate to shoot either their victims or the cops—you guys need to be on your toes."

"I hear you sir. I'll let Joe know and you'll have your answer shortly. And Captain Steele, thanks for this opportunity."

Steele smiled and said, "Pete, I don't know if I'm doing you a favor or not, giving you this assignment. I hope that you guys are up to the task."

"We won't let you down sir." I shook his hand and walked out the door with Mac.

"Holy cow Mac! Me and Joe on the Tac Team...I'm psyched!"

"You guys earned it Pete; you're both good cops, but remember what the Captain said, these guys are ruthless killers. Their last job they shot the homeowner even though he was cooperative. That type of thug won't think twice about dropping the hammer on you."

"I agree.   Joe and I will have to use all of our street smarts to lock these guys up."

Mac walked up the steps to resume his position at the front desk. "Let me know what you guys decide sometime tonight so that I can get back to Steele. In the meantime, here's the folder on the last three jobs these guys pulled."

"Okay Mac." I took the folder and headed toward the garage. "Hey Mac...thanks brother for thinking of us."

He looked at me like I remember my Dad used to whenever he was concerned about me.

"Pete, I'm praying for you and Joe every day. You two guys are more than just two cops working for me; you are like my own boys. May God bless you both."

"Amen Mac."

I headed down the steps, my eyes tearing up. I hadn't thought about my Dad in some time. Those few words with Mac had brought back some memories....

4
Leaving Home

"Why do you have to go son? Can't you get your college in first and then enlist?"

My dad wasn't happy about Joe O'Hara and me having just signed up for the Army.

"Dad, we're young, we're healthy...we love our country. What better way to show it than to help defend our freedom?"

I tried to assuage his pain. I knew he would not be overjoyed about what I had done, but Joe and I had talked about this all through our senior year at St. Laurence. We were both good athletes, but not good enough to get an athletic ride to college.

"Besides Dad, this is going to help foot the bill for school—the G.I. Bill is what I need to pay the freight for college. You and Mom can't afford to send me, and I don't want to get mired in school loans that will take me 20 years to pay off."

"Son you know that I don't care about bills. Your Mom and I have always paid our debts, your schooling would just be another one added to the pile."

My Dad was one of the most responsible people that I knew. He never missed church on Sundays; he never turned his back on a friend. He was a man of his word. He married my Mom right out of the Marine Corps, after having served in the Pacific Theatre. He never talked about what he did or saw, and I never asked. My Mom showed me a few pictures that he had sent while he was overseas—Dad was a lean, mean, fighting machine. He epitomized the Marine slogan, "No better friend; no worse enemy."

When he came home, he worked a few odd jobs until he had saved enough money to start his own business. Dad said that he didn't want to work for someone else his entire life. He built a food supply service over the years that allowed him to make my sister, Lisa, me, and my Mom all very comfortable. We weren't rich, but Dad always seemed to be able to give us everything that we ever wanted or needed. The Catholic schools they enrolled us in cost a pretty penny. I always told my folks that I would be just as happy in public school, but they wouldn't hear of it. In retrospect, I'm grateful that they didn't take my advice. My education and the discipline that I learned in the Catholic schools put me far above my contemporaries in the public school system.

My Mom stayed home with us kids until we were in our third year of high school. Later she told me that she and Dad had made a pact—no one would raise their children but them. They refused to farm us out to daycare, or relatives, or turn us into "latch-key" kids. I never told them, but to this day I am ever so thankful that they did that. To have had my Mom there when we got home from school each day was the best feeling ever.

Dad gave me that look.... "Son I'm afraid of what might be going on in the Middle East in the near future. Reagan just got the hostages released in Iran, but I don't know if he will send troops in there or not."

"Dad, you were in the military. You came back safe. You know that I will get the best training ever, and besides, Joe and I enlisted with the guarantee that we would always be in the same unit. We'll have each other's backs like we always have."

"I know son. I guess that I still think of you as my little boy...."

Two weeks later Joe and I were off to Ft. Leonard Wood, Missouri, where we did our Basic Training, then on to Ft. Lewis, Washington for Advanced Infantry School. All through those six months of training, Dad sent letters to me inside of care packages that Mom had put together. She knew that Joe and I would be missing her cookies and brownies, so there was always a couple dozen each that arrived every month.

When we got our orders to go overseas, Joe and I landed Military Police (MP) assignments in Korea. Seems the 2nd Infantry Division was reinforcing the border on the DMZ, standing up a whole new MP unit.

Joe and I would be a part of that effort. On my two week leave at home before going over, Mom and Dad were the happiest that I had ever seen them. I think that they were finally convinced that everything was going to be okay; their boy was now a man—a man that could take care of himself. Nevertheless, when they took me to O'Hare Airport for my flight overseas the tears fell like rain.

"I can't bear not seeing you for a year son," Mom cried. "Please be careful and I will be praying for you every day." She handed me a medal and chain. "This is St. Michael the Archangel. He is God's principal warrior. Say a prayer to him every day that he will be by your side and no harm will befall you."

I took it from her, put it around my neck, and gave her a kiss. "I love you Mom; I won't ever take this off."

I headed toward the gate, kissed Mom goodbye, hugged my sister Lisa, and turned to Dad.

"Dad, don't worry about me. If I can be half the soldier that you were, I'll have no problems."

"I know that you'll be fine son. I've been praying. The Lord told me last night as I was reading the Bible that you will return to us unharmed. In Jeremiah 29:11 He said, "*For I know the plans I have for you, plans to prosper you and not to harm you, plans to give you hope and a future. ...*""

"Thanks Dad, I love you."

"I love you too son." His eyes were tearing up as I walked to the gate...so were mine.

<u>5</u>
Beth's Secret

Walking into the coffee shop at work, Beth was thinking about that night in Boston. She had closed the deal that eventually earned her promotion to Executive Accounts Manager, but the price that she paid had been much too high. Even though it had occurred three years ago, that night was still as fresh in her mind as if it had happened yesterday.

How could she have allowed herself to spend the night with Bill? Sure she could blame it on one glass of wine too many, or being out of town alone and finding herself with a stunningly handsome man in a hotel, but those are flimsy excuses. The fact is there was no reason for her adulterous behavior. The deal that she made turned out to be a deal made with the devil.

As soon as Bill had left her hotel room, Beth had become violently ill—and not from the wine. Realizing what she had done to her marriage, her betrayal of Pete, her damaged self-worth, made her sick to her stomach. Her desire for material gain and pleasure had obfuscated the morals and values that her parents had inculcated in her from early on.

Moreover, just as devastating as the illicit relationship with Bill, was the fact that she had betrayed her faith. She had committed a mortal sin, one that could condemn her to hell. Her faith had always been strong; at least that's what she thought. Now she had not only deceived her husband, but even more importantly she had turned her back on the Lord.

How was she ever going to make things right? How could she expect anyone to forgive her when she couldn't even forgive herself? She hadn't yet formally admitted her sin at confession. She continued to attend Mass on Sundays, but couldn't bring herself to confess to the priest what she had done. She certainly couldn't tell Pete what had happened—he would be devastated. He may even want to end their marriage.

Beth found that a couple of months after the incident, the Lord was intent on teaching her a lesson. She had been experiencing nausea in the mornings, along with some dizziness. On one of those mornings, the pain had become intense. Pete was out of town that week; he and Joe had driven to Detroit to compete in the Police Olympics. She couldn't rely on him for help. However, the pain continued and got worse once she arrived at work. Then she began to bleed.

Beth decided to have one of her co-workers drive her to Rush University Medical Center, which was only about 10 minutes from her job. By the time they arrived she was barely conscious. They immediately took her into the ER. An hour later they had her stabilized and she was resting comfortably. To her astonishment, the ER nurse later explained to her that she had miscarried!

For a moment, she couldn't believe what she was hearing. But when she regained her composure and thought it through, it all made sense. Bill Reynolds that night at the hotel...and now the ultimate punishment from above. The Lord was making her pay for her sin. She was falling deeper and deeper into a pit that she felt she could never crawl out of. So many people were adversely impacted by her moment of weakness and infidelity...how would she ever make this right again?

Paying for her coffee, she took the elevator to her office. Her close friend and colleague, Patty, greeted her, "Good morning Beth".

"Good morning Patty. How are you today?"

"Great! Someone brought in bagels and crème cheese this morning, care to join me for a quick breakfast?"

"No thanks Patty, I've got my coffee."

Patty frowned and said, "Beth is anything wrong? You are really looking thin lately, and you seem to be down in the dumps quite a bit."

"No Patty, I'm fine—just fighting a little cold, not much of an appetite..."

"Okay.... Listen Beth, I want you to know that if you ever need someone to talk to, I'm here for you. I love you as a sister, and if you need me please reach out for me."

"Patty I will, believe me I will. I've got some 'stuff' that I'm working through that I can't share with you right now, but thank you for being there for me."

"Alright Beth, just know that there's always One that is waiting for you to ask for help."

Patty walked out of Beth's office. Beth knew that Patty was right; she should be asking God for help in freeing her from the bonds of guilt that had shackled her these past three years. But she felt that God had turned his back on her. After she lost the baby, she couldn't bring herself to spend any private time with the Father. She was humiliated— she had forfeited her Christian birthright to eternal life when she allowed Satan to rule her thoughts instead of the Lord. That one night with Bill was turning out to be the worst night of her life.

As far as her appearance was concerned, Beth didn't see herself the same way that Patty did. Sure she was thinner than she had been, but that was of her own doing. Her thinking was that her life was out of control in many ways, but the one thing that she could control was her weight. She would determine if and when she would eat or drink and no one could take that power from her. She needed to be in control of at least one thing.

Just then the phone rang. "Hello, this is Beth Shannon at Prudential."

"Hi babe! You'll never guess what happened last night...."

Regaining her composure she said, "Let me think...you and Joe arrested a serial killer, then wrote three moving violations each, and brought home two curfew violators."

"C'mon Beth, get serious."

"Okay, I can't guess Pete. What happened last night?'

"The WC called me into his office and offered me and Joe spots on the TAC Team! We start next week."

Beth took a sip of her coffee. "That's pretty dangerous stuff isn't it—plain clothes work?"

"Not any more than what we've been doing already. It's a big step for us; it could really help us make a name for ourselves in the District and the Department. Joe and I are psyched about it."

"Honey that's great. Will you still be on mids?'

"Oh yeah, that's where all the action is. Besides, I still have to go to school during the day. Hey, we're all going to dinner tonight at Palermo's to celebrate."

"Whose we?" Beth inquired.

"You, me, Joe and Susan."

Beth hated going out to dinner anymore. She had to play games in order to hide the fact that she had been cutting back on her food consumption. No one had said anything to her yet, but she sensed that people had been scrutinizing her during meals lately. She felt that maybe they had been keeping track of her alcohol intake as well. Last time they went out, Joe's wife, Susan, seemed to be paying a little too much attention to Beth's plate.

"Okay babe. I'll see you after work. Get some sleep...love you."

"Love you too Beth; see you tonight. Bye."

<u>6</u>
The Devil Man

Pulling out of the parking lot of the "The Lawn" on their first night as Tac guys, Pete and Joe figured they would keep an eye on the area that Mac had alerted them to previously. The intersection of 63rd & Western Streets was a high traffic area; both streets were main arteries for city traffic. At night, the area around the intersection attracted a mix of folks for different reasons. There were lounges and all-night restaurants, some of which were mostly of the one star variety. Lots of seedy characters and street people emerged like fireflies after the sun went down. It's not unlike many big cities in America today. Some neighborhoods take on two different personalities. By day, the working class folks and business owners go about their normal activities. Once the "9 to5ers" go home a sub-culture claims the turf for their own nefarious business.

Prostitution is one of those elements of the sub-culture that has been an integral part of society for ages. The practice pays no mind to laws, policies, and norms put in place and followed by most of us. An enduring "profession," it is unfettered by the attention given to it by the law. The irony is that hookers and cops have co-existed for years, regardless of laws—local, state, and federal. A quid pro quo exists in their unlikely alliance. Hookers need the cops to protect them from johns that would stiff them for their "fee." They also depend on the cops to intercede if a pimp goes too far in disciplining them for perceived disrespect, or attempting to withhold any monies from them.

Since these "ladies of the night" know most everything that is happening on the street, befriending one, or having one as a" hip-pocket informant," allows a cop to get info on the bad guys that he wouldn't normally be able to get. Hip-pocket informants have existed for a longtime in police work. They are unofficial informants—no paper work exists for the 10 or 20 dollars that a cop will give a person for useful information. Most times the money comes from the cops' own pocket, thus the term hip-pocket.

It's quicker and less complicated than going through official channels. In exchange, the cop may look the other way when a lady is "on the stroll", or may let them "walk" instead of arresting them for their transgression. The downside is that most of the hookers are on drugs, and some of the intelligence they provide sometimes hardly qualifies as such. Regardless, a good cop cultivates informants—it's still the best way to know who the players are and to make collars.

Sliding their unmarked Chevy into a parking spot on 63rd St, Pete and Joe were able to watch a couple of ladies at work. While they were watching, they were rewarded about forty five minutes later when a car pulled over to the curb near the two women. After a brief exchange one of them got into the vehicle and it pulled away.

"Joe, let's head over there and see what's up."

"Okay, no question about it—they're definitely working this area. Mac was right."

Pete pulled the unit into the curb where he and Joe got out. Pete and Joe, although in civies, were clearly identifiable as cops. They both wore their "Stars" on their belts next to their weapons.

"Police Officers," Joe said in an authoritative voice. "I'm Officer O'Hara, and this is my partner, Officer Shannon."

"Sorry officers, I'll move—I don't want no trouble."

"What's your name?" I asked her as I eyeballed her up and down. No weapons on this gal—she barely had enough clothing on to be legal in public.

"Blaz. Please officers just let me go and I won't be out here no 'mo tonight. I'm gonna be straight up with 'yall, I'm on probation for drugs, if I get busted again judge say he gonna lock me up. I got a 'lil baby at home that need me."

"Put the cuffs on her Joe."

We cuffed her and put her in the back of our unit, drove down

Western Avenue for about half a mile and then pulled over. We didn't want to "heat the area up"in case we wanted to continue working it later.

Joe turned around to the now sobbing hooker. "Listen, we're going to run your name through records. If you're not wanted on any beef, maybe we can work something out here. Give me your info straight up Blaz, no street jive"

A few minutes later, the computer terminal showed that she had no outstanding warrants, but that she was indeed on probation.

"Alright Blaz, you were straight with us—you're clean, but you are on 'pro.' Let's talk. What can you give us that would justify giving you a play tonight?"

"I ain't got too much really, we only been out here maybe a couple a weeks now. But I can tell you what been goin 'round on the street."

"Okay," said Joe. "You tell us what you've got and we'll see if we can let you walk on it or not."

"Well...'bout two weeks ago my sister, Deelilah, was tricking with me and had a car date wiff some white dude. He drops her back after about 20 minutes...she was scaaaared! She say dude tol' her that he an' a black dude been bustin into white folks' homes takin' all they computers and what not, and then she say dude tol' her he capped one cuz he not movin' fast enough. She say he was laffin 'bout it."

Pete and Joe looked at each other with the same thing going through their minds...it had to be the home invasion gang working in Morgan Park

"What did this guy look like? What kind of car was he driving? I need more," I said.

"She didn' say much 'bout em...cept his hair was slick back and greasy wiff long sideburns. Had a devil ring."

"What?"

"Deelilah say he had a ring on his finger wiff a devil on it, that what made her scared first."

Joe looked at her and said, "We need to know the car...what kind of car?"

"Dee don't say nuffin 'bout it, but I 'member when she got in it—it was a black Enscalade."

"You mean Escalade, a Cadillac Escalade?" Joe asked.

"Yeah, that what I said—a Enscalde."

"Okay Blaz, that's good stuff." I handed her twenty bucks and told her that she was good to go for tonight, but that she should go back and talk with "Dee" to nail down some more details on this guy.

"Thanks officers. I sure dint want to get locked up tonight. I owe y'all."

We took her out of the car, uncuffed her, and told her, "We're going to be working this area a lot from now on. If you want to stay right with us, you need to get me as much as you can on the 'Devil Man'."

"I like dat—the Devil Man! I'll do that y'all, thanks again."

She made her way back to her corner.

"Oh man Pete, this is a big break. We've got to stay on her—make sure that she doesn't drop the ball on this one."

"Yeah, folks like her have short attention spans." We drove off down Western Avenue content with our first contact with the ladies

"Hey Pete, can I ask you something?"

"About what?"

Joe turned to me and said, "The other night at Palermo's...I noticed that Beth hardly touched her pasta. Has she been feeling okay?"

"I think so...she hasn't complained about anything. Why?"

"Well, don't get mad at me or Susan, but we were discussing Beth on the ride home after dinner. You know that Susan got her nursing degree at St. Xavier before we got married."

"Yeah, Joe I know. So?"

"Well, Susan thinks that Beth might have an eating disorder, maybe anorexia, or bulimia. She looks awfully thin."

"Wow...she said that? I guess that I haven't really noticed, but now that you mention it, she does seem to be getting thin. I just assumed it was from her running program. This past year she's been running around Xav's campus at night before I leave for work. I thought that she should use the treadmills inside, I mean we're both members there, but she said she prefers being out in the fresh air."

"Pete, something else, the last few times we've all gone out together, not only does she not eat, but she seems to be pounding down the drinks."

"Are you serious? You guys think that she might be an alcoholic *and* an anorexic?"

"I'm not saying anything Pete, other than Susan is concerned about Beth's behavior. Her nursing education tells her that she exhibits signs for both problems. I just think that you should keep your eye on her. You know that we love you both."

"Oh man...I've been so wrapped up in my own world—school, midnights, working out.... I've been pressuring her lately about having a baby too, and she has been unwilling to even talk about it. Thanks Joe. I have to do something quick; I can't let this go on. If you and Susan are right about this, there's something wrong in her life that I need to help her with."

"So you're not mad?"

"Joe, you and I are like brothers, we're family. If you *didn't* tell me, then I would be mad!"

"Thanks. Joe promise me that you and Susan will pray for Beth...and that you'll ask the Father to give me the wisdom and counsel to discover what she needs to get past this."

"Pete, we pray for you both every day already, but we'll add that intention."

"Thanks brother. I love you guys."

7
Home Invasion

"That's it man...that's the house my boy told me about," said Devil Man. "Said it's got lots a trees and bushes so nobody can see us."

The two thugs had found the house that would be their target tonight, thanks to their accomplice working in the "straight" world.

"Dude said the back o' the house got like a screen porch with a door that don't have no locks, and the back door o' the house got that flimsy lock we can open with the screwdriver—no deadbolts."

Devil Man eased the car in between a couple of already parked cars just down the block from the house—didn't want to have it sticking out by itself—too easy for cops to spot. He and his partner in crime, Maurice, got out of the car, looked around for any "Five O", and then began to walk nonchalantly down the block.

"You sure they'se black folks in this hood", Maurice asked?

"Yeah, my boy said house next door got black folks livin' in it. Don't worry 'bout it man, ain't nobody out now no how."

A few seconds later they had walked up the drive and were at the back porch door. Opening it quietly, they found the back door just as their comrade had told them—nothing but a flimsy lock on the knob. Within seconds they were inside.

They quickly made their way up to the second floor, first door on the right, where they were told that they would find the master bedroom. Kicking the bed hard and flipping on the light, Devil Man shouted, "Get up muthas, get up 'less you want to get shot!"

The terrified man and his wife hopped out of bed quickly, horrified at the sight of two armed intruders that had shattered the safety and serenity of their world.

"We ain't gotta lotta time—I want money, wallets, jewelry—NOW!"

"We don't keep much cash at home," the man pleaded.

"You fulla shit! You open that closet safe now 'for I have your wife doin' things she never dreamed she would ever do. MOVE!"

Devil Man smacked him across the face with his gun, causing his cheek to split open—his wife screamed at the sight.

"Shut her up man."

Maurice drew back and hit her with a right hand that sent her crashing to the floor.

"That good 'nuff bro?"

"Old man you better move fast or you ain't gonna see another sunrise."

The terrified and now bleeding homeowner opened the safe which was quickly emptied of its contents. Next, they dragged him downstairs where they grabbed a laptop computer, camera, and both of their wallets.

"Man unless you wanna die, I better not find out that you talked to the poleece 'bout this. You unnerstand what I'm saying?"

The man nodded, barely able to stand now and just praying that they would leave. The two thugs strolled casually back to their car, putting their loot in the trunk and driving off.

"This is gettin' too easy man," said Devil Man mockingly. "Ooooee ! You smacked that bitch so hard...."

"Yeah, that one coulda put Mike Tyson on the mat, know what I'm sayin?"

"Let's go by my boy's and see what we got. Then I might get me some 'strange' later on."

<u>8</u>
Beth

"Mornin' babe, sleep well?" I gave Beth a kiss then sat on the bed to watch her finish applying her makeup as she prepared for work. I had hoped to get home a little earlier to catch her before she got dressed, but Joe and I stopped a guy that had a gun in Marquette Park; we wound up working a little longer than usual. I wanted to see for myself how she looked, maybe catch her coming out of the shower. How could Joe and Susan notice this health problem and not me...her husband?

"Yeah, I slept fine...watched the news as usual then drifted off."

She was combing her long red hair that made her green eyes even more attractive as it framed her face. She was a beautiful woman, both inside and out. It seems like she hadn't changed since I first laid eyes on her at a dance in high school. She was there with another guy, but when I saw her I was drawn to her like steel to a magnet. I finally got enough courage up to ask her to dance before the night was over. After that I couldn't get enough of her.

Beth attended public high school; her parents couldn't afford the tuition at the Catholic schools. They were good people that worked hard for everything that they had, and thanked God for all of the gifts He had bestowed upon them. They regularly read the Bible together as a family. They made sure that their daughter had a close relationship with the Lord, even though she was educated in the city schools.

"How was work last night? Are you and Joe enjoying the Tac Team job?"

"Well, it's only been a week, but how could you not love being a cop in Chicago, working in plain clothes, and being able to pick and choose what you want to do? Joe says that he doesn't think that he can ever wear the uniform again, he loves working every night in jeans and t-shirt."

"How about your fellow cops—any jealousy from them over your new assignment?"

"No, everybody is cool with it...well except Sal Rosato."

"Is that the guy you call The Hammer?"

"Yeah, that's him. Says Joe and me kissed up to Mac so that we could get the assignment. Sal said that he should have been picked since he is a former sergeant."

Beth was finished getting ready for work now. "Pete you need to watch yourself around him, there's something about that guy that gives me the creeps. It's almost like I sense an aura of evil surrounding him."

"I agree. He's been involved in some questionable things. I'm actually surprised that he's still on the job after that last brutality beef that he had. Mac told me that the bosses are watching him close, one more misstep and he's gone."

I followed Beth into the kitchen. She picked up her coffee mug and was finishing it—I took a close look at her arms—they did seem thinner than I remember.

"Did you already eat breakfast?"

"No, either I'll grab something on the way like I usually do, or somebody always brings bagels or donuts to the office and I'll have one of those"

"You sure?"

"Yeah, don't worry about me I'll be fine."

"Beth, can I ask you something. Is everything okay, are you doing alright?"

"I'm fine Pete, what do you mean?"

"Well, I don't know. With the both of us working different shifts we don't get much time to talk, or even have much opportunity to be together. Sometimes I feel like we're drifting apart, that maybe we're losing that intimacy that we had."

She leaned into me for a hug and gave me a big kiss. "Listen babe, I love you now just as much as when we were first married. You're the only one for me; the only one that I want."

"I love you too honey. It just seems that we're on different pages all the time. I'll be glad when I finish my degree so that I can get off steady mids."

"But you love mids, you told me that's where all the action is."

"It is, but it's not worth staying on that shift if it has a negative effect on our marriage."

"Well I guess in another year you will be able to make that decision."

"Wouldn't you rather have me home at night?"

"Sure."

"I just feel like sometimes we're leading separate lives. You'd tell me if something was bothering you, wouldn't you Beth?"

"Of course honey. Hey, I've got to go or I'll be late. Love you."

She kissed me and headed for the garage. I felt guilty about the hug that I had given her—it was more of an exploratory move than an affectionate one. I was certain that I could feel her ribs through her clothing. She did seem thinner than before. Maybe Joe and Susan were right...maybe Beth does have a problem.

<u>9</u>
Ask Father Mike

I hit the bed as soon as Beth left for work, but tossed and turned for a couple of hours hardly getting any sleep. Thoughts of what could possibly be affecting her to the point of placing her health in danger would not leave me. I felt so restless that I decided to walk over to St. Xav's for a workout. Maybe a good run and lift would wear me out to the point of exhaustion—then maybe I could sleep.

Finishing my three-mile run around the campus, I walked into the gym and spotted Father Mike from Queen of Martyrs parish. Queens was right across the street on 103rd; Beth and I have been members since we moved into the neighborhood. Father Mike was not only a great priest, but a close friend as well. Whenever we could arrange it we would go for a run together. It was a great opportunity to discuss the Catholic Faith. It also afforded me somewhat of a free counseling session. I could bounce things off Father Mike; he would come up with a solution to my problem more often than not, and we would both get in a great workout.

"Hey Father Mike!"

"Pete, how are you? Just get off work?"

"Naw, I've been home for a couple of hours, but I couldn't fall asleep. I thought I'd come over here, wear myself out, and then give it another shot."

"That's a good plan—I hope that it works for you. I'm just finishing up my weight workout now, and then I'll put in 15-20 minutes on the elliptical."

"Do you have a minute Father?"

"For you, always. I'm going over to Little Company of Mary Hospital at two o'clock to visit a sick parishioner, but that's all that I really have on my plate today as far as scheduled things go. What's up?"

"It's about Beth."

"She sick?"

"In a way…yes. Let me ask you a question…Do you think that she is looking a bit too thin these days?"

"You know Pete, since the weather has finally warmed up, and people have shed all the heavy clothing, I have noticed that she is looking very thin. I didn't want to mention anything to you, but since you asked, I would say *most definitely*. In fact, I think that she is looking almost anorexic."

"As much as I hate to say it, I think that you're right Father. Joe and Susan O'Hara are actually the ones that pointed it out to me. I've been so self-absorbed that I failed to recognize the fact that my own wife was in trouble. I feel horrible about it, like I'm almost complicit in her health problems."

"When you say problems, is there something else?"

"Yes. Joe and Susan also said that they have noticed an uptick in her drinking as well."

"Pete, when something like the problems that you just described begin to manifest themselves, there is almost always a mental component involved. Granted, there are hereditary predispositions for both disorders, but in many cases the genesis is traceable to some traumatic event that they now feel guilty about, or that they have no control over. They become depressed and feel a need to regain control over their lives, or at least one aspect of it. In the case of females, disorders like anorexia and bulimia are most often the behaviors that they turn to so that they can regain control over something."

"Father if that's the case, the only thing that I can possibly attribute it to would be our inability to get pregnant. I have been after her about the two of us going to get tested, but she flatly refuses to go or even discuss the problem."

"That could be it Pete, or maybe that's just a part of whatever it is that is causing her all of this uneasiness. Do you both want to come and see me to talk about it...?"

"Not yet. I'm going to see Dr. Grossman at Little Company Hospital about my shoulder—it's been giving me some pain whenever I do bench presses. I'll see what his thoughts are."

"Isn't Grossman an ER doc?"

"Yes, but we've become pretty close the last couple of years. I had a shooting victim in there one night; Grossman saved his life. I was amazed because this guy took a bullet to the head and barely had a pulse. Within ten minutes he had the bleeding stopped and the guy regained consciousness."

"He served in the Middle East didn't he?"

"Sure did, he said that was some of the best training that he has ever had. He loves trauma so much that he's Chief of ER, doesn't want to leave it."

"Okay. Keep me updated. In the meantime I will include her in the intentions at tomorrow's mass. They say that laughter is the best medicine, but Psalm 107 tells us that, '*He sent His Word, and healed them.*' Pray Pete."

I resolved that I would. Even though I thanked God for her every day I needed to ask Him to show me how to help the woman that was my whole world.

<u>10</u>
Blonde In The Red Car

The radio blared: "All units in the 8th District and on City Wide Radio, we just had a report of a hit and run accident at 59th and Kedzie. The wanted vehicle is described as a red sports car; the first two digits of the plate are 'SR' Sam Robert. That info comes from an eyewitness at the scene. The vehicle was last seen travelling southbound on Kedzie"

"Hey we're close to Kedzie, let's drift over and see if we spot it Joe."

We had just finished the paperwork on a couple of "juvies" that had broken into a "Mom and Pop" store on 69th Street. These two fifteen year olds had already amassed numerous arrests for theft and other anti-social behavior. We caught them as they made their way out the back door, their pockets stuffed full of lottery tickets. That's what results when kids are out past curfew, nothing good happens at that time of night. It was obvious that these two were headed for adult court in a couple of years when they turned seventeen.

"Pete that might be our car!" Joe pointed to a red car that just flew through the intersection at 63rd Street.

"Let's go take a look."

I turned south on Kedzie and floored it. The red car was really moving fast, judging by the speed this had to be our wanted vehicle. If not we were going to stop it anyway for reckless driving. I hit the emergency lights that were hidden behind the grill, and activated the flashing headlights and siren. We didn't get the driver's attention for about a mile, where we finally pulled it over.

"860 Squad...We're pulling over that suspected hit and run vehicle at 79th Kedzie. The plate number is 'Illinois SR 8311'. Can you run that number for us?"

"10-4 Eight Six Zero, Sam Robert 8-3-1-1"

"I've got the driver Joe."

"Roger Pete, I'm on the passenger side. Right now all I see is one occupant—looks like a woman, blonde hair. Wanna call her out with the PA?"

"No, let's approach. I think what we may have here is a lady that's had a little too much to drink. She probably wouldn't understand our commands over the speaker anyway if she's hammered."

I walked up to the driver's side of the vehicle, scanning the inside as I approached. I put my thumbprint on the tail light and trunk lid to mark it in case this thing "broke bad" on us.

"Looks like only the driver inside Pete."

"Roger that Joe."

He took his post on the passenger side of the vehicle, just to the rear, to act as my cover man while I contacted the driver.

"Pete, I've got what looks like fresh damage on the right side of the vehicle—the whole side's been damaged, like a sideswipe."

"10-4 brother."

I went up to the driver's door. "Ma'am, I'm Officer Shannon. We have a report that this vehicle was involved in a hit and run accident a few minutes ago. We also observed you driving in a reckless manner. I need to see your license, registration, and proof of insurance."

"Don't you know who I am?" said the blonde driver.

Her hair was bleached blonde—*really* bleached blonde and worn puffed up high like they used to wear it in the '60s. She had blue eye shadow on and candy apple red lipstick, so garish looking that her appearance was rather clownish. Her skirt, if you could call it that, was much too short and rode up her legs to the point of exposing her underwear. She topped that ensemble off with lots of jewelry on her neck and wrists. And, she was loud.

"No ma'am I don't know who you are, but as soon as I see your identification I will probably have a better idea. Now please—license, registration, and proof of insurance.”

“Hey, don’t pull that crap on me. Get Sal over here right now, he’ll tell you who I am!”

“Sal...Sal who?”

The odor of alcohol was beginning to waft out from the car, along with stale cigarette smoke and cheap perfume. Glancing over at the passenger seat, I spotted a vodka bottle.

“Sal Rosato you idiot! He‘s your boss; he works nights here. Get him over here...now!”

“Did you hear that Joe?”

“Yeah, I think she’s going to be trouble.”

“Ma’am it doesn’t matter who you may know at this point. I am going to tell you once more...give me your driver’s license, vehicle registration, and proof of insurance!”

“I’m not giving you anything until Sal gets here.”

She folded her arms across her chest and looked straight ahead, giving me the cold shoulder. Reaching inside, I quickly snatched the keys out of the ignition. This was the type of person that would roll her car window up before you could do anything about it, and then quickly drive off.

“Hey asshole, what do you think you’re doing? Gimme back my keys!”

“Step out of the car Miss—do it now!”

“Go to hell.”

I opened the car door and grabbed her left arm. Pulling her out of the vehicle, I worked her arm into a “come-along hold” and led her back between her vehicle and ours.

“Get your hands off me....what the hell do you think you’re doing? Sal is gonna’ kick your ass!”

“Joe, let’s get her cuffed and we’ll bring her in for sobriety tests.”

"This could be trouble Pete. If she does know Sal, who knows where this might go. Let's get a supervisor here, and get a wagon to transport her."

"Good idea brother." I grabbed the mike..." 860, send us a supervisor, a wagon, and a female officer for a prisoner search."

"10-4, and 860 that plate comes back to a Sally Ruggeri."

"10-4 squad, order us a tow truck also for a 2007 red Ford Mustang."

"860, what's the reason for the tow?"

"Suspected hit and run."

"10-4 sir, on the way."

I didn't like the way this was going, but we were too far into the incident now to change course. Even though everything was being done by the book, I had a feeling that The Hammer was going to want revenge when he found out that his girlfriend was being arrested. We loaded her into the wagon and headed for the station.

<u>11</u>
Longing To Forget

Beth stepped out of the shower, dried herself off, then stepped on the scale—102 pounds. Just two more pounds to go to reach her goal of 100. Tonight's run was a good one; she ran six miles—that's further that she had ever run before. She'd really been vigilant about her weight; she was in total control and it made her feel good.

Looking at herself in the mirror though she still saw areas that needed help. She felt like her stomach needed more work, maybe some more crunches and leg raises to get rid of that little "pouch" of fat sitting on her lower abdomen. Still...being able to get down from 130 pounds to this weight gave her a sense of accomplishment and a feeling of happiness.

She had not really felt much happiness the past couple of years. The last year in particular had turned out to be the worst year of her marriage, well except for that night in Boston. Pete had been relentless in his desire to start a family. Truth be told, Beth wanted children just as much as he did, but she couldn't risk getting pregnant while she was keeping her dark secret. What if Pete somehow found out? Would he want to stay in the marriage? Would he even be attracted to her anymore once the truth was revealed that she had been with another man? No, she couldn't let it happen until this problem was resolved. But how? How could she extricate herself from this web of deceit that had entangled her?

Now she was experiencing depression anytime that she even thought about her predicament. She went to the kitchen and poured herself two fingers of vodka. One good thing about Pete working mids was that she could drink as much as she wanted before going to bed and not have to worry about him finding out.

Two or three quick glasses usually "relaxed" her, allowing her problems to disappear at least for a while. She treasured the time when she could move those concerns off center stage. She was tired of thinking and worrying about them every day. They had consumed her forever it seemed, and she just wanted to be free from the fear, the worry, the shame and humiliation.

"Help me Dear Lord...I don't know where to go or who to turn to. Please help me. I don't like who I've become. I need you back in my life. Please hear me...please...."

She quickly downed two more glasses, and then stumbled to the bedroom. Sleep was her only escape from her pact with the devil.

<u>12</u>
The Hammer

Sal Rosato stormed into the station like a tornado ripping across the Midwest plains, "What the fuck is goin' on here Shannon? Why did you lock up my girlfriend; haven't you ever heard of 'professional courtesy'?"

Right or wrong, a practice known as professional courtesy exists that involves cops giving other cops and family members a break if they are stopped for minor traffic offenses.

Sal was mad, well that was putting it mildly—he was steaming, like a boiler that had just reached its capacity.

"Settle down Sal..."

"Fuck you—you settle down! I should kick your ass right now. You knew Sally was my girl but you stopped her anyway!"

Joe piped in, "Sal hold on. First of all we didn't know that she was your girlfriend until after we stopped her—but that wouldn't have made any difference. She was involved in a hit and run; there was an 'all-call' out on her vehicle."

"What did she hit?"

"She side-swiped two parked cars on 59th Kedzie. There were three guys on the corner that saw her do it. They happened to be coming out of Tracey's Bar after it closed. They called 9-1-1 right away with a description of the car."

I could see that this explanation wasn't penetrating Sal's rock hard attitude. The fact that he was up at four o'clock in the morning on his day off wasn't helping matters either.

"So Einstein, you do a traffic accident report then let her walk. She's got insurance; happens all the time!"

"It's not that simple Sal, she was drunk—she blew a .14 on the breathalyzer."

"Shannon…you fucking buried her man! Now she's gonna have to hire a freakin' mouthpiece to go to court with her—that's gonna cost her five grand! She don't have that kinda dough!"

Just then Mac walked in.

"What's all the commotion about in here? Sounds like a bunch of street idiots trying to out-yell each other."

"Sarge these two assholes just locked up my girlfriend!"

"Keep your voice down Rosato, I'm standing right next to you. Is the blonde woman in the red car your friend?"

"Yeah, we been goin' together for almost two years. She owns a beauty shop right on Kedzie there around 82nd St—she lives above it. She's a business woman, an upstanding member of the community."

"Well, she wasn't very upstanding tonight," Mac said. "In fact when they brought her in she had a very difficult time standing at all."

"Okay, so she had a couple o' drinks, we all do that once in a while."

"Some of us, yes. But most of us don't hit parked cars afterward, and if we do, we know that the proper thing to do is to stop and report the accident. Most of us also don't curse and spit at cops"

"Oh man, this is goin' nowhere. Let me take her home Sarge, what's the bond?"

"Sal, you know the procedures around here. Bond is $500 cash, but she's going to sit for a couple of hours until she sobers up a little."

"I can't believe you Mac. I would never treat one of your people like this…."

"Listen Sal, if any of *'my people'* acted in a manner like your friend did, I would expect that you would be professional and handle the incident according to the law."

"Yeah, whatever… Can I go see her?"

"Sure, you know where the lockup's at. But Sal, if you cause any trouble I will not let her bond out. Understood?"

"Yeah Mac, yeah."

Mac walked back to the desk area leaving Joe and me standing there with Sal.

"You haven't heard the last of this Shannon. I don't know who the fuck you think you are...just 'cause you're on the Tac Team now you think you can go around lockin' up anyone you want? Payback is a bitch pal—watch your back!"

"Are you threatening me Sal?

"I'm just telling you the way it is, '*brother*'...."

It had been a long night. Joe and I checked our equipment back in— radio and shotgun—we gassed up the car for the next crew, and then headed to our personal cars.

"Guys, wait up a minute."

"What's up Mac, more trouble from Sal?"

"No, he's gone. He finally took his friend home; I'm glad to see both of them out of here. Don't quote me, but I don't think this is going to go away any time too soon."

"I agree," said Joe. "I think that both of us need to watch our backs."

"I hope that was all bravado in there—that he's not stupid enough to do anything to retaliate. Keep me in the loop on that."

"Will do Mac, that it?"

"No, while you guys were finishing up your paperwork, a beat car took a report of a robbery/ home invasion."

"Where at?"

"85th and St. Louis, right here in The Lawn."

"The guys from Morgan Park?"

Mac read from the report in his hand: "Two subjects, one black, one white, hit the husband with a gun and cracked the wife with a vicious right. Both had to go to Little Company Hospital; the husband took 21 stitches to his cheek, the wife had a fractured eye socket and a concussion."

"Anyone see the vehicle?"

"No Joe, but the wife noticed something peculiar."

"What?"

"She said the white guy wore a ring with a devil on it."

13
The Consultation

I walked into the ER at Little Company Hospital and spotted my friend at the desk.

"Hey Jeff, how are you tonight?"

"Pete, it's only ten o'clock what are you doing here so early? Did you bring in a shooting victim?"

"No, I don't start my shift for a couple of hours. But I was wondering if you might have a minute to take a look at my shoulder."

"Sure, no problem. You came in at a good time—there's a lull in the action. What's the problem?"

I explained to him that I had pain there the past couple of weeks whenever I bench-pressed. He did a hands-on exam then ordered an x-ray. While I was waiting to go to x-ray we talked guns. Jeff was a gun nut and he loved police work. He owned several handguns and an M-4 Assault Rifle. I had taken him shooting on several occasions, allowing him to fire the same qualification course that Chicago cops shoot. He loved every second of it.

"Jeff, let me ask you about something. Are you familiar with anorexia?"

"Sure, I'm a doctor remember?"

"Yeah, yeah. But seriously, what causes an otherwise healthy person to become anorexic—is it caused by medication or an allergic reaction to something?"

"Well, it's complicated. It can have a genetic component, meaning someone can have a predisposition for the disorder, or it can be the result of a traumatic incident that leaves the person with little control over his or her circumstances. When that's the case, people feel a sense of anxiety. One of the ways that they try to ameliorate that anxiety is to try to gain control over at least one thing in their lives. More often than not if it's a woman, and 90% of those that suffer from anorexia are women, she will turn to her weight. That is something so personal and private that when she is able to gain control of it, it erases some of the uneasiness that she feels.

Unfortunately, when the numbers on the scale start to go down, it becomes an addiction. Then that person must continue to lose weight in order for them to feel any happiness or success. When they stop losing, they become depressed. Depression will sometimes cause them to pick up other addictions like alcohol or drugs. It's a downward spiral that is difficult to stop."

"What are the signs Doc?"

"They're fairly noticeable symptoms. They obsess about food and limit their intake; they exercise a lot, even when they are sick. They become secretive. They may pull away from family and friends, and make excuses not to eat around other people. They may even lie about their eating habits."

"Do you know someone that's anorexic Pete?"

"I guess I do—my wife…"

"I'm sorry to hear that. I will tell you this—it's rare that someone who is anorexic can beat it without professional help. If you want, I can refer her to a specialist in the field."

"I may take you up on that Jeff. To be honest, I just realized what has apparently been fairly obvious to others around me. I don't know what's happened to Beth, but I'm determined to find out. When I do I'll get back to you for that referral. Thanks Jeff—you're a true friend."

"No thanks needed. C'mon, let's get you up to x-ray."

I finished up with the x-ray people, and thanks to Jeff they read them right away. No muscle tears, just a strain that required rest and aspirin. I had a few minutes to kill so I made my way to the Chapel at the hospital. I took a pew in the front row.

"Dear Lord, you told us in the Bible,' ask and you shall receive'. I come as your humble servant and ask that you will give me the wisdom and understanding that I need to help Beth. I pray for forgiveness for having been so self-absorbed in my own life that I failed to minister to my wife's needs. Please continue to watch over and bless us. Amen."

Fifteen minutes later I met Joe at the station.

"Pete, let's roll. Mac took a call from Blaz—she's got some info for us on whoever's been ripping off the johns."

"That's great brother, I could use some good news right now."

"Is it anything that I can help you with?"

"No. I guess the full impact of Beth's condition just hit me. I spoke with Father Mike and Dr. Grossman about her. They confirmed what you and Susan thought...she's showing the symptoms of anorexia. Joe she must be feeling so lonely... Why didn't she come to me with whatever it is that's been bothering her?"

"I thought that it was the 'baby thing'."

"I don't know Joe...maybe it's that, maybe not."

We pulled out of the station lot and headed east on 63rd Street toward Western Avenue. I made a right on Western and pulled over about halfway down the block. I didn't want to heat the corner up for the trade. Blaz spotted us and took her time making her way over to our location. She slipped into the back seat.

"How y'all doin' tonight?"

"We're good Blaz. The desk sergeant gave us a message that you called, what's up?"

"It's some bad shit man. Look here...I'm over by the tracks last night 'bout nine o'clock takin' care o' some old white dude in his big Caddy. I just get into it when dis ride pulls up—I thought it was ya'll—the pohleece. I can't hardly see wiff the lights shining bright at us. 'For I know what's hap'nin, dude yanks open the doh and tells my trick to give em all his money!"

"What did he look like Blaz?"

"Who?"

"The bad guy!"

"I'm gettin' to that man. Anyway, my trick is an older dude, he scared and ain't movin' fast 'nuff, so the dude smacks him upside the head wiff a gun! He put a knot upside his head like I ain't never seen."

"Blaz, please, what did he look like?"

"That's what I'm tryin' to tell ya'll—it was the Devil Man!"

I looked over at Joe and said, "I thought we got reports that it was pimps ripping these guys off."

"Man, my pimp ain't gonna rip no customer off—they ain't never gonna come back if he do."

That made sense to me. The ladies would never get repeat customers if they couldn't be trusted.

"Blaz, one more time, what did the Devil Man look like?"

"Just like Deelilah say—he a white dude wiff slick back black hair and he got dat ring. An' his ride is that Black Enscalde like I tol' you b'foe."

"You have made our day Blaz, this is great information." I reached into my pocket to give her some cash...

"Hey man, you ain't heard it all."

"There's more?" Joe said.

"Hell yeah...I got the number on his tag man! It was easy to remember—DBS 1—and it had dat handicap chair on it."

I pulled out a twenty-dollar bill, but quickly added another one to it. Handing it to her as she began to leave I said, "Blaz, we're going to be concentrating on this area for a while. The Devil Man knows that he's got an easy score here so I'm positive that he'll be back. Do you feel safe working here now that you know he's around?"

"Baby, he ain't gonna hurt us. We his meal ticket man, 'sides, Dee already took care o' him, she know what he like."

"Okay. We'll be around the rest of the night."

"I'm on'y givin' it 'bout one more hour. I gotta get home to my baby."

"Alright, we'll stay close for another hour. Will you be out here again tomorrow night?"

"Baby, you know we ain't got no life. My man spect me to work ever' day. Don't get no days off like you pohleece, lessin we's sick."

"Okay, we'll see you tomorrow. Blaz...thanks."

"Hey man y'all doin us a favor. Devil Man's a sick dude."

14
The Confession

Taking another gulp of vodka from the flask, she quickly put the top back on it so that she could put it back in her purse. But she wasn't quick enough—just as she was about to hide it, Patty walked in.

"Beth, I..."

"Just a moment..."

"Beth, what are you doing? I saw that—it's a flask! You can't hide this any longer; you're damaging your health. Your weight continues to alarm me; you look like a skeleton! And don't think that you've been fooling anyone; we've all smelled the alcohol on your breath for some time now. Honey, you need help...let's talk about it, please."

"Patty, it's personal—it's my problem."

"It's not just *your* problem anymore. It's affecting your job, and the way that people think about you. Do you want me to tell you about some of conversations that I've overheard? You wouldn't like it. You've gone from one of the brightest stars in the company, to someone who is sometimes unreliable and distant. Your head's no longer here at work, it's like you're in a fog much of the time. You need help Beth, can't you see that?"

Beginning to sob, Beth realized that Patty was right. Carrying this burden alone for so long was killing her. Her life was in turmoil. Her relationships as well as her health were deteriorating. Maybe it was time to take a step toward easing this unbearable pain.

"You're right, I do have a problem—I do need help. Maybe you're the one that He sent to release me from the prison that I've been in. Do you have time to talk right now?"

"Of course I do. Let's go into the far conference room; we'll talk, we'll pray, we'll do whatever needs to be done to bring back the Beth that's been missing for much too long now."

They talked for several hours. It proved to be a cathartic experience for her, one that seemed to reawaken her soul from a deep sleep. She vowed to tell Pete everything, regardless of what might come of it, but first she had to confess her sins to God. On the train ride home she called Father Mike at Queen's.

"Queen of Martyrs, this is Father Mike, how can I help you?"

"Father, this is Beth Shannon."

"Beth, how are you?"

"Well, I haven't been well lately, that's why I'm calling. I really need to see you; I need to go to confession. I need to unburden my soul and be honest for the first time in several years. Can I come in now? I'm on the way home from work."

"I'm just finishing my dinner. I'll be waiting for you in my office, just come right in when you get here."

"Thank you Father."

Beth was feeling better already with the first step having been taken toward healing. She didn't know which was going to be more difficult, confessing to God or to Pete, but she was adamant about doing both. Pulling into the lot at Queen's, she walked into the rectory.

"Beth, I am so pleased that you are here!"

"Father Mike, I've been a horrible wife and a horrible Catholic. I need to rid my soul of Satan's evil works; I need to tell God how sorry I am that I let the devil rule my heart."

"Beth, you are a child of God. Just as a parent forgives his own child, there is nothing that you can do that the Father will not forgive. Our Lord and Savior forgave the apostle Peter, the one who denied Him three times. He gave him a second chance, just as He is waiting to give you one. In the Bible, John tells us, *"He is faithful and just to forgive us and to cleanse us from every wrong.*" Now, let's begin..."In the name of the Father, and of the Son, and of the Holy Spirit."

By the time she had finished getting it all out, she was exhausted and *hungry.* She felt renewed and refreshed both spiritually and physically. No longer having to fear that someone would discover her dark secret, she felt awash and alive in the Spirit of Christ.

"Thank you Father Mike. This sin has been like an anvil that I've carried around for the last several years, sapping every bit of energy that I had. It has caused me to feel undeserving of anyone's love and attention."

"Beth, you've confessed your sins to Him—believe me when I tell you—you are forgiven. Now you need to focus on the here and now. Pete needs to know these things as well. He has been very concerned about your health and spiritual well-being. Now go to him. He will be hurt, but if your love for each other is as strong as I think it is, you will both eventually move beyond this."

"I hope that you're right Father."

"You have no choice. May God bless you, may He fill you with His Spirit and give you the strength and the courage that you need to finish the task."

"Amen..."

<u>15</u>
Making Plans

"Two medium black coffees please."

In the drive thru at White Castle Hamburgers, Pete and Joe waited for their order. Even though they had been on mids for a couple of years now, the body never fully adjusts—it naturally wants to sleep at night. Coffee and cops have had a symbiotic relationship for decades.

"Susan and I are going on that couple's retreat in Wisconsin that Father Mike was talking about last Sunday. We leave in three weeks."

"Who's watching the kids?"

"Susan's mom will stay the weekend at our house. She just doesn't have room at her place for all four of the boys to sleep, and Joey has baseball practice on Saturday so it's more convenient if she stays over."

"Isn't that your 10th Wedding Anniversary?"

"Yeah, we thought this would be a good way to celebrate, we can renew our faith and our relationship with each other at the same time. It's been hard for us to really spend any time together. Susan's time is spent mostly keeping track of the boys, and I'm out here with you every night. Even on our days off there's not much time for just her and I."

Joe was a good man. His ten-year marriage to Susan was one that they could be proud of. They were a team, both focusing on their four sons: nine year old Joey, Pete, seven, who they named after me, and the twins, Mike and Billy both five. Joe helped coach Joey's baseball team; Susan was the team mom—scheduling practices, bringing refreshments, and doing any other miscellaneous jobs that needed to be done. You could see them at mass every Sunday in the front pew at Queen of Martyrs. They were a beautiful Christian family that served as a role model for many families in the parish.

"Beth and I went to that retreat on our 5th Anniversary. You will love it Joe, it's a beautiful setting, quiet and serene. It's just a great way to reacquaint yourselves with each other and really get closer to God."

"Yeah, we're looking forward to it. My only concern is you."

"What are you talking about brother?"

"The Devil Man Pete. If he's still out here breaking into people's homes, my sense is that he is going to become more vicious each time he commits another robbery. He may even start shooting his victims, rather than just hitting them with that gun he's carrying."

"I agree. He seems to have become emboldened by his successes thus far. There has to be some connection somewhere... How is it that he and his partner know which homes to hit, and then they seemingly know the layout of the place before they get inside?"

"I know; it's eerie... I just hate to be gone for a few days and have you teamed up with someone else. It's been the two of us backing each other up for years."

"Don't worry about me Joe; remember I've got St. Michael watching my back too."

"The radio came to life. 860...Beat 8-6-0..."

"This is 860 squad."

"860, head back to the barn. Your desk sergeant advises that Area 1 Robbery dicks are waiting to meet with you."

"10-4 squad."

Area 1 Robbery detectives investigate crimes that occur in Districts 2, 7, 8, 9, and 21. After the initial police reports are completed at the scene of the crime, the "dicks" are called in to do any follow-up investigation. They conduct interviews with the victims, and if they have a suspect in mind, they show "photo spreads", a series of photos of the suspected offender and others that are similar in appearance to him. They may also have a victim come into the station to view an actual police lineup. The lineup includes the suspect and others who are similar in age, height, race, weight, etc.

We walked into the squad room to find Mac was already in a conversation with both detectives.

"Pete, Joe, this is Joe Miller and his partner Bob Lett."

We shook hands.

"Hey Joe, didn't I meet you last year at the Police Memorial race on the Lakefront?"

"Sure did Pete. That ten-miler is a heckuva race; I almost collapsed at the finish. You seemed to be fine though."

"Yeah, I felt good. I trained hard for it. The 8th District had a team entered—we took first place!"

"Well, this year I'm going to pace myself a little better than I did last year so that I have something left at the finish."

Miller's partner, Bob, said, "If you guys ever see me running anywhere, take a look behind me because there's probably some jealous husband chasing me!"

"Bob's not much of a fan of working out as you can see," Miller said.

"Yeah, I'm allergic to sweat."

Mac quickly jumped in, "All right guys; let's get down to business here. Bob, tell these two what you have so far on the home invasion pair."

Bob took a police memorandum pad from the pocket of his sport jacket. "As you know we had a home invasion/robbery in your district several days ago. The residents got pretty roughed up, even though they were fully cooperative with the bad guys. We interviewed the husband and wife who both said that these two seemed to know the layout of their home, as well as some of the things that they had inside the house."

Miller opened a folder. "These are reports from Area 2 Robbery. They've had four similar home invasions. In all four of those incidents the residents said the same thing—these guys knew the layout of their house and knew what to look for. They also gave the same description of the bad guys—one white, one black. They describe the white guy as menacing, with black hair that he wears slicked back. The black guy's only distinguishable feature is that he wears his hair in corn rows"

"What about a ring? Any mention about a ring from any of the victims," I asked.

"Yeah," Bob read from his pad. "This is one of the common threads that run through each incident. They all say that the white dude wears a devil ring on his right hand. It's gold, with two ruby red eyes."

Joe was taking his own notes and asked, "You say that's one of the commonalities, what's the other?"

"Well, Bob and I re-interviewed all of the victims," said Miller," especially regarding their daily patterns—when they leave for work, or go shopping, who they regularly have in their homes. Nothing really struck us as being a pattern or out of the ordinary. But there was one thing that all of the victims had in common...they all recently had carpet cleaners in their homes."

"We went to Clean Carpets America and spoke with the owner, nice guy, very cooperative, didn't want to lose his contractor license over an employee's misdeeds. We reviewed the personnel files and one guy stood out—Jessie Trout. This guy's on probation for drugs, both sale and possession. He's a small time punk, been in and out of County Jail the last eight years on some theft charges too, but no robbery or assaults in his background. He was on the crew at each of the homes that had been robbed."

Miller joined in, "We picked Trout up this morning at the carpet office for questioning...wouldn't you know he's holding a nickel bag of weed! So we bring him to our office and lean on him about the robberies. I can see that he wants to deal with us, but he wants to speak with the State's Attorney about it before he gives up the names."

"Yeah, so we're holding him on the possession beef and violating his probation—he's not going anywhere."

"Bob, what did you guys come up with on that handicap tag?"

"That comes back to a car on the North side. It was stolen a few weeks ago. It's a front plate, so most people don't notice that it's gone right away—gives the bad guy a few days grace period to ride around with it before it shows up on our Hot Sheet. We figure that the Black Escalade is hot too, but Devil Man is probably stealing front tags all over the place every couple of days, that's how he's able to drive around without being stopped."

"Sounds like it's coming together guys, what's the plan?" Mac asked.

"That's the other reason that we're here. Once Trout gives up Devil Man's name and address, then we'd like to put a surveillance/arrest team together to grab him and Maurice. We'd like to use Pete and Joe if that's alright Mac."

"Definitely, they've developed some good intel already on this crew."

"I know, that hooker...Blaz is it? She's the best source we had before Trout surfaced," Bob said.

"That's for sure. We're going to see her tonight; maybe she'll have some additional info for us. Joe and I are keeping an eye on her."

"Good and I'm pretty sure that Trout's going to flip by tomorrow. The prosecutor will give him a deal that he can't refuse. As soon as he gives it up, we'll get paper on both Devil Man and Maurice and get those guys off the street before they kill someone."

"Listen you guys, I probably don't have to say this but I will." Mac got that serious look in his eyes; I felt like he was speaking only to me, even though the others were standing there. "This Devil Man strikes me as the type that has no soul, no conscience. The fact that he's armed and smacking people around with that gun, tells me that he won't hesitate to shoot if he thinks he's going to be taken down. You guys need to be ready once you make the decision to move on him."

"I hear you Sarge," replied Miller, "that's why we've assembled a team to serve the warrant. We hope that a show of force will convince him that he has no choice but to comply. Bob and I will leave a message with your WC as soon as we have the paper in hand."

Lett and Miller headed toward the door, "We'll probably be hooking up tomorrow night; be ready guys."

"Okay brother, see you both tomorrow."

<u>16</u>
"10-1" Officer Needs Help!

"Those guys sound pretty confident that Trout's going to flip tomorrow."

"Yeah Joe, we could be involved in some heavy police work." I eased the unmarked car out onto 63rd and cruised toward Blaz's location.

"If they haven't thought of it already, I want to make an arrest plan so that all of us are on the same page when we hit this guy's house tomorrow. If we get there early, say around six o'clock in the morning, we should catch him in bed."

"I agree Pete. Every time that we've surprised someone that early we've never had much resistance."

Joe grabbed the computer terminal and punched in some data. "I just want to run Trout's info and see what kind of rap sheet he has."

Seconds later Joe had the results. "This guy's small time, nothing real serious on his record that makes him a threat. He avoids confrontation; his pedigree is mostly drugs and property crimes. I'm guessing that he met one of our guys in jail, or sold them drugs."

"He's not small time anymore. That conspiracy rap is going to net him some hard time in the joint—no more County Jail. He's in the big leagues now."

"You have to admit though Pete, they had a pretty good scam going. Trout cases each target while he's legitimately in the houses on business. No one get suspicious as he eyeballs every door, window, and all the expensive toys that people have."

"Yeah, that explains how those guys get in and out so quickly."

I slid in behind two cars already parked near the intersection of 63rd and Western. Blaz and Deelilah were out walking back and forth hoping that someone in need of their services would pull over. We had a clear view of all the activity so we sat and waited.

It had been almost an hour—it was getting close to three o'clock.

"I'm getting drowsy sitting here Pete; want to grab another cup o' joe?'

"I would, but the girls usually wrap it up around this time. Let's give it another ten minutes. If they haven't packed it in, we'll roll over there and tell them to close up shop. I don't want anything happening to them before we take down Devil Man tomorrow."

A couple of minute later, a vehicle pulled over next to the ladies.

"Pete, do you see that?"

"Yeah brother, is that our guy?"

"It looks like the Escalade!"

Deelilah walked over to the passenger side of the car and leaned into the open window. After a few minutes, she signaled for Blaz to join her.

"I wonder what's going on...I thought this guy liked Dee."

"Maybe he's looking for a change."

Blaz started to walk away from the car, but suddenly stopped. She had a frightened look on her face as she turned and walked back to the Escalade and got in. Dee stepped back on the sidewalk as the Escalade drove away.

"Pete, we need to follow this guy and see what's going on."

"Yeah, I know. Blaz could be in danger—no telling what this guy will do."

We took our time, keeping back a good distance so that we wouldn't be "made". The worst thing that could happen now would be for this guy to get spooked and take off on us.

"I think this guy is just taking his time Joe—I think he's going to wind up over by the railroad tracks with her."

"You're probably right. I don't think that we should try to take this guy down tonight Pete. I say we just stay close by and make sure that he brings Blaz back to her corner. Tomorrow we'll grab this guy at his home when we've got the cavalry with us."

"I agree brother."

The Escalade pulled into a work area with piles of old railroad ties and stones next to the gravel road. It was dark and secluded—definitely an ideal spot for the type of work that Blaz was engaged in. There was no activity for several minutes, then suddenly the passenger door flew open and Blaz came flying out, minus her top, and screaming. Devil Man quickly followed and within a few steps had her by the arm.

Joe was looking through binoculars—"Pete, he's got a gun! We need to take this guy—now!"

I slammed the car into gear and mashed so hard on the accelerator that I thought my foot would go through the floor.

"Joe, give the squad operator our location—hurry..."

"860...10-1...Officer needs help...63rd & Oakley, railroad tracks...10-1!"

Within seconds I had closed the distance on the Escalade. Our approach and the headlights bearing down on him startled Devil Man. He maintained his hold on Blaz as he made his way back near his vehicle. I slammed on the brakes, the car coming to rest about 20 feet from the nose of the black vehicle.

Joe and I opened our doors and leaned out, guns drawn.

"Police! Drop the gun. Do it now!"

Blaz was screaming—"Help me officers, please help me..."

"Let me get back in my ride, and I'll let this bitch go," screamed Devil Man.

"Put the gun down...do it now!"

Joe reached over to the spotlight, adjusting it so that it would blind the Devil Man and give us an advantage.

Reacting to the light, Devil Man fired directly at it.

Thanks to Joe, I had my sights right on the now illuminated Devil Man's head—I took the shot. Bam, Devil Man dropped like a man whose bones had just been repossessed...and then more screams from Blaz as she started running toward me.

"Officer Pete, Officer Pete...he hurt me...thought he gonna kill me...Oh my God...my baby, my baby."

"Get down behind my car Blaz—now!"

I had to make sure this guy was down and no longer a threat.

"Cover me Joe!"

I inched my way toward the front of the Escalade and peaked around the bumper. Devil Man was on his back, not moving, blood running down his face.

"Joe, I think we got him—there's no movement. Joe...Joe!"

I turned and looked back toward our vehicle. Joe was on the ground lying on his right side.

"Joe! Are you okay...are you hit?"

He was barely conscious, but there was no blood visible.

"Joe what happened..."

"Shot Pete...losing it buddy...dizzy...can't feel my arm..."

I ripped his shirt off and removed his vest. I saw a trickle of blood near an entry wound close to his right underarm. Devil Man's shot must have hit him as he had his gun arm raised—exactly where there is no coverage.

Grabbing the radio I sent out the call, "Officer down, 860—Officer down!"

Police cars flooded the area around us, responding to Joe's original call for help.

"Pete, tell Susan...love her...the boys...won't make retreat..."

"Joe, hang in there brother. You're going to be okay, you have to be okay! Joe...Joe—please Father in Heaven don't take him from us."

Just then the paramedics waded into what was now a sea of blue uniforms.

"Let us do our job officer; we'll take care of him."

They quickly loaded Joe onto the gurney and headed toward Little Company of Mary Hospital. As I watched the flashing lights of the ambulance disappear, I sensed that my faith would be tested like never before...

<u>17</u>
Reverend Dean

I don't even remember driving to the hospital, except that it took forever. I ran into the ER hoping to see Grossman taking care of Joe, but that was not the case. I quickly spotted one of the nurses that Joe and I had become familiar with having brought so many shooting victims here.

"Chandra, where's Dr. Grossman?"

"He's off today Pete."

"No... Joe needs him. If anyone can fix him, Jeff can do it."

"C'mon Pete, you know that all of our ER docs are the best. Joe is in good hands with any one of them. They have a team working on him now."

Just then, Rev. Dean walked into the ER. Dean was the Police Chaplain. I had known Dean for several years now; he was a compassionate, kind man that had a knack for comforting people when they needed it most. The Chaplain prowls the streets, ear tuned to the police radio ready to respond to offer support for cops and victims when they are in the throes of crises.

"Dean..."

"Pete, how's Joe doing, and are you okay?"

"Dean...I don't know. I think he's in bad shape. He was losing it when we were at the scene, he took a round right above the vest at the arm hole." Those types of gunshots are the worst; you don't know what kind of damage they will do inside the body cavity.

While Dean and I talked, a parade of people began to show up at Little Company: the WC, the Chief of Patrol, the Chief of Detectives accompanied by Detectives Joe Miller and Bob Lett, the two dicks who had briefed us earlier and of course the ubiquitous news media.

The two Chiefs and the WC walked over to Dean and me.

"Officer Shannon, I'm Bob Downey, Chief of Patrol, this is Chief Collins from Homicide. I know that this is a bad time, but we need to get some information on exactly what happened. I will tell you that preliminarily, based on the witness Blaz's statements, the shooting appears to be a justifiable homicide."

"Chief, no disrespect meant here, but right now my partner is in there fighting for his life with a bullet inside of him. I don't know that I really care about anything else but what happens to him."

"Officer Shannon..."

At that moment, Mac walked through the door with Joe's wife, Susan. She was pale and unsteady and was quickly swallowed up by a mob of TV reporters and cameras. Mac spotted me through the sea of pariahs and worked his way towards us.

Through her tears Susan said, "Pete, Oh God Pete what happened? How is Joe? How could this happen...?"

The mob of news people surrounded us.

"Officer Shannon, tell us what happened..."

"Is this the wounded officer's wife...?"

"Who was the man that was shot over by the tracks...?"

The horde of reporters pressed in, suffocating us, backing us into a corner, unrelenting in their quest for answers. Seeing what was happening, Rev Dean deftly pierced his way into the amoeba of people, guiding Susan and me to the Chaplains office.

"We'll be safe here Pete, it's off limits to the press. Susan, I'm Reverend Dean, the Police Chaplain. I've know your husband and Pete for several years. I don't know much of what has happened this evening, except that Joe needs our prayers at this moment. If you will agree, I would like us to say a prayer before we do anything further."

"Yes Reverend, please, I need Him now more than ever."

The Reverend began... "Dear Father in Heaven, we humbly come before you, asking that you hear our prayers offered up for your son Joseph. He was struck down as he toiled to save others in your name, working as a warrior sworn to defeat Satan and his evil influence on those that are weak in spirit. We pray that you will have mercy on Joseph and heal him. Father we know that if it is your will, our brave brother Joseph will fully recover and resume his position as your warrior here on earth. In Jesus' name we pray...Amen."

"Amen."

"Pete what happened out there? Did you see him after the shooting?"

"Susan, it all happened so quickly...we had planned on taking this guy in the morning on a warrant with an arrest team, but we were forced to confront him tonight to save a life."

I went on to explain in full detail to her what had transpired. When I had finished Mac walked in.

"Just so you know, Shirley is over at your house now Susan so that your neighbor can go to work. Don't worry about the boys; she will stay there for as long as you need her."

"Thank you Mac, you are a blessing."

I looked at my friend, "Mac I don't know..."

"Pete stop, you don't need to explain anything right now. Our focus is on Joe's situation—nothing else. I know you did your best son, you always have. Get any negative thoughts that you may have out of your head, you and Joe are two of the finest cops that I have ever had the pleasure of supervising."

"Thanks Mac."

Turning to speak with Susan, I was interrupted by the door opening...

"Mrs. O'Hara, I'm Dr. Herrara. Joe sustained a gunshot just under the armpit on his right side. It was high enough, and the trajectory of the bullet was such that it severed the subclavian artery. The EMTs were unaware of the internal bleeding, and by the time your husband arrived he had sustained a massive amount of blood loss. When we got Joe on the table we tried to stabilize him, but he was going into shock. We performed an emergency invasive procedure to locate the source of the bleeding, and Joe's blood pressure dropped so low that he suffered a heart attack."

"So is he going to be alright doctor, did you stop the bleeding?"

"Mrs. O'Hara, I'm sorry to tell you this, but we couldn't save him."

Falling onto the floor, Susan wept uncontrollably. "No, no, no...please God no...don't take him...we need him...the boys..."

I couldn't control my tears and got on the floor and held Susan tightly as her body writhed in emotional pain. I asked God why, I asked Him how, and I felt that Satan had won a battle this night.

<u>18</u>
No Greater Love

It was close to noon by the time I got home from the hospital. Before I left I sat down with Captain Steele and gave him an informal statement as to the facts surrounding the incident. Police S.O.P. dictates that all officers involved in shootings be placed on administrative leave with pay while the investigation takes place. The involved officer's duty weapon is also taken for ballistic testing. Even though an officer can be 100 per cent right, it is still an uneasy feeling to have to surrender one's weapon and be told to stay home.

I drove Susan home. Her parents had arrived and were waiting to comfort their daughter. Joe's boys didn't quite know what to make of what was happening, but they sensed that something was horribly wrong. When they saw their mother walk through the door they rushed to her side, clinging and sobbing, not really knowing why except that their mother was in pain. The whole scene was emotionally draining, so surreal that I almost felt that I was a spectator. This could not have happened to us... I'll wake up soon and discover that it was all a bad dream.

Shortly after we arrived, Father Mike came over to offer his condolences and lead all of us in a prayer for Joe. A few minutes later, Susan and her mother retired to the bedroom. Father Mike and I stepped out onto the patio.

"Pete, how are you? What can I do to help?"

"Father, I don't know how I am—I can't believe that Joe is gone. I feel I let him down, we always prided ourselves on having each other's back."

"Pete, I spoke with Mac on the phone. He told me what happened— you couldn't have done anything any differently. You saved that woman's life."

"Yeah, but Joe saved mine by shining that spotlight on the guy so that I had a perfect shot."

"Pete you know that guy fired blindly. It was a lucky shot that hit Joe; neither one of you did anything wrong."

"I want to believe you Father; I really want to believe you."

"You and Joe knew the dangers of police work Pete. You both accepted the challenge knowing that something like this could happen at any time. You both trained hard on your firearms and tactical skills, but many times the Lord calls us home when we least expect it."

"Father, that's the only thing that is preventing me from losing my mind right now, the fact that I know that Joe walked with Jesus every day. We prayed together before each shift."

"Joe is where we hope to be some day—he has received his eternal reward. Remember Christ taught us in John, Chapter 15, '*Greater love has no man than this, that a man lay down his life for his friend.*' Joe did just that, he did it without reservation, just as you would do Pete. Don't beat yourself up over this—you did nothing wrong."

"I just don't know Father. At this point, I'm not even sure that I want to be a cop anymore...not sure that I can ever allow anyone to look to me for backup. I feel like a failure. I can't look Susan in the eye. I didn't keep Joe safe for her and the boys..."

"Pete I'm telling you again—it's not your fault. Go home to Beth and get some rest, you've been up over 24 hours. Come to church tomorrow and let's talk some more. Will you do that please?"

"I'll try."

I walked back through the house and made my way home. Beth was waiting for me and quickly took me into her arms and started to cry. "Oh Pete, it's so horrible what happened to Joe. I've been crying since Mac called to tell me the news... How are you babe?"

"How am I? How do you expect me to be? My best friend in the whole world is killed standing next to me, and I let it happen. Why couldn't it have been me...?"

"Don't talk like that Pete, it wasn't your fault. You did everything you could—you saved a life."

"Joe was Susan's whole world. He was like the sun shining on his family every day, lighting their way. Now what does she have? She's a single mom with a broken heart and four boys to raise. Why".....why?"

"Pete, we will never know why He does things, except that it's all in His plan. He won't abandon Susan. He is a benevolent God, one that will watch over her and the boys. You know that. Don't let Satan get into your head over this, please."

But I had let him into my head. He was in there planting seeds that he hoped would take root. I always knew that the evil one was still roaming the earth, and I did my best to keep my shield raised in defense. But tonight he had won a major battle. He had defeated St. Michael and me, and he had taken a fellow warrior and a brother in the fight.

One part of me just wanted to throw in the towel, yet deep down I knew that I had to step up for what was sure to come. He had defeated Joe; *he was after me next.*

<u>19</u>
The Morning After

It was the morning after Joe's death and Beth had not slept well. She was in a quandary about what to do about confessing her infidelity to Pete. Before the shooting had occurred, she had been prepared to tell him everything, but now with him in a terrible state of mind from losing his partner and friend, Beth wasn't sure if now was a good time or not. She needed to talk with Father Mike again, get some advice on how long she should wait. She put the coffee on and heard Pete stirring in the master bedroom.

"Pete...want some coffee hon?"

He walked into the kitchen and sat down at the table.

"Yeah, I can use something this morning. I didn't sleep well at all last night. I kept seeing Joe lying on the ground, wounded. I hoped that when I awoke I would discover that it had indeed been all a bad dream."

"I know babe, I tossed and turned all night too. It is just so hard to believe that he's gone..."

"The only consolation is that I am positive that he's with the Lord. Now we need to help Susan as much as we can. She and the boys will need as much prayer and emotional support as we can offer."

Beth poured two cups of coffee and put one down in front of Pete. "What are your plans for today? Are you going over to Susan's?"

"Well I thought that I would get over there this afternoon. She's probably in much worse shape than we are—probably didn't sleep a wink. I know that her folks probably stayed the night, so there will be someone with her. I need to work out—get rid of this stress and anxiety that I'm feeling. Then I need to speak with Father Mike."

"What about?"

"Just a bunch of things Beth. I feel that I let Joe down...what I should do about my future...our relationship...."

"Our relationship...what about it?"

"Beth you know what about it. You and I have been going opposite ways, we don't share like we used to. I hardly see you anymore...and there's a couple of other things also."

Beth was worried now. Did Pete know about her affair and her miscarriage?

"What are you talking about Pete—what other things?"

"I can't talk about it right now."

"Wait a minute, aren't' you the one that told me that we needed to talk? You've been after me for weeks to sit down and talk."

"That was before Joe was killed."

"So when do you want to talk?"

"Beth, I don't know! I need to get through this whole thing with the shooting first! That's a whole other huge event. In a couple of days the Department will have me report to headquarters to give an official statement. I have to get myself together before I make any sworn statements. What you and I have to discuss is only going to distract me from what I need to do."

Beth was scared now...*is it possible that he knows?* As good as she was feeling a couple of days ago, she now felt herself losing that sense of well-being. All the good intentions and promises that she had made to herself about mending her ways, her intention to start eating and stop drinking, all that was now gone. She was once again on edge, in need to have control over something.

"Since you will be busy all day babe, I may as well go to work. I need to get my mind on something else. Besides, I'm working on a proposal for a new company out in Evergreen Park. I should probably put some time in on that."

Pete got up from the table. "I'll put my sweats on and head over to St. Xav's; I'll see you tonight."

That sounded distant...not good she thought. This isn't going as I had planned. Maybe I'm not meant to confess my sins to Pete. Maybe the Lord wants us to go our separate ways. Maybe the Devil Man killed more than a friendship...*maybe he killed a marriage too.*

<u>20</u>
Roll Call

"Fall in!" Mac walked into the squad room and had the early watch line up for weapons inspection. Afterward, he read off the assignments for the night...

"...and Beat 831, Johnson and Perez. Okay, listen up. The weather's getting warmer so keep your eyes open for public drinking problems around the parks and playgrounds. Let's make sure we stay ahead of the problem this summer and ensure that folks know that we won't tolerate any drinking parties—no open containers on the street. Remember, block parties must be approved beforehand. Also, Holy Cross Hospital ER is closed for the next few hours—they can't accept any more patients due to lack of bed space. If you have to transport anyone, take them to Little Company or to St. Francis in Blue Island."

Once it gets really hot we aren't going to wait to bring in Special Operations to Marquette Park. Last year we called in SOG a little late and got behind the eight ball. This year I'm calling in both the Mounted Unit and Bike Patrol. They can be all over that park and prevent any little skirmishes from even beginning.

Ford City Mall has had an upsurge in burglaries lately...Simmons and Hardesty I want you to concentrate on patrolling that area for the next few nights. Unless you get a radio assignment, I want you to saturate the place—high visibility patrol—use your blue lights if you want."

"Okay sarge."

"One other item...Officer Tameeka Swanson has reported in tonight for her first tour of duty here at The Lawn. Swanson graduated from the Academy last week, and will be working Beat 811 with Officer Stone as her Field Training Officer. Anything you'd like to say Officer?"

"I'm just very happy to be a police officer, and glad to finally be out of the Academy. I am looking forward to working with all of you. My only concern is trying to stay awake all night!"

Mac looked over his glasses at her from the podium, "I don't know what they told you at the Academy officer, but you won't have any problem staying awake. Your FTO, Officer Stone, has always had one of the highest arrest totals in the District. He'll make sure that sleeping will be the least of your concerns. That's all I have—any questions...?"

The Hammer spoke up. "Yeah Sarge, I've got one...What's the deal with Shannon lettin' his partner get killed? Shouldn't they have waited for backup or maybe got a warrant and used an arrest team to go after the guy?"

Not wanting to lose his temper, Mac paused. "Wait a second Rosato, first of all, Officers Shannon and O'Hara went up against a vicious thug who had no qualms about hurting or killing people—he had no conscience. Secondly, they were confronted with a hostage situation, one in which they were able to save the victim. Their original plan was to have an arrest warrant issued, and then serve it at the guy's home early in the morning with an arrest team. Before that could happen, things went sideways on them. The investigation is still pending and Officer Shannon has not given his official statement yet. Ostensibly, the shooting team tells me that it looks like a good shooting—both of them performed admirably, they saved a life and I will more than likely recommend them both for Citations of Valor. I am not going to allow you to make any disparaging remarks about a man that is mourning the loss of a dear friend and fallen fellow officer... You should be mourning his death as well. Do I make myself clear?"

"Yeah...it just seems odd to me that here's these two guys that get on the Tac Team because they're supposedly such great cops, and then a couple of weeks later one of them gets killed. I thought they had each other's backs," he remarked snidely.

"Rosato if I have to tell you again to keep your mouth shut, I'll be making a call downtown to OPR (Office of Professional Review). Now if you don't want to have your life put under a microscope, heed my warning. You have enough on your plate after your behavior with your friend and her drunk driving arrest; your behavior and attitude that night was less than admirable. Do you read me Officer?'

"Loud and clear sarge."

"As far as any burial arrangements and the like, Headquarters will keep us informed so check the bulletin board before your tour of duty each night. There will also be a ceremony to retire Officer O'Hara's badge, and then further down the road we will have his named inscribed on the Police Memorials both here in Chicago and over in Washington, DC at the National Memorial. I expect that we will send an official contingent to accompany his wife and children. That's it...dismissed."

Rosato breezed out of the squad room, making sure that he avoided Mac. He'd had a bad taste in his mouth from Shannon and O'Hara ever since they got the Tac assignment, which should have been his, and then pinched his girlfriend for DUI. They were lucky that Mac was around the night that he came in to confront them. He was all set to smack Shannon around and teach him a lesson. But he meant what he said when he told Pete that "payback was a bitch." Rosato would wait patiently for the opportune time, but revenge would happen—sooner or later. No one screws over The Hammer and gets away with it.

<u>21</u>
Mom and Dad

"Hello."

"Pete, this is Mac, am I calling at a bad time, how are you son?"

"Hi Mac, I'm doing okay...I guess. Beth decided to go to work rather than hang around the house with me. I guess that I'm probably not the best company right now."

"Well, I hope that you are doing as well as can be expected; Shirley and I have been praying for you ever since the shooting occurred. You know that our door is always open if you need anything—anything at all—but especially if you need a place to escape or need to talk. These last few years with both of us being on mids together has given me the opportunity to see the kind of person that you are. I respect and admire the manner in which you conduct yourself on the job and in your personal life as well. I don't know if I'm out of line saying this Pete, but you are like a son that I never had. In fact, you and Joe made being on mids enjoyable. Just remember...I am here for you."

"Thanks Mac, I appreciate that more than you will ever know. Joe and I felt the same toward you and Shirley. Before all of this happened, it's somewhat eerie yet comforting at the same time, but the way that you sometimes look at me reminds me of my dad."

"You know Pete, I know that you parents are deceased, and if I'm prying please stop me, but what happened?"

"No, you're not—it's okay to ask, you're like family. A few years after I went on the job my parents finally decided to take the honeymoon that they never had. When they were married my dad was working full-time at his business and couldn't really be away from it for any period of time. My mom was trying to finish her degree and couldn't be gone more than a weekend, so they just went to the local Holiday Inn for a couple of nights. The years passed by so quickly that before they knew it, Lisa and

I were grown and out of the house. They decided to go to Hawaii; my mom had always wanted to visit there anyway, so they celebrated their 25th Anniversary by taking the trip. They had a great time in Waikiki and decided to visit Maui as well. Unfortunately the shuttle plane from Oahu to Maui got caught in a horrific cloudburst and was hit by wind shear. The flight plunged into the ocean killing all 19 passengers aboard."

"Oh Pete, that must have been terrible for you and Lisa."

"It was; we were both devastated by the fact that we lost both of them at them at the same time. But our faith helped us through the hard times and frankly, we looked on the bright side—they both went to be with the Lord together, neither had to mourn the loss of the other."

"Your faith sustained you. I can tell that it plays a pivotal role in your life. I wish that more of our officers were like you."

"Well, I've had so many supportive friends…in particular Joe. We had known each other for so long, having gone through school together and the Army, and then eventually going on the job together. His loss is so difficult to accept. Yet I feel that I am being selfish when I think of how Susan and the boys must be feeling."

"Don't think that way son, we're all hurting. But death is part of the plan that our Lord has for all of us. It's not easy to accept, but we must grieve and then move on."

"I'll try."

"I took a call from Reverand Dean, the Police Chaplain. As you know he's part of the Department's Post Critical Incident Program. You're free to call him and set up a time to sit down and talk about the shooting and its aftermath. It's all sponsored and supported by Headquarters. You can avail yourself of his help now or anytime in the future. I suggest that you take him up on that offer."

"Yeah, I think I will. Dean is a good man; he's always been there for us cops when we're down. I don't know how he keeps his own head on straight with all of the carnage and evil that he must see each day."

"The Reverand is strong...I've talked with him several times, he's one of us."

"Mac, when am I supposed to give my statement?"

"Well, that's another reason why I'm calling. I got a call from the Chief of Patrol's office; they want to know if you're ready yet. If so they will send a team out from HQ to take your statement. They realize that it's only been a couple of days since the incident, and they want you to know that if you need another day or two to compose your thought you've got it."

"No, I'm ready...I really want to get it out of the way."

"Okay. You have the option of either going to HQ or having them come out to the station."

"Will they come out on mids? I'd like to have you in the room while I give the statement. Besides, I haven't been sleeping at night."

"I'm sure they will accommodate your request. Let me put a call into them and I'll get back with you on the details."

"Thanks Sarge."

"Call me if there's anything else I can do for you son...it doesn't have to pertain to the job."

"I will Mac...I will."

Mac's call put me in a better frame of mind. I got dressed and headed over to Queen's; I needed some quiet time with the Lord. I walked inside the church and made my way to the front pew. Getting down on my knees I closed my eyes...*"Lord, I know that I've had questions about my faith these last few days—forgive me for doubting that You are the one in control, not me. I pray that you will strengthen my faith and resolve. Help me to comfort my dear friend Susan and her family. Lord, I am having second thoughts about my life right now. Should I even continue with police work, or was this incident a sign from you that I should move on to other things? I'm confused Lord; please clear my mind...set me straight on whatever path will lead me to You and the Father. And if it be your will that I remain a police officer, I pray that you will keep St. Michael in front, in back, and beside me at all times. Amen."*

$\underline{22}$
Office Intervention

"Beth, do you have the file on the Evergreen Park client? Beth...?"

"Oh...sorry Patty. Uh, yes, I have it; I'm working on the numbers for the monthly deductions. I should be finished with it by later today."

She had dozed off while working at her desk. The past few days with Pete home at night life had been miserable. The both of them hardly slept. There was an uneasy silence that was as deafening as the roar of the ocean. They walked around the house trying to stay out of each other's way, speaking only when necessary. To Beth it seemed like the strange vacuum that was created just seconds before a tornado was about to touch down. She was certain that he knew something, but he wasn't giving her any clues.

Last night she had gone over to Susan's house and stayed for about thirty minutes, but Susan's parents had decided to stay to help with the boys and there was what seemed like an impenetrable shield that surrounded the family. They had turned into themselves to protect everyone from the terrors of the outside world.

After she left, she stopped at the liquor store and bought a pint of vodka. She was no longer comfortable drinking around others, or even wanting anyone else's company while she drank. She sat in her car in the lot, finishing half the bottle before she even knew what happened. That was enough to give her a buzz. By the time she got home, Pete was in the shower so she hopped into bed without having to talk to him.

Patty jolted her back..."Beth, what's wrong? You seem to be slipping away from me again."

"Sorry, I thought that I was on the road back Patty. After our talk, I resolved to tell Pete everything; I even talked with our pastor about it. But then Joe was killed and it swept everything up into a windstorm that has completely blown away my plans. I tried to talk with Pete but he refuses to discuss anything until he clears things up with the shooting.”

“Do you want to talk now?”

“Yes, but not with you! Wait...that didn’t come out right. I want to talk with Pete and just get all of this off my chest. At this point I don’t know how it can get any worse than it already is. We live in the same house, but separately if you know what I mean.”

“Is that alcohol I smell on your breath...are you drinking during the day again?”

“Just a couple to steady my nerves—I’m so on edge over all of this.”

“That’s it. Let’s go!”

“Where?”

“Down to the coffee shop for coffee and a sandwich...and I’m not taking no for an answer. I love you Beth, and I am not going to be complicit in you ruining your health and your career. If I have to threaten you with going to Mr. Bingham, I will. You either straighten out your life and not show up here with booze on your breath, or I spill the beans. Deal...?”

“Yes...deal.”

“Okay, let’s go.”

She sat with Patty for over an hour; it was good medicine for her. She had half a sandwich and several cups of coffee, which made her feel much better. She decided that as soon as Pete was done with giving his statement, for better or worse, she was going to tell him. If it meant that it would end her marriage, so be it. Their life was in a shambles now; it had never been worse than it had been the last few months. She was tired—just so sick of the pain, the hiding, the lies, the shame. If it was God’s will that she and Pete split, then nothing that Beth could do would change that now.

When she got off the train and found her car in the commuter lot, she was tempted to stop and buy a pint of vodka. As she headed in the direction of the liquor store she sent up a prayer...*"Father please take this urge from me. Help me to stay sober and be the woman that I need to be for my family and myself."*

The store was now a block away on her right, but at that moment the need to have a drink passed. Thankfully Beth drove by the store and continued home.

<u>23</u>
Traffic Court

Sally and her boyfriend, The Hammer, exited the Dan Ryan Expressway enroute to the Daley Center Traffic Court. Sal had a plan that would save his girl "big bucks" by not needing to retain a lawyer to represent her. This was to be Sally's first appearance to answer the DUI and other traffic charges. Normally a prudent person would have a lawyer present to answer such serious allegations, but Sal had a scheme in mind that he was confident would clear Sally of all charges.

They parked at an expired meter on the street, The Hammer liked to use his police sticker in the windshield to keep from getting parking tickets written on his vehicle. It was both unethical and illegal, but Sal figured that he was deserving of special treatment. They walked two blocks to the building on Washington Street, and as they made their way up to Room 402 Sal gave her last minute instructions.

"Remember, you have to *demand* that the judge hear the case today. With Joe dead, and Pete on administrative leave, there's no officer present to testify against you—no officer—no case. He has no choice but to dismiss the charges!"

"What if he refuses? "

"He can't, he has to hear it—it's your right as a citizen to have your case heard. Remember, be forceful about it and don't' forget to tell him that your insurance company has taken care of all of the damages. I'm tellin' you, it's open and shut...you're going to walk on this one."

It was nine o'clock and the courtroom was about half full of defendants, the other half were lawyers. The first cases that were called were those in which the defendants, all represented by attorneys, were requesting continuances. This is the normal sequence of events. The first couple of court dates are for the attorneys to file motions, either motions for continuance or perhaps even motions to dismiss. It's rare that in Major Violation/DUI Court a case is heard on the initial appearance.

The next group of cases involved those in which the lawyers had previous discussions with the prosecutor and both parties have agreed upon a plea. Generally a defendant will admit to a reduced charge, just to get a disposition on his case. He may admit to reckless driving, which carries a heavy fine and maybe thirty to sixty days license suspension, rather than plead to DUI which can mean his license can be taken for a year or more, depending on how many previous charges he may have had.

It was getting close to eleven o'clock and both Sally and The Hammer were becoming impatient. The Hammer walked up to the clerk. "Hey brother, how you doin'? "

Hammer pulled his police ID from his back pocket. "I'm Officer Rosato, 8th District; I'm here with my friend who has a DUI. I'm on mids man, any chance of her case getting' called pretty soon?'

The clerk, an elderly black gentleman with almost thirty years seniority in the Courts, took umbrage with The Hammer's approach.

"Sir, this area is off limits to the public; it's reserved for attorneys and officers. Please go back to your seat. Your friend's case will be called in the order that is most convenient to the judge."

Becoming indignant, The Hammer raised his voice, "Hey man, I told you, I am a cop. What's goin' on here?"

"Sir, I believe you when you say that you are an officer. However, you also told me that you are here with your friend, meaning that you are not here in an official capacity. Please return to your seat, this area is off limits to you."

At that moment the judge looked over to see what the commotion was all about. "Mr. Randolph, is there a problem there?"

"No sir, just this gentleman inquiring about a case."

The judge looked over at Sal..."Sir this is my courtroom, I don't appreciate interruptions. I have a full case load to get through. Unless you are either an attorney, or a police officer testifying in one of these cases you need to return to the seating area."

"Sir, I am a cop, that's what I'm trying to explain to this guy."

Now the judge was becoming very distracted. "For your information, that 'guy' is a Clerk of the Court, one who has been in the service of the City of Chicago for thirty years. He is an invaluable part of this process, but more importantly, he is a dear friend of mine. I will not tolerate any disrespect toward him or this court. Are you testifying in a case today?"

"No your honor, I'm here with a friend."

"Then if you are not here testifying on behalf of the State, you need to clear this area immediately and go back to your seat. If you fail to obey, I will hold you in contempt and order the Sheriff to put you in a holding cell. Is that clear officer?"

"Yes sir."

"Good. Mr. Randolph proceed calling the rest of the docket."

"Yes your honor."

Two hours later, after the court had recessed for lunch, the clerk called Sally's case..."State of Illinois vs. Sally Ruggeri."

Sally wasn't feeling as confident as when they first arrived at the court this morning. Sal's big mouth had probably hurt her chances of ever getting any kind of break from this judge. With much trepidation, Sally put on her best face and approached the bench. She hoped that maybe the mini-skirt, low cut blouse, and spiked heels would make an impression on the judge—maybe distract him enough to make a call in her favor.

"Miss Ruggeri, you are charged with DUI and leaving the scene of an accident. How do you plead?"

"Well your Honor, the cops that arrested me aren't here so can I be dismissed?"

"Miss Ruggeri, I'm not interested in anything right now other than hearing how you plead to the charges—do you plead guilty or not guilty? Do you have an attorney ma'am?"

"No judge, my boyfriend said that I wouldn't need one because the cops aren't here to testify against me."

"Who is your boyfriend?"

Sal got up from the chair and made his way to the front. "That would be me judge."

"What is your name officer?"

"Sal Rosato, sir—8th District."

"Well Officer Roasato, do you have a license to practice law in the State of Illinois?"

"No your honor, but I've been to traffic court enough times to know that if there are no witnesses present to testify against the person charged, then the case must be dismissed."

"Counselor, what's the status on the arresting officer?"

The prosecutor looked at her case file and after several seconds of review answered. "Judge we received a call from 8th District Desk Sergeant Ed McNamara. The sergeant advised us that the officers involved in this arrest were recently involved in a shooting. The incident took one officer's life; the other is on routine administrative leave. Sgt McNamara requested a 30 day continuance so that the surviving officer could resume active duty."

"Counseler, inasmuch as these are extraordinary circumstances surrounding the testifying officer, I will grant that request by the State for a 30 day, no, make that a 60 day continuance. Mr. Randolph, set a date for two months from today. Miss Ruggeri in the meantime I suggest that you retain 'competent' representation. My brief review of your file indicates a need for professional advice. As for you Officer Rosato, in the future if you cause any other disruption in my courtroom, I will most definitely hold you in contempt. That's all; see the clerk for your next court date."

On the drive home The Hammer was steaming like a lobster in a pot of boiling water. "Damn that judge...damn Mac. Now we're in it for the long haul. You're gonna have to get a mouthpiece, who knows how much the shyster will charge us."

"Don't you know anybody Sal?"

"Yeah, but not good ones...somebody that can represent you in front of that guy. Now he's going to be out for blood."

"I don't have the money for a lawyer, what am I going to do? The beauty shop hasn't been exactly pullin' in big money lately."

"I know...listen, I'll think of something. At least we've got a couple of months to get our act together."

"You know that judge is liable to take my license away..."

"Yeah, I know. Damn that Shannon... But if he's not around the next time your case comes up, then the judge has no choice but to throw it out."

Sal's evil mind kicked into overdrive for the remainder of the trip to the South Side. The Evil One found an opening in this mortal and was slowly planting seeds of hate and destruction. Satan found this one to be easier than Devil Man—this one was focused on one thing—*Revenge.*

"The thief (Satan) does not come except to steal, and to kill, and to destroy" (John 10:10).

<u>24</u>
Detective Robert Gusberti —The Inquisition

I was looking forward to this day, the one where I would finally give my statement regarding the night of Joe's death. The last week had been one of the worst in my life. The death of my friend and partner was just now becoming reality for me—he was gone—forever. I visited Susan a couple of times since the shooting, but she seemed distant, out of touch. Not that I could blame her. One day her life was that which dreams are made of; the next day everything that anchored her life was gone. Sure the boys were still there, but the glue that held all the pieces together was now missing. The logical now became illogical, dreams and hopes for the future were now just like burning candles trying to survive a strong draft. There was no more safety net for Susan, no more blanket for her to wrap around herself when she became anxious or afraid. She now faced the world with two small boys in tow who still wondered when daddy was coming home.

The funeral and burial were a blur. The crowds at the church and at the cemetery were just overwhelming. As Beth and I sat in the front pew with Susan, her four sons and both sets of parents, I still felt a sense of responsibility for having caused all of the sorrow that crushed us all like a humid Chicago day in August. We all broke down several times during the ceremonies, particularly at the gravesite. The finality of it all hit home when they lowered Joe's casket into the burial plot. St Mary's Cemetery was teeming with cops from all over the region. There were even contingents from New York and Boston. When the Emerald Society Bagpipers played, there wasn't a dry eye to be found anywhere. And then, just as quickly as it began, it was over. We were alone again.

I felt guilty about not paying much attention to Beth. She was trying her best to comfort me, yet I knew that she was battling her own demons. I didn't have a good feeling about our future, something was amiss...something that had hold of both our souls. Was it Satan, or just both of us not listening to each other and to God? I'm not sure, but whatever the reason was I had to face it head on.

It was ten o'clock when I walked into the station. "Hey Shannon, how are you doing?" asked the desk sergeant from the third watch. The afternoon shift was still on duty. The early midnight crew would relieve them at eleven and midnight.

"I'm okay sarge. I've got an interview tonight with the homicide dicks from headquarters. Are they here yet?"

"Yeah, they're in the conference room with Mac—they're waiting for you."

"Thanks sarge."

"No problem. Hey listen Shannon; I just want to tell you how sorry I am about Joe. I know that you two were close and that his death is a tremendous loss. Just so you know, I think that you guys did a helluva job that night. We're all proud of you."

"Man...that means a whole lot. I've been beating myself up over this ever since it happened. Thank you for your kind words...God bless you brother."

I made my way down the hall to the conference room. I saw Mac sitting with two suits that I didn't recognize. Mac jumped up and grabbed my hand to shake it.

"Hi Pete, are you feeling up to this tonight?"

"Definitely Mac, I need to move on. I think sitting around has been the worst thing that I could have done. I've got to get back to doing something before I lose my mind."

"Good. When we're done here don't leave before you see me. I have to talk to you."

"Okay Mac."

Mac pointed to a male detective, "Pete, this is Detective Bobby Gusberti."

I shook Gusberti's hand. He was mid 30s, Italian, lean runner-like build with thick curly hair and a firm handshake. He looked like a guy that could take care of himself.

"Good to meet you sir."

"And this is Detective Angela Montoya."

"Nice to meet you ma'am."

Montoya was older, looked like late 40's, a little plump but definitely a cop. She exuded confidence from her handshake to her demeanor. Montoya spoke first...

"Officer Shannon, we're here to take your statement about the events that took place on the night that the subject, Richard Hatch, and Officer O'Hara were killed. We can do this one of two ways, whichever you are most comfortable with. You can just tell us what happened, starting from the time that you initially saw Hatch on that night, or we can ask you questions and lead you through the process."

"I prefer to just tell the story from start to finish. Afterward you can ask for any details that I may have not made clear."

"That will be fine Officer. Just so you know, we will be recording this interview for the purpose of accuracy and transcription at a later date. Once the statement is transcribed, you will be asked to read the entire document, initialing each page, and then signing and dating it at the end."

I sat down next to Mac, and began my statement from the point when we first saw Devil Man pull over to where Blaz and Dee were working. Once I began to tell the story, I felt as if I was actually re-living the events. I must have talked uninterrupted for close to an hour. When I got to the point where I found Joe lying on the ground, I lost it.

Mac put his arms around my shoulders to comfort me. "Pete, it's okay son, it's okay. You did your best. You reacted based on your training and your instincts. Any one of us here in this room would have done the same thing. Joe's death was an unfortunate event that was no one's fault except the shooter. Let it go now Pete...let it go."

Detective Gusberti spoke up. "Officer Shannon, was it your intention to wait to arrest the subject on a warrant?"

"Yes. We had tentatively arranged to serve the warrant along with Area One once they had the paper in hand."

"So this shooting was avoidable or unavoidable in your opinion?"

"Wait a minute."

I looked at Gusberti hard, wondering what angle he was trying to work here.

"What are you driving at?"

Gusberti put his pen down on the table, "It just seems to me that you would have been better off waiting and hitting this guy with more bodies and firepower on the following day."

I was getting angry now, and turned my body so that I was facing Gusberti directly. "Did you read any of the reports from that night Detective?"

"Yes I did."

"Then you know that this guy had a gun and was holding a female hostage, threatening to shoot her. We had to take action to save her life."

Gusberti squared off toward me in his chair.

"Was this female a hooker?"

"Yes she was," I said. "She was instrumental in allowing us to develop intel on this guy to begin with. We would not have had any vehicle or physical description on this guy if it was not for her help."

"Did you know that Area Two detectives arrested Jesse Trout?" asked Gusberti.

"Yes, he's the guy that worked for the carpet cleaners, and he was the common thread through all of the robberies."

"That's right Officer. He gave us all of the information that we needed to solve this crime spree, including Hatch's partner, Maurice

Lucas. We could have taken them both down the next day."

Mac stood up. "Detective Gusberti, I don't like the direction in which this interview is going. You and your partner are here to take a statement. This is not an adversarial proceeding, but you are attempting to make it one.   Officer Shannon has given you all of the facts surrounding the night in question. He's answered your questions. As far as I'm concerned he has complied with what our police procedures require him to do."

Mac started to push his chair into the table. "Detective Montoya, do you have anything further to ask this officer?"

"No sergeant and I apologize for my partner's inappropriateness. He has been in the unit a total of five months, and apparently he has yet to discover the difference between friend and foe. We are done here. Officer Shannon, my condolences on the death of your partner. I looked through his personnel file—he was one of our best."

Gusberti and Montoya gathered their equipment and walked out into the hallway. Just then The Hammer was reporting in for the early midnight shift. He spotted Gusberti down the corridor.

"Hey Bobby, how u doin'?"

Mac and I walked out of the conference room and saw Rosato and Gusberti shaking hands. It was obvious that these two knew each other well.

"You all done taking the 'hero's' statement?"

Lowering his voice, Gusberti replied, "Cool it man, it's not a good time. I'll call you later."

Rosato took the hint. "Yeah, right, see you later."

The Hammer ducked into the next hallway and Mac steered me toward the Supervisors' Room.

"Well it's obvious to me that Rosato and Gusberti were up to no good, and that Rosato must have encouraged his pal to give you some grief in there. I will call Montoya later to get a handle on this whole thing, but right now I've got something to give you."

Mac opened the gun safe, took out my Glock pistol, and handed it to me. "The Chief told me to tell you that you're cleared to return to duty. It's your call. If you want some more time, he's authorized another five days admin, otherwise I've got you back on the schedule for tomorrow night."

I took the gun from Mac and slid my belt through the loops on the holster. "Mac, I'm ready. In fact, I'll start tonight if you can work that out."

"No, tomorrow will be fine Pete, but there's one more thing."

What's that?"

"I've got to put you back in uniform for a while until Captain Steele picks a partner for you on Tac. He's at the Academy all week at a management school so I haven't been able to sit down with him and draw up a matrix."

I had not even thought about that angle. Going to work without Joe was going to be a huge hurdle that I would have to get over.

"Who am I working with?"

"I'm teaming you up with Officer Marilyn Benson. She's worked mostly afternoon shift, but she went on mids a couple periods ago so that she can work on her MBA down at UIC Chicago during the day. She's a good cop; been on the job about ten years and did a couple years in the Army beforehand."

"Oh yeah, I've seen her a few times. In fact, the last time we had that big disturbance at Marquette Park with the skinheads, I saw her take a guy down with a rear choke and cuff him like she was roping a steer at the rodeo."

Mac headed out toward the desk area to relieve the afternoon sergeant. "It will work out Pete, you might even find that you like working with her. If not we'll make a change. The important thing is to get you back in the saddle so that you can move forward."

"I agree Mac, thanks."

On the drive home I felt a wave of relief wash over me. I had been dreading giving this statement, but other than the episode at the end, it actually proved to be somewhat cathartic. Obviously The Hammer had tried to have his buddy trip me up on my statement, but I got through it. What was wrong with Rosato? Was he that vindictive that he would want to cause me grief or harm? I made a mental note to be vigilant around him in the future. The Hammer was a loose cannon that could go off unexpectedly.

My immediate challenge was now to fix whatever was wrong with Beth and me. I needed to right my sail now; I was adrift and needed someone to throw a line to. Beth had always been that person, but now I had my doubts. Would the choppy seas we've been sailing prove to be too much for us, or could we ask the Lord to calm the storm just as he did in the boat with the apostles?

<u>25</u>
Time For The Truth

I plopped down on the sofa to get a few hours sleep. I didn't want to disturb Beth; it was her morning to sleep in. She enjoyed Saturdays, taking her time waking up and reading the Sun-Times over coffee. I started a pot and turned on the news. One of the lead stories on Fox concerned the latest search for a new Superintendent of Police. The search was apparently over; a replacement had been found, someone from the FBI. I had mixed emotions, hoping that someone from within the department would be chosen. But this guy's background was solid; maybe his new ideas would breathe fresh life into the job. At least we had to give him a chance.

"Mornin' hon," Beth appeared in the kitchen and made her way over to the counter to pour herself some coffee. "Want me to throw on some eggs and turkey sausage?"

I wasn't really hungry, but the fact that she wanted to eat seemed like a good thing. "Sure, that sounds great."

Beth busied herself with cooking while I continued to watch the news and drink my coffee.

"Oh, how did it go last night...did you give your statement?"

"Yes. And except for a near confrontation with one of the dicks, I feel pretty good about it—especially the fact that it's over with."

Beth brought the two plates over to the table. "What do you mean confrontation?"

Well, I didn't know it at the time but one of the detectives, a guy named Bob Gusberti, was apparently a friend of Rosato. He must have known that his buddy was going to be there for my statement, and convinced him to give me a rough time. He was trying to get me to say that the shooting could have been avoided if we just would have waited to take the Devil Man down the following day."

"That's crazy Pete. You and Joe saved that woman's life by taking action when you did."

"I know. Thankfully Mac was there and diffused the whole matter before it turned ugly."

"Well I'm glad that's over for you. I was praying that once you gave your statement you could return to some sense of normalcy." She leaned in and gave me a kiss.

"Thank you Beth. I'm going back to work tomorrow night. Mac gave me the word last night. The only change is that I'll be back in uniform for awhile until the WC finds a replacement for Joe, but I'm thankful to be getting back to doing something useful."

Beth began to get anxious and although she had eaten only a few bites, she immediately lost her appetite. Was now a good time to tell Pete, or should she wait a couple more days?

"Beth...now that I've got most of the admin stuff surrounding the shooting out of the way, I'd like to focus on you and me. I think that we need to put all of our cards on the table and see where we stand with each other. We need to talk; we can't go on like we have been. Are you comfortable with doing that now?"

Beth had her answer. Dear Father in heaven, strengthen me, let me speak the truth to the man that I love, but whom I've hurt. Let your will be done, not mine, and help me unburden myself of all the lies and deceit...now.

"Yes Pete, we do need to talk...I need to talk."

"Good. I have been worried about you lately. I want to tell you that I was wrong for hounding you about having children. I never should have pressured you like that. I was so busy with the job and school, that I missed a lot of things that others picked up on."

Beth gave me a quizzical look. "What do you mean?"

"Joe and Susan told me that they sensed that you had developed an eating disorder. When I asked Father Mike about it, he said that he also felt that you did...that you were looking anorexic. I talked with Dr. Grossman at Little Company about you as well—he said that it sounded like anorexia."

"Pete, I can't believe that you would talk about me behind my back."

"Beth, they brought the subject up; it came totally out of the blue. But once they started telling me what they'd observed, you hardly eating anything when we all went out for dinner or at cookouts, and your increased use of alcohol, it all made sense to me."

She shifted uncomfortably in her chair now looking like a hurt child...

"I don't blame you Beth, I blame myself. I know that I'm the reason why our marriage hasn't been the best lately. I have been ignoring you and your needs. I used to look at Joe's kids and wish that we had our own. Their family seemed so happy and full of love. I wanted that for us. Now, I'm not so sure. After the pain and sorrow that I witnessed after Joe's death, I don't think I could bear for you and any of our children to have to go through something like that. If you don't want to have any children, I can live with that. All that's important to me is that you and I find the love that we somehow misplaced—that we get back to the partnership that we once enjoyed."

It was clear to Beth that Pete was on the wrong track, blaming himself for all of their marital woes. This would be the perfect opportunity for her to take the easy way out and not admit to her infidelity. She hesitated for only an instant before she felt the resolve to speak up.

"Pete, it's not you honey, it's not any of your fault. It's all my fault. All the problems that we've been having lately, the arguments about getting pregnant, none of it has anything to do with you."

"What do you mean babe?"

"You're going to hate me when I tell you this, and I can't say that I blame you. And if after what I have to say you no longer want me in your life, I will understand. Remember when I went on that business trip to Chicago, and you and Joe went to Detroit for the Police Olympics?"

"Yes, what about it?"

She talked without interruption for fifteen minutes, not holding anything back. She saw the pain in his eyes, the tears, and she felt his heart breaking. By the time she was finished, she was exhausted, crying, her body totally spent.

"Beth, no...how could you...? I never expected that you would do anything like that to me—to us. I have never even thought about being with anyone else, and I thought that you felt the same way. "

"Pete I do, I love you more than anything. You don't understand...I've regretted that moment from the time that I allowed myself to be duped into that situation. I was weak; I didn't turn to the Lord for strength. I let myself be tempted and lost every ounce of self-respect that I had. I couldn't face you after that. Anytime that you brought up getting pregnant, I thought about the miscarriage and that brought back all the horror of that night. I have been dreading this day for so long... My only escape has been through drinking, and now even that has become a problem and it no longer comforts me. I had no direction and no control over anything. I tried to gain some peace by controlling my weight and that just turned into another cross to bear. Pete...I'm lost, I don't know where to turn, who to go to for help. Without you my life has meaning or direction, how can I ever regain your faith and trust?"

I was reeling. I couldn't process what my wife had just revealed to me. I was mad, but not at her. I was mad at whoever it was that had the nerve to sully our marriage. I felt disappointed in Beth, that she would disrespect the vows that we made to each other in front of God. How could she have done this to me...to us?

Beth got up from her chair. "Pete, can you forgive me? Can we somehow work this out and start over again? I'm so sorry about everything...you're my whole world. Please help me to somehow make this better for us."

She tried to put her arms around me but I shrugged her off.

"I don't know what to say. I can't believe that you would do that. Are you still in contact with this guy?"

"No, no, I haven't' seen or talked to him since that night. He's evil...he's Satan. I curse the day that I ever met him!"

"I just don't know Beth. You drop this bombshell on me after Joe's death and expect that I'm just going to say...fine, apology accepted? No, it doesn't work that way. I need some time to sort through all of this."

"So what does this mean for us Pete?"

"It means that I need some time—some space."

"I understand," she said. "Tomorrow I'll pack some things and stay with my folks for awhile. If I stay here, I know that it will make you uncomfortable. You have nowhere to go; I have my parents. I will stay away for as long as you want me to Pete. If that means forever, I will very regretfully accept that. I know that I broke your heart babe, but just know this: *I broke mine too.* I've been slowly dying inside since that night. I lost everything, including my faith. But I've recently found my voice again, and I've asked Him for forgiveness, just as I've asked you. I don't know if our marriage can be saved, but I'm asking God for his help so that I can climb out of the abyss that I've fallen into. Just know that I never stopped loving you Pete, and I never will."

I was crushed. The world had no meaning anymore. I walked out the door and just wandered around in a daze for several hours. The one thing that had always been a rock for me was my marriage. It gave me joy and comfort whenever everything else in life made no sense. I could always come home to Beth, and just hold onto her shutting out the static of everyday life. Marriage was our refuge, our safe place. Now that was gone. Now my best friend and my wife were gone. It was dark, and although I could see people in their homes as I wandered down the neighborhood streets, I felt more alone that I had ever felt before in my life.

26
The Overhear

The "Evil One" wanders the streets of the world looking for opportunities. He is especially vigilant for those that are weak or experiencing problems in their life. Once he gets inside their soul, it's difficult for any mortal to resist his power. He's relentless; he will smother his target with temptation until he wears them down. Once they accept or relent, Satan has gained another disciple. His goal is to create an army large enough to battle St. Michael and his contingent of angel warriors. He holds a grudge. He is full of resentment and hatred toward the Almighty, and will stop at nothing to get revenge for having been cast out of Heaven and damned to the fire forever.

The Devil is evil personified. He sends others out of hell to prowl the earth for more converts. They constantly test human faith in an effort to turn them away from God. Satan set his sights on what should have been one of Michael's Warriors—Officer Sal Rosato. He was certain that this weak human being was now under his control. He would use him to hunt and destroy another believer.

Sal and his girlfriend were out for the night. They were frustrated and upset over Sally's traffic court appearance. They had been at Fox's Pub on 99th and Western for the past two hours drinking more than their share of beer; and neither Sal nor his girlfriend were feeling any pain.

Sal ordered another round for them both. "I've had it with those guys in the 8th District man. Mac has been out to get me forever. That last shooting that I was involved in should have earned me an Award of Valor, instead it got me busted back down to street cop. Shannon, Mister Super Cop Hero, gets his partner killed and everybody wants to make him Cop of the Year!"

Slurring her words, Sally tried to comfort her man. "Sal honeee, why don't you just transfer out of there? Why don't you go over to the 22nd District, they'd respect you there?"

"Those guys aren't any better," Sal said as he chugged half his glass of Coors Lite. "They're all goodie two shoes types, they're all afraid to bust heads. I don't know what kinda cops we got around this city anymore."

Fox's was a popular bar on the South Side of Chicago. It was a great restaurant also, serving some of the best pizzas and beef sandwiches in the area. A lot of cops liked to use it as their watering hole. For a bar owner in a city like Chicago, if the cops liked your place, you were set. You had a steady clientele with built in security as well.

This particular night, Lt. Eric Ottney from the Training Academy happened to be seated at the bar having a sandwich and a beer with his son Mark; he was within earshot of The Hammer. Ottney was a 25 year veteran cop who earned his bars on the street, having been involved in many dangerous, high-profile cases. After riding the seat of a cop car for 20 years, his expertise and knowledge of firearms resulted in the job as head of the Firearms Training Unit at The Chicago Police Academy. For the last five years he supervised and instructed every new recruit coming on the job, as well as all of the in-service training. Lt. Ottney knew Rosato only too well. He was head of the shooting review board that investigated The Hammer's last shooting incident.

Ottney had weighed all of the evidence and wrote the investigative summary, concluding that the circumstances surrounding it were questionable. Rosato used poor judgment and lethal force was not justified in that particular incident. Somehow The Hammer had called in "favors" from some influential politicians after the recommendation came down to fire him. He wound up with a thirty day suspension and demotion to police officer. Now Ottney was tuning in to what this "problem child" was spouting off about to his girlfriend.

"So what are we gonna do at the next court date baby? Am I gonna have a lawyer or not?"

"I'm workin' on that...I gotta cousin that chases traffic cases out in

Markham, been doin' it forever. He knows all the tricks on how to beat these a'holes at their own game."

"I can't pay him much..."

"Yeah, I know, I know—enough with the whining already. You're a broken record for chrisakes. I got some markers I can call in with Mario, and besides, I'm lookin' for the next court date to be the last one."

Sally fired up another Kool cigarette, and tilted her head back, blowing the smoke away from Sal. "What are you talkin' about, that Shannon's gonna be back to work by then?"

"Shannon don't know what's comin' his way. When he comes back to work, he's not gonna have his old buddy lookin out for him anymore. He's needs to watch his back—I mean really watch it from all sides. I told him that payback's gonna be a bitch. I'm tired of that holier than thou son of a bitch makin' me look bad all the time. The sooner he's gone, the better off we'll all be. Besides baby, I told you before—no cop, no case."

"Yeah...whatever. Hey, I gotta check my makeup in the ladies room, I'll be right back."

"Naw, forget about it, let's get outta here. I gotta drop you off. I know there's a card game at Bob Richard's joint tonight over on 59th Street, maybe I can make some dough."

The Hammer and Sally strutted out of the bar right past Lt. Ottney without even realizing that he was there. Ottney made a mental note to contact Pete Shannon and give him a heads up on this nut case. It could just have been the alcohol talking, or the danger may in fact be real. In any case, Shannon needed to be made aware of what Ottney had overheard this night. That kind of talk coming from a guy like Rosato could only mean trouble. Tomorrow he would call over to the WC and leave a message for Shannon to give him a call.

<u>27</u>
A New Partner

The house was quiet which I had become accustomed to before the separation, but it was a different quiet now, one that was not soothing or welcome. Beth had taken many of her things and was staying at her parents' home in Beverly. I had always liked that area on Longwood Drive where they lived. On my many runs through the varied neighborhoods on the South Side, heading down Longwood was always one of the most enjoyable areas to run. With their long driveways leading back to homes surrounded by big, beautiful trees, each house seemed like the perfect oasis in the midst of a busy, bustling, metropolis. Now the once admired avenue represented a shattered life and love.

I readied my police gear and got my uniform out of the closet. I hadn't worn it for a while, but I felt good about being back on the street in a patrol car. With so many major changes occurring in my world the past few weeks, getting back in uniform was comforting—like putting on an old pair of sweats that I had worn for years. I checked my duty bag for the tools that I might need during my tour of duty: two extra .40 caliber magazines for my Glock pistol, ASP Baton, OC Spray, two pairs of cuffs, disposable gloves, tactical mirror, two flashlights, and ballistic vest. On many days I only used a couple of these items, but the others were all at the ready in the event that I needed them.

I walked into the kitchen to make a sandwich before I headed out for the station. Glancing at the telephone I saw that there was a message on the answering machine. ***I wonder who that could be...*** Hitting the play button I heard the following message: "Pete, this is Lt. Ottney from the Academy; I got your home number from Capt. Steele. Give me a call before you go on duty tonight, I have some important information for you."

I copied down the number and dialed... "Hello."

"Lt. Ottney, this is Pete Shannon from the 8th District; you asked me to call you."

"Oh hi Pete, first my condolences to you on the loss of your partner. I reviewed the shooting report that our team made on your incident, and I think that you both did a great job. The shot that the subject took was pure luck, but that seems to be our lot as cops. We train and train and still have a tough time hitting what we want to hit in the heat of battle. These knuckle draggers whip out a gun that they've never even shot before and hit us with no problem."

"Thanks Lew."

"You're welcome. The real reason that I called was that I was in Fox's last night having a sandwich with my son. We happened to be seated at the bar, down from Officer Rosato and some blond gal with loud makeup and a short skirt. I don't think that he ever saw me because my boy was seated in between me and his friend."

"Yeah, that's his girlfriend. Unfortunately, Joe and I had to arrest her for DUI a while back; Rosato blew up at us like *we* had done something wrong."

"Well now it makes a little more sense," said Ottney. "I overheard their conversation Pete, and I have to tell you that he sounded like he was out to get even with you in some form or fashion. Now it may have been just the booze talking, they both had a few too many, but I wouldn't trust that guy to be a back up for me. In fact, if I were you I'd watch my back around him."

Great I thought, that's all I need is to have The Hammer after me. "Thanks for sharing that with me Lew, I'll be sure to be careful around him."

"No problem Pete. If you need anything from me at the Academy, don't hesitate to ask. Are you doing okay?"

Being honest I said, "Not yet, I still can't believe that it happened— that Joe is really gone. And I've got some other issues, but I'm dealing with them."

"Well, from what I know about you Pete, I'm certain that you have already asked for help, and that the first one that you probably turned to was God. I will include you in my daily prayers and ask that He comfort and strengthen you in the days ahead."

"Lieutenant..."

"Call me Eric."

"Eric, you don't know what that means to me," I said. "I do need prayers, and if I may ask, please pray for my wife as well. We are going through a rough patch right now. Thank you for everything."

"No problem, I'll pray for you both, God bless you son."

"Good-bye."

I finished my sandwich and packed some water and a couple of energy bars. It seemed odd not to look in on Beth and whisper goodbye before I left. Would we ever get back to where we were? For that matter, would we ever get back together? I still felt hurt and betrayed that she had spent the night with that guy, I don't know that I could ever forgive her for what she had done. How could she do that to me? At least I had my answer about why she was avoiding the whole "baby" issue. In retrospect, it's probably a blessing that we didn't have any kids, just more people to be hurt.

I wondered what it would be like working the streets without Joe. How would I get along with my new partner Marilyn? Would she have the instincts that Joe had, could we work in harmony? Tonight would be the first test to see if I could regroup and move on. Was police work still a viable career for me, or should I look for another one? At least I still had St.Michael in my corner. He would be my backup when all else failed. As I pulled my truck out of the garage I said the prayer to my glorious partner...

St. Michael the Archangel defend me in battle. Be my protection against the wickedness and snares of the devil. May God rebuke him, I humbly pray. And do thou, O Prince of the Heavenly Host, thrust into hell Satan and all the evil spirits who prowl about the world seeking the ruin of souls. In Jesus' name I pray...Amen.

Mac was concluding the early midnight roll call, "Before we hit the street, one more thing. Officer Shannon is back on duty tonight. The Shooting Review Board has concluded its investigation, as has the Chief of Patrol's Office. Their conclusion is that the shooting that occurred that night was justifiable, and well within our department's deadly force policy. The Chief's office also advised me that both Officers Shannon and O'Hara are recommended for the Department's Award of Valor, and Officer O'Hara will receive the Blue Star Award posthumously. Congratulations Pete. I know that our joy is tempered by the sorrow that we all feel about losing Joe. I know that I speak for the rest of the guys on mids when I say that Joe will be greatly missed."

"Thanks sarge."

"Okay, dismissed. Check your equipment and gas tanks and hit the streets."

I headed toward the rear door to go find our car. Beat 813 was a fairly large beat that included Midway Airport, businesses along 63rd Street, factories, and residential areas. It was a nice mix of many things that required good police work. Marilyn found me in the lot as I went through the vehicle. A good cop never takes his car out on the street before he does a thorough check of all the emergency equipment—lights and siren—makes sure the gas tank is full, tires are full, and then goes through the car to make sure no prisoners from the afternoon shift hid anything in the back seat area, like weapons or drugs.

Marilyn came up with her duty bag in one hand and shotgun in the other, "Well partner, for better or worse we're on graveyard shift together."

I extended my hand to her, "Marilyn, I'm glad to meet you and look forward to us working together. Mac wouldn't have put us together if he didn't think that we would make a good team. It will take some getting used to I'm sure, but if you enjoy police work as much as I do I'm certain that things will go smoothly for us."

"Thanks Pete. What the sergeant said in there about Joe goes for me also. I'm sorry for your loss, and won't even attempt to take his place. But I will tell you this—you can depend on me to have your back and to work hard each and every night. I know that you and Joe were on the Tac Team, which means you are good, aggressive cops. That's what I am as well. Just know that I'm expecting the same from you Pete. I need to know that you'll back me up when I need it."

I liked her already, putting her cards on the table and not trying to take Joe's place. "You've got it partner. I like the way this is beginning. Now let's get that shotgun in the rack and find out what's happening on Beat 813."

<u>28</u>
Officer Marilyn Benson

We rolled out of the lot heading westbound on 63rd Street. I took the wheel for the first four hours; Marilyn had the paperwork. "How 'bout a coffee?" I asked. I was about to say that's how Joe and I always started our tour, but caught myself before the words came out.

"That's a great idea," she said. "I've only been on mids a few periods; I need that caffeine in my system to stay alert. I know a Dunkin Donuts at 65th and Pulaski, the owner's name is Tommy Morse—good guy. He likes to take care of the cops when they come in, you know free cup o' joe and a donut, but I don't feel comfortable doing that. I pay for everything out here, especially when I'm on duty."

Man, so far so good I thought. Marilyn is so much like Joe and me that it's scary. "I agree. I don't think it's right for cops to use their badge to get any freebies. Besides, it looks bad to the folks in the store when they see cops getting their goods for free."

I turned south on Pulaski and headed toward Dunkin. "I'm surprised that you drink coffee, you look like an athlete; I can see that you are definitely into the iron from the look of your arms."

Marilyn smiled and said, "Thanks Pete. I do work hard at it because I think it's important that cops have a fitness program that will help keep them alive if they get involved in a situation on the street. I work out every day, regardless of the shift I'm working, or if I'm in class down at UIC. I think that being fit is just as important as being proficient with my firearm. Besides, how many people do we shoot versus how many we have to put our hands on?"

"You're a nut."

"What?"

"I said you're a nut. That's what some of the guys here call me because I place so much importance on working out and staying fit. For some reason, those of us that place a high priority on physical fitness are looked upon as strange. Are you involved in any sports?"

"Oh yeah, I compete in lots of road races—you know short ones like three and five mile distances—I also compete in bodybuilding contests a couple of times per year. I've won a couple of Police Olympic titles, and last year I placed fourth overall in the Miss Illinois Bodybuilding Contest."

"Wow, fourth....that's great!"

"Thanks Pete, after the contest I asked the judges why I didn't place any higher and they told me that I wasn't big enough. The problem is that I don't want to get too big; I think that it would interfere with my ability to do the job. I also think that some of these women are going way overboard to put on size—some of them are beginning to look like the guys. I prefer to be unquestionably feminine. I'm sure that there's steroids involved with some of them as well, but I'm not about to risk my health for that. Besides, with all of the running that I do, I burn so many calories that unless I stopped I'd never put on much size anyway."

I pulled into the lot at the donut shop. "Where do you work out?"

"Well, I live up around 111th Street, so I work out at Bally's in Oak Lawn. My training partner is on the fire department; if you think I look good, you should see her!"

"Pete, I already know that you work out religiously too. I did some checking on you when Mac informed me that you and I would be teaming up."

"Oh you did...?"

"Sure, didn't you check on me?"

"Yeah, I would have been surprised if you hadn't checked on me too; it's the sign of a good cop."

We walked into the donut shop and Marilyn introduced me to the staff; Tommy had already gone home but his wife Lisa was there to run the store until the drive thru only service became available at two am.

"Bens! How you doin' girl?" Lisa called out to Marilyn as we walked through the door. "You're still working graveyard?"

"Yeah Lisa, probably for a long while until I finish that MBA down at UIC. Hey, meet my new partner, Pete Shannon."

I shook Lisa's hand, "Nice to meet you ma'am."

"You don't need to ma'am me Pete, Lisa will be just fine."

"Okay, Lisa it is. I need two coffees to go." I threw my money on the counter and we said our goodbyes.

I looked at Marilyn quizzically, "Bens?"

"Yeah, that's my nickname; all of my friends use it. Two years ago I handled a robbery here. Tommy got beat up pretty bad, but he gave me a great description of the guy. The next night I see a suspect that's a good match for what Tommy gave me. I cuffed him and put him in the back and went over to the donut shop where Tommy made a positive ID. By the time the case was adjudicated, we had become good friends. I try to stop there a couple times per week just to check on them and to say hi."

"So, should I be calling you Bens or Marilyn?"

"Even though it's early yet, it kinda looks like Bens will be fine."

We walked back outside and got into our car. I checked the traffic on Pulaski, and then headed north. We both decided that for the first couple of days, if we didn't have a call to respond to, we would spend the time getting familiar with our beat. We needed to know the alleys, the parking lots, any parks or rec areas where there might be any gang or drug activity. We had to scope out shopping areas where car thefts or car jackings might be a problem. We also needed to talk, just to so that we could get to know each other.

"Any kids Pete? I know that you're married."

"No, no children...not yet."

"Are you planning on them?" asked Marilyn.

"I...uh... Marilyn, I'm going to be honest with you. Right now my wife and I are separated; we're going through a rough time and I'm just not sure where we're at in our marriage. We talked about children, well, mostly I talked about them. But recently something's come up that has pushed that issue way down the list of things that are important."

"Was it Joe's death?" she asked.

"That certainly didn't help matters, but no, it was something else. I'd like to say that we're working on resolving the problem, but the truth is that we're not. Or maybe I'm not. I'm just not sure where I stand right now."

She turned and looked at me, "I'm sorry to hear that. I don't know if you are a Christian, but I am. I was raised in the Catholic faith, but I'm not a very good one when it comes to following the rules like going to mass and confession. I'll occasionally attend Mass at St. Christina's on 111th. But I do have a personal relationship with Jesus Christ—I pray morning and night that He will walk with me each day, and if you'd like me to, I will include you on my prayer list each day."

Her words were like a shot of adrenaline to my tired soul. She barely knew me, but she realized that a brother officer was in trouble and in pain, and she unselfishly offered words of comfort and her prayers. This partnership was truly one ordained by Him. I was amazed that she came into my life at exactly the time when I needed a buffer against the brutal winds that were threatening to blow me off course.

"Marilyn, I would very much like for you to pray for me, and if you don't' mind, for my wife also. I just realized that she is probably hurting as much as I am. She needs prayers...*yours and mine.*"

"It's done partner."

"Beat 813, Beat eight one three."

"Go ahead squad," said Marilyn as she grabbed the clipboard to copy.

"813 check on the burglary at the factory, 5013 W. 65th Street, owner's on the scene, offender already gone."

"813, 10-4." Marilyn finished writing and prepared the incident report required for each call for service. "I guess we'll have to finish our beat recon after we check out this break in."

"One thing's certain in this area," I said as we cruised past the intersection of 63rd and Cicero, "With all of these planes landing and taking off all the time at Midway Airport, the noise is going to mask some of the burglary activity around here."

"Yeah, good point. I never thought of that Pete. You might actually be pretty good at this stuff!"

"Thanks partner...back at ya." This new partner might just work out fine, I thought.

<u>29</u>
Mac's In Trouble

We rolled through the rest of the shift without much excitement. We spotted a couple of curfew violators trying to make it home through the alleys before any cops spotted them. We wrote them up and brought them home, but their parents seemed already used to the drill and didn't seem to be very disturbed about their sons being brought home by the cops, other than having to get out of bed to answer the door. We'd likely be seeing more of their boys in the months and years ahead.

After that we prowled a few alleys along Cicero Avenue and recovered a hot car that had been partially stripped. It was an SUV sitting on cinder blocks in the middle of the alley. It probably had the fancy spinner type wheels and premium tires that many of the young kids love to put on their vehicles. It never ceased to amaze me how quickly the thieves are able to get the wheels off without being detected. If they ever thought about working legitimately, they probably had a job waiting for them in the pits at NASCAR.

We wrote a couple of tickets—one red light violator, the other an illegal u-turn. We finished up around the airport, watching throngs of still sleepy commuters park their cars and rush to catch the trains heading downtown. I guess that subconsciously I was hoping to spot Beth possibly leaving for work early, but that didn't happen. We headed back to the station, checked out with the sector sergeant, and said our goodbyes.

On the ride home I reflected on my first night back without Joe. Although tinged with some sadness and guilt, I was at least sure that this was where I needed to be—police work. It was different to be sure, working with Marilyn. She was proving to be another wise decision by friend Mac, and it proved to me that my desire for the job was still there. For the near future at least, my career would be something that gave me satisfaction and direction. I could depend on it to give me strength and motivation. My drive to help people, to save them from evil, was still strong. Now I needed to focus on my personal life. Was I going to be able to save my marriage, or had it gone so far off the track that fixing it was not possible?

I pulled into the driveway, only to be surprised by Beth's car parked inside the garage. *"What's all this about?"* I wondered aloud. I grabbed my gear and walked into the kitchen through the garage door.

"Hi Pete," she said somewhat taken aback. "I forgot a couple of things that I needed for work, so I thought that I would stop by on my way to pick them up. I hope you don't mind. I was just about to leave; I didn't expect to see you."

"You made coffee..."

"Yeah, well...I needed some. You know my folks don't drink it so there's none around the house. Besides, I thought that maybe you might like a cup when you got home."

This all came out of left field. The last thing I expected was to see Beth...here in our house... I was thrown off guard. And she made me coffee...

"Well, thank you for thinking of me. How are your folks?"

"They're upset and confused about what's going on. I told them everything; told them it was my fault and that we needed some time apart to see where we're at. Lots of crying, you know they're old school, they don't understand separations... How was your first night back?"

"It was okay Beth. I think that I can pick up the pieces and move forward."

"Good, I'm happy for you. I'm afraid that I have to leave now before I miss the train. Good bye Pete."

She walked past me to the door and I saw the tears in her eyes. She was hurting. I heard the engine start and stepped out to watch her pull away. *Why Lord, why? How could this have happened to us? Wasn't it enough that you took Joe from me... now Beth? What do you want from me...help me, please!* I resisted the urge to wave to her, and then regretted it. Ego...pride, sins that I still haven't conquered.

I felt totally exhausted now and stripped off my clothes. I fell into bed, forgetting all of my plans to work out and get some other things done. All I could think about was Beth and how we used to be. How could that have fallen apart? Was I so blind to everything that I couldn't have prevented it from happening? Was any of her infidelity my fault? I thought that I had been a good husband, but apparently I was missing something. A million questions invaded my head. I needed to find out what was wrong with me, but right now I was just too tired to do anything but sleep.

A few hours later I awoke to the sound of the phone ringing. I groggily reached over to the night stand to grab it and see who was interfering with my sleep. "Hello."

"Pete?"

"Yes, this is Pete, who's calling?"

"Pete, this is Shirley. Mac's in trouble," she said, her voice trembling, "we're at the ER at Christ Hospital. Can you please come...now? I'm afraid for him Pete; he's had a heart attack."

"Oh my God, Shirley, yes, I'll be there as quickly as I can."

I hung up the phone and threw on a pair of jeans and a tee shirt. Christ Hospital wasn't far away, 95th and Pulaski, and I could be there in ten minutes. I jumped into my truck and headed that way, praying that Mac would be okay.

I ran into the ER to find Shirley and the grandkids seated in the waiting room. She got to her feet when she spotted me and I immediately went to her and held her.

"Oh Pete, it was so quick," she sobbed. "One minute we were seated at the table with the babies for lunch, and the next thing I knew Mac was on the floor, unconscious. I called 911 right away. As soon as they got there they checked his heart and put the paddles to his chest. I couldn't watch, and I didn't want the babies to see..."

"How long have you been here?"

"About thirty minutes. I called our daughter; she's on the way. And I told her to call Fr. Bill from our church. Oh Lord...our poor grandbabies are so scared, they don't know what's going on."

I looked at the two little towheads huddled together in one chair, their arms around each other—they didn't have a clue about anything except that their Papa was sick.

"Shirley, has anyone come out to give you an update?"

"No Pete, that's what worries me."

"Okay, you take care of the two little ones. I'm going to go ask some questions and see what I can find out. We bring injured folks here all the time; chances are I may know someone on duty here now."

"You know Pete...it's funny...Mac cares so much about others, including you, that I think the events in the past few weeks have put too much of a strain on his heart."

"Shirley, Mac is one of the finest men I've ever know. Both of you are like family to me," I said as my eyes started to well up with tears. "He's one of the big reasons that I'm the man that I am today."

I walked toward the nurse's station to find out what I could. The nurse didn't look familiar to me, but I needed information quickly so I decided to ID myself.

"Ma'am, I'm Officer Shannon from the 8th District," I said as I showed her my Star. "Sgt. McNamara and I work together, is there any update on his condition? How is he doing?"

"Well officer, his vitals don't look real good at this point. Dr. Wolanska is the ER doctor on duty today. If you want to wait around here until she comes out, you can ask her yourself."

"Thanks, I'll do that."

I waited for about fifteen minutes, praying the entire time. Finally the doctor came out of the room and headed toward the nurses' station with Mac's chart.

"Dr. Wolanska, I'm Officer Pete Shannon...I work with Sgt. McNamara. Can you tell me how he's doing?"

"Are there any family members here?" she asked.

"His wife is in the waiting room with their two little grandbabies."

She was scribbling something on the chart, and when she finished she looked up at me. "Your friend has suffered a serious heart attack. The paramedics didn't have a pulse when they arrived on the scene. They were finally able to revive him after several minutes, but on the way here his heart stopped twice. He's weak and barely holding on."

It was worse than I thought. Was it possible that Mac wouldn't make it? No, I couldn't think that way—Mac was strong, he was a Viet Nam vet and a warrior on the streets of Chicago. It would take more than a heart attack to kill Mac.

"Can I go in and see him?"

"Let me suggest something," the doctor said. "I can't say with any certainty that he will survive this episode. If you would like to bring his wife in here right now, I think that would be appropriate."

I hurried back out to the waiting room and saw that Mac's daughter had arrived along with Father Bill Tindall, their pastor.

"Pete, what did you find out?" Shirley was very upset now, probably because she had relinquished control of the little ones to their mother. Caring for them had at least diverted some of her concern about Mac. She was now feeling the full impact of what had happened to her husband and best friend.

"Shirley, we need to go in there right now and see him. The doctor said that he's in bad shape, his heart stopped several times."

After hearing this Shirley grew weak and needed support from Fr. Bill. We got on either side of her and escorted her into the cubicle where Mac was at. He appeared to be semi-conscious and was tethered to several machines that were monitoring his vitals and giving him fluids.

She went up to the side of the bed and began stroking Mac's forehead..."Mac honey, it's me Shirl, can you hear me dear? You're going to be okay, everything will be fine."

The nurse spoke up, "Mrs. McNamara, he may not be able to hear or understand you. He has been drifting in and out of consciousness."

Shirley tried a couple more times to reach him, but Mac was unresponsive. Fr. Bill put on his stole and prepared to administer the Sacrament of Anointing of the Sick. He made the Sign of the Cross with blessed water, reminding us of our baptismal promise to die with Christ so that we might rise to new life with Him. He then read from Scripture and anointed Mac's head and hands with oil while he prayed over him. Fr. Bill then had all of us join him in praying the Lord's Prayer, and ended by blessing all of us.

The priest turned to Shirley, "Mac has been a good steward of the faith, and he has truly been a child of God. His life is now in the hands of the Almighty; may His will be done."

We stayed for several more minutes before the doctor had us return to the waiting room. The minutes turned into hours, and eventually the waiting room turned into a gathering of family and friends that soon overflowed into the adjoining corridors. I slipped out to the chapel to lift up my own prayer for my dear friend. I knelt down and focused on the crucifix...*Dear Lord, I know that I have doubted your sovereignty lately. I've been questioning your authority and your will, focusing on what I want, rather than what you expect of me. I humbly come to you now as your child, asking for forgiveness and imploring you to show mercy on my friend Mac. I pray that you will make Mac well again, so that he can give you praise and glory in all that he does.*

I finished at the chapel and went outside for some fresh air. I looked across the parking lot and saw Marilyn heading my way. She came up to me and hugged me..."Pete, it's terrible. How is he doing?"

I was surprised that she reacted so strongly, but Mac had that type of effect on everyone that knew him. "He's not good Bens, the doctor was not optimistic about his condition."

"I don't know him well, certainly not as well as you do Pete, but just in the short time that I've known him I've seen qualities in him that I admire and want for myself. He is like a father figure, a protector to many of us on the shift; he's fair yet firm, and he knows the job inside and out."

As we turned to walk back toward the ER, I saw Joe's wife, Susan, standing at the door. My wife Beth was with her.

<u>30</u>
The New Woman?

Susan looked at Beth and asked, "Who's that with Pete?"

"I don't know," she replied, "I've never seen her before."

"Well, she's probably a cop judging from her looks," said Susan.

"Maybe," said Beth, "but she's awfully attractive..."

Marilyn was wearing a dark pair of capri pants, and a form fitting sleeveless black top with a scoop neckline. The shirt in particular showed off her female muscularity quite well. The definition in her shoulders and arms was evidence of her hard work in the gym. She looked pleasingly athletic, rather than blocky as some female bodybuilders have a tendency to appear. Her dark hair was down, just off the shoulders. Her olive complexion complimented her lean, fit body, which she topped off with a thin gold neck chain and bracelet. The off duty Marilyn was a stark contrast to the one in uniform.

Beth was worried. Who was this woman that Pete was with? They obviously knew each other, maybe even knew each other too well since she went right up to him and gave him a hug. Was Pete already seeing someone? Were things worse than she imagined? Was this just another brick in the wall that was getting higher and higher between her and Pete?

Pete and Marilyn reached the door to the ER where Susan and Beth were standing. "Hi Beth, hi Susan, I'd like you to meet Marilyn Benson—she's my new partner."

Marilyn extended her hand to them both and exchanged greetings. She sensed that the moment was uncomfortable and quickly excused herself, "Pete, I'm going to go inside and see how Mac is doing and say hello to some of the people that I know. Nice to meet you both."

I turned to Susan, "How are you and the boys doing?"

"I guess as well as can be expected Pete. They're still in a fog, not able to understand why daddy isn't coming home. The Hundred Club of Cook County came over to the house and gave me a check for $15,000.00. That should hold us over for a while until I can figure out what money we have and where all of the paperwork for the accounts is located. Joe took care of all the money and bills; I took care of the children and the house. But knowing how organized Joe was, it shouldn't be hard to figure it all out."

The Hundred Club was a blessing to all police families that suffered a loss of their mother or father. Within 24 hours of the death, they present a check to the spouse. Later they review the family's debts and will pay up to an additional $50,000, to include up to $30,000 in mortgage or real estate. Furthermore, they provide educational assistance to spouses and children for vocational schools and college. Started in Detroit in 1950 by a single businessman, the program has spread across the nation and has provided help to over 230 families.

"That's great Susan, thank God for organizations like that. And please remember that I'm only minutes away for you any time that you need anything."

"Thanks Pete. So many people have been by to offer support and prayers... We'll be fine. Beth has been a big help the last couple of nights. My parents had to go back home; I'm afraid the boys wore them out. I don't know what I would do without her; she has a knack for making the boys feel safe and loved."

No doubt I thought. Beth would be a wonderful mother for any child; she has the qualities that are inherent in every mother, love, compassion, and an unselfish attitude that would ensure children live in a wonderful love-filled home. If only...

Susan turned and said, "I'm going to sit with Shirley for a while," and went back inside. That left Beth and I alone, and admittedly I felt a bit uncomfortable.

She brushed a strand of hair from her face and said, "You didn't tell me that your new partner was such a stunning looking woman. How is she working out?"

I didn't know how to take that question; didn't know if she was probing me or not. "She's good Beth, she has a lot of experience—she's a tough cop."

"Well, I don't know how tough she may be, but she's a beautiful woman isn't she? You looked pretty comfortable with her when she gave you that big hug over by the driveway."

As soon as the words came out of her mouth she regretted them. Who am I to read anything into a hug between two co-workers greeting each other as they visit an ill colleague? But, what if it wasn't just an innocent hug? What if she's more than a partner? The possibilities mounted in Beth's mind and she imagined the worst outcome...

"Beth...what do you mean?"

"Nothing Pete, I'm sorry...I shouldn't have made that remark."

"Listen; if you think that Marilyn is anything more than a partner you're wrong. I have way too many problems in my life to add another one. So much has happened recently that my head is still spinning. I find it difficult to concentrate in class; my mind is off in space somewhere. The job is different now that Joe's gone; I'm back in uniform working a beat. And I think that Rosato is out to get me for writing the DUI to his girlfriend. Amidst it all I'm trying to adjust to a new partner. The last thing on my mind is getting involved in any new relationship."

"What about us Pete? Is that on your mind at all?"

She hit a nerve with that one. Was it on my mind? Only every minute of the day! And while I think that we need this time apart for some introspection, I hate every second that we're apart. "Beth, I think about you all of the time. The house isn't a home without you. There's no longer any sense of needing to go home because you're not there. It's just a place to shower and sleep. But the thought of you and that other guy is also on my mind, and I can't shake it. You destroyed a beautiful pact that we had created and lived with for all these years. The trust that we used to have in each other was so strong, that I never imagined that one day it would be shattered. I'm having a hard time dealing with it. Every time that I see a couple walking down the street holding hands, it saddens me because it reminds me of us—how we used to be. Just seeing Mac's grandbabies in the waiting room today again reminded me of how much I wanted us to be parents. But I guess that I'm being selfish thinking that way."

"No Pete, you're not selfish; you have a right to be upset. I did something that I'll have to live with forever. I don't know that I can ever forgive myself for hurting you. And what bothers me most of all is that I've done something that you'll have to live with as well—either with or without me."

She looked so sad and forlorn that I almost wanted to take her in my arms and hold her, tell her everything would be alright I looked at Beth and noticed that her color seemed much better, and that hollow look that had begun to detract from her beautiful face was now gone. "How are you doing on eating, are you back to normal? You look well."

"Thanks Pete, I' m trying hard, very hard to get back to where I was before I let us down. Father Mike set me up with a psychologist and I had an appointment with her already. But I think that what's helped me the most is that I got honest with myself and with God. I finally just stopped and listened to what He was trying to tell me."

She didn't mean to, but she was becoming emotional, starting to tear up. In just the past couple of days, she had felt better than she had in almost three years. She was welcoming every emotion—happiness and sadness—not running away from anything or masking it with booze. All it took was to bring the Lord back into her life. And although she and Pete were separated, Joe was gone, Susan was left with the four babies, and Mac was in the ER fighting for his life, she felt strangely at peace.

"The biggest piece of the puzzle that I had been missing for these past years was honesty. I couldn't be honest with you or myself; I had to invent reasons and excuses why things were going downhill between us, and why I kept putting you off about having a baby. I'm not saying that you would have liked it anymore that you do now if I had told you when it happened, but at least we could have either worked on the problem or made a decision to end it."

"I'm glad to hear that you are doing well Beth, and I hope that you continue to improve. But can you see things from my perspective? Can you possibly understand the hurt and betrayal that I feel? We were best friends babe, everything revolved around us and no one came between us. To one day have that totally blown away is life-changing." I rubbed my eyes now, as I was beginning to feel the emotion of the past sap my strength and steal my optimism.

"I know Pete, I know. You have to make a decision on what road you want to travel," she said. "I pray that we can get past this and start anew. I can't tell you enough how sorry I am for deceiving you and disrespecting our marriage. I will abide by whatever decision that you eventually come to, and with any conditions that you may attach. You are the only one that I've ever loved Pete, and you are the only one that I ever want to love."

My heart was breaking now; I had to get out of there before I started sobbing like a baby. "Okay Beth, I need some time, and I need help. I can't get through this myself. Until this happened today with Mac, I was prepared to get some counseling to help me through the pain. But now I need to know that Mac is going to be okay. I won't be able to focus on very much until then. It's like He keeps loading me up with one challenge after another, trying to see where my breaking point is. I don't know how much more I can take."

Beth reached out and put her hand on my arm..."He won't give you more than you can handle babe, but he will test you, just as he tested me. Remain focused on what really matters in your life, and don't for one second close your eyes and ears to His message. I'm praying for you every day; you will always be in my heart."

"Thanks babe." I quickly turned and headed down the block. I needed some private time to absorb what just happened. The old Beth was somehow back, the one that I knew before the evil one had tempted her. But could I trust her not to succumb to his evil ways again? Was that one brief episode to be the only one? I needed help—some direction. I was about to make an important decision that would affect two lives—hers and mine. Could our marriage weather this storm or not?   At this point, I wasn't sure.

<u>31</u>
Sgt. Mike Castro

By the time I got back to the ER from my walk, most of the people had already left.

Mac hadn't gotten any better, but he hadn't gotten any worse either. I left to go home for a few hours sleep so that I could make it through the shift tonight. Shirley went home briefly to shower and grab a few things to get her through the night. She wasn't about to leave Mac alone, they had been together too many years and been through too much for that team to be split up now. I found myself questioning Him again...why did bad things happen to good people? Why did scumbags seem to prosper despite their evil ways, yet folks like Mac and Shirley are constantly asked to bear not one, but several crosses? It didn't seem fair...

I woke up groggy. Three hours sleep, after all of the emotional turmoil of the day was woefully short of what I needed to recharge my batteries. By the time I got my equipment together and headed to the station, I barely made in time for roll call. I walked in just as the sergeant was ordering everyone to fall in. I stood in the front row next to Marilyn.

"Hi Bens, did you get any rest?"

"I got a few hours, how about you?"

"The same," I said, "but I could have used another eight."

"I heard that," she said. "We're pointing that car straight to Dunkin Donuts after roll call. I need an extra large cup tonight if I'm going to stay awake."

Mac's replacement was a guy named Mike Castro. I remembered Mike from when I used to work day shift. We both came on the job about the same time, but he eventually got the day shift because his wife Casey was a nurse on afternoons at Christ Hospital. Mike was an aggressive, no nonsense cop that didn't pull any punches. He wore his heart on his sleeve; no one ever had to guess where Mike was coming from. He loved police work and he was good at it...so good that in his early days on the job the undercover unit used him for a lot of temporary assignments. Mike was a good schmoozer, particularly when it came to drug deals. He could play any role, be it big time dealer, money man, or simply going on a controlled buy. He eventually got burned out doing the UC stuff. He told the bosses that he preferred being in uniform so that the bad guys knew exactly who they were dealing with.

"Morales, where are you cuffs?' asked Castro as he inspected the troops.

They're not in the case sarge?"

"No, what are you going to do, ask the crook to provide his own? See me after roll call and sign for a pair until you locate yours. I hope that we don't have some schmuck running around with your cuffs on."

"Or some babe chained to a headboard," someone added.

"Alright, enough of that. You see that mirror over there by the lockers? See the sign above it...? It reads, *Does your appearance command respect?* Check yourselves ladies and gentlemen before each shift, make sure your uniform is clean and pressed and that all of your equipment is present and accounted for. Right Morales?"

"Right Sarge."

"Okay at ease; take your seats. For those of you who don't know me, I'm Sgt. Mike Castro from the 2nd Watch. I've been volunteered to fill in for Mac until he's well enough to come back to work. I know Sgt. McNamara...he's a good man and he's tough. If anyone can beat a heart attack, it's Mac. I know a little bit about his background, including his time in Nam. He's had worse setbacks than this, but if any of you have a connection with 'The Man Upstairs,' that will certainly help speed his recovery."

Castro gave out the assignments, talked about the admin items that needed addressing, and then got down to the real business at hand.

"Ladies and gentlemen, I know that we will be feeling each other out the next few weeks. You'll want to know how much 'crap' you can get away with before I come down on you. Let me dispel any notions right now. I'm a no-nonsense cop that loves you if you work hard, and despises you if you don't. We get paid by the citizens of this town to keep them safe, and they expect us to lock up any knuckle draggers that may try to do them harm. If I find out that any of you fail to take action, or as is sometimes the case on midnights, if anyone tries to grab a nap, I'll write your ass up. If you want to sleep, you should be working another shift. I don't have any sympathy for those of you that have second jobs during the day and then show up here for work exhausted. Your private life is yours; your tour of duty is mine. Any questions?"

Mac had been firm but not this vociferous. As I looked around the room, I saw everyone focused and alert, except one person—Rosato. He spoke up quickly, "Sarge, are you threatening us?

"What's your name officer?"

"I'm Officer Sal Rosato, people call me 'The Hammer'."

"Well Rosato, or Hammer, or whatever you call yourself, you make your own interpretation about what I just said but know this: You and I will get along famously as long as you do your job. If that sounds threatening to you—so be it. If you don't like what I said, make a phone call to whoever your 'Chinaman' is and see if you can get rid of me. In the meantime, work your beat, make arrests when needed, and back up your colleagues. That's all I ask."

Hammer didn't have any comeback. He wasn't a real bright guy, having just put a target on his back for Sgt. Castro to zero in on. He'd know Rosato well enough if he stayed on mids for any length of time. My hunch was that the two of them would cross swords in the near future.

"Okay, if there's nothing more, hit the streets."

We filed out to the lot, everyone pretty much doing the same things...checking equipment and vehicles. Ten minutes later, the early midnight shift was on the street and the afternoon guys were preparing to come in for check off. It was Marilyn's turn to take the wheel for the first four hours, and true to her word she headed straight for the coffee shop. We pulled up to see Rosato inside at the counter.

"Want to wait a few minutes Pete before we go in?"

"No, let's just get in real quick and get out."

We parked and went inside. "Hi Lisa!"

"Hi Bens, you and Pete doing alright tonight?"

"A little sleepy Lisa, but we'll get by as long as we get some caffeine in us—give us two large black please."

Rosato turned and faced us, "Well, look who's here, the hero and his new gal pal. If I were you Benson, I'd make sure that all my insurance policies were paid up—this guy could be bad for your health."

I stepped a bit closer to Rosato. "Listen brother, I don't appreciate your remarks, nor does anyone else. If you have a problem with me, you and I can settle it in private."

"I'm not your brother Shannon, and I'll say whatever I wanna say. You don't have your guardian angel, Mac, here anymore."

Marilyn stepped in between us. "That's enough Rosato, how the hell old are you anyway? Grow up and just do your job. If you have a problem with my partner, then you have a problem with me. Understood?"

I was impressed with her. She stepped right up to the plate and knocked it out of the park. Most guys just let Rosato get away with his arrogant remarks. Marilyn let it be known that she would not be intimidated; she wasn't going to take any bull from him.

"Take it easy Miss America, I got no beef with you," said Hammer as he raised both hands in a gesture of surrender. "All I'm sayin' is that you gotta watch your back around this guy. You know what happened with his old partner, right?"

"Yeah, I know what happened," she said. "He and his partner saved someone's life by putting their own on the line. I'd go through any door with Pete; I'm not so sure about you though." What do I owe you Lisa?"

"Four twenty five."

Bens put the money on the counter. We said good bye to Lisa and got back in our car.

"Bens, I don't need anyone to fight my battles, but you sure kicked his butt in there. I don't think that he was expecting that. Most guys just keep quiet and take it from him; you threw it right back in his face. Anyway, thanks partner."

She pulled the squad out on Pulaski..."Let's go earn our keep, *brother*!"

<u>32</u>
The Chase

We started cruising our beat, looking for everything and anything. "Pete, do you mind me asking, what's the beef between you and Rosato? In the short time that I've been your partner he's like on you all the time."

"I know. It's a long story, but it boils down to two things: he thinks that me and Joe jumped over him for a spot on the Tac Team for one thing, and we also wound up writing his girlfriend a DUI one night after she was involved in a hit and skip with three or four eyeball witnesses. Then I guess that he showed up with his girlfriend for her first appearance at traffic court, looking to get it thrown out because Joe was gone and I was on admin leave. It didn't happen though because Mac had called and talked with the State's Attorney's office requesting a continuance. He had it all figured out that she was going to walk, and when she didn't it just angered him even more."

"What a schemer," she said.

"Yeah, what's worse is that I guess that he got into a beef with the court clerk, and the judge threatened to lock him up for contempt."

"Wow, this guy is bad news....no wonder he got busted down from sergeant."

"That's another thing...that wound has been festering too—he blames Mac, me, and Joe for some crazy reason. I had someone call me the other day, telling me that he was in the same restaurant with Rosato one night and overheard him say something about getting even with me."

Marilyn turned west on 59th Street. "I think that we should watch out for this guy Pete. I don't trust him one iota. He's probably got me in the crosshairs now too, since I 'dissed' him at the coffee shop."

"Whoa...let's not use that kind of descriptive language partner, lest it come to fruition."

"Sorry, she said, "but I don't put anything past this guy. Pete look at that car..."

She had spotted a Nissan SUV travelling in the opposite direction.

"Pete, that door lock's been punched. Run that tag partner; I'm going to pull it over."

Marilyn made a quick u-turn; I grabbed the radio and gave the squad operator the plate info. Bens hit the blue lights and shined the spotlight on the vehicle. There was no reaction from it at first, so she hit the siren. With that the vehicle sped up and took off.

"813 squad, looks like we've got a chase on our hands. We're following a white Nissan SUV, we're eastbound 59th Street approaching St. Louis Avenue."

"All units in the 8th District and on City-Wide...Beat 813 is in pursuit of a white, Nissan SUV...eastbound 59th Street, approaching St. Louis, any units able to assist?"

"Beat 813, what's the vehicle wanted for?" asked the operator.

"Right now it's suspicion of stolen vehicle and traffic violations."

"10-4"

Marilyn hung back just far enough to ensure that we kept the vehicle in sight, but gave us a cushion to safely navigate through intersections. One of the biggest dangers cops face when involved in pursuits is smashing into each other in their fervor to catch the offenders.

"813, eight one three..."

"Go ahead squad, we're approaching Kedzie now."

"10-4, all units, still westbound 59th at Kedzie...that plate comes back s*tolen* 813."

"Roger that," I said. "Southbound turn now squad, southbound Kedzie approaching 62nd Street."

These guys are looking for a place to bail out I thought. "Bens, when these guys find a spot they like they're going to dump the ride and take off in different directions. We don't split up; we both go for the driver—agreed?"

"Got ya partner…"

"813, we're through 63rd Street now, still southbound Kedzie approaching Marquette Road."

The SUV made a quick left on Marquette and then the first left into an alley behind a row of apartment buildings. Halfway down the alley the vehicle skidded to a stop and the doors flew open in a cloud of dust and smoke; all three males took off in different directions.

We got as close as we could and Bens slammed on the brakes. We both jumped out and hit the ground running. "Pete, he's eastbound in the alley—white tee shirt, blue bandana, cutoff jeans."

"I'm with you Bens…813, we're on foot eastbound in the north alley along Marquette Road…chasing a male Hispanic, white tee shirt, and cutoffs."

"Copy that…all units foot pursuit eastbound in the north alley along Marquette, just east of Kedzie."

Bens was faster than I expected her to be and was closing the gap on this guy. Having to work the radio to keep everyone apprised of our location slowed me somewhat, but I was only a few steps behind her. Our bad guy reached the end of the alley and turned to run across Marquette Road into the park, but his timing was bad. He wound up running right into the side of a passing car. Bens quickly grabbed the guy as he bounced off the car, and took him down to the ground. I drove my knee into his back, holding him down while she cuffed him.

"Good job Bens, you okay?"

"I'm great partner, how 'bout you?"

"Never better! 813 to all units…driver's in custody, we're still looking for two male passengers, but other that both being Hispanic, we have no further physical on them."

"10-4, 813."

We marched our arrestee back to the scene where a wagon was standing by to transport him to the station. We'd more than likely have him flip on his two passengers. As usual he had no ID, and of course "a friend" had allowed him to use the car. He had no answer as to why both the door lock and ignition were punched, but hey, we're not dealing with huge intellects out here.

By the time we got the vehicle towed, the paper completed on our guy, and all the notifications made, it was almost time for our shift to end. We were just finishing putting our prisoner in the lockup when Sgt. Castro approached us.

"Hey you two, nice job out there. I was listening in on the radio; that was great teamwork. Pete I like the way you worked the radio, and Benson, you did a good job with driving the pursuit and then running the dude down on foot. You guys make a good team."

"Thanks Sarge. It all came together rather well," I said.

"Well it should when you have two hard working cops like yourselves. That's exactly what I was talking about at roll call. If I had a shift full of cops like you and Benson, my job would be a breeze."

I shook his hand and said, "Having a supervisor like you makes it even easier. I wish that we had more leaders like you."

"Thanks Shannon, but truth be known I'd much rather be in your shoes. Being a cop on the streets of Chicago is the best job in the world."

"Amen brother,"

"I'll see you both tomorrow, get some rest."

He went back to the desk to brief the incoming day shift sergeant. Bens looked at me and said, "Pete, that was some great police work wasn't it?"

"It sure was Marilyn, and it was fun. I think Joe must have had a hand in choosing my new partner; I think that he still has my back in some way."

"Maybe he does, but I hope that I convinced you tonight that I've got it too."

"Yes you did Bens, yes you did..."

On the drive home Marilyn felt good about the night's activities. Being able to drive the pursuit, and then chase the guy down had her energized and looking for more. She only had one class today later in the afternoon, which would give her plenty of time for sleep. But she was so excited about the arrest, that she knew she would only toss and turn if she tried to get some rest right now.

She got home, fed the cat, then threw her workout clothes in her duffle bag and headed for the gym. Besides the obvious need to be strong and fit for her job, the simple act of exercising gave her joy, satisfaction, and tons of confidence. She had always compared herself to other women around her, checking their bodies out and frankly, feeling a little superior to most of them. She prided herself on being fit, and as a result more attractive. She constantly scrutinized herself in the mirror during her workouts, and after her shower. And she was used to the whistles and catcalls from guys when she ran down the street on her daily training runs.

Now, with this new dynamic in place, partnering with Pete Shannon, she had all the more reason to be in shape. Pete was obviously a hard charger, and a guy who valued his fitness as much as she did. She was quickly realizing that they had a lot in common, and she was looking forward to going to work each day much more than she used to. It helped that Pete was a handsome guy as well and had a great personality. She liked that he was a Christian also, one that was unashamed to let people know of his belief in the Lord. His only flaw seemed to be his marriage. What could be wrong there she wondered? She wouldn't pry, but she was going to pray that he and Beth would resolve their differences. Having Pete's mind clear and focused would benefit them both while they worked the streets.

She was feeling good about her life right now. The only concern that she had was Rosato. If this guy was as bad as he sounded, both her and Pete could find themselves in trouble. Time would tell, but she made a note to herself to be vigilant around him. But right now she cleared her mind and got down to the business of working out. It was good to be alive.

<u>33</u>
Forgiveness

Feeling refreshed after a quick run, shower and sandwich, I headed to the hospital to check on Mac. I automatically made my way to ICU where Mac was at when I last saw him, but the nurse on duty advised me that Mac had been moved to a semi-private room. A few minutes later I walked into a room so full of flowers and balloons that I thought I was at some kind of party. Mac was sitting up in bed talking with Shirley and their daughter Leslie, looking a little pale but happy nonetheless.

"Mac! It's good to see you brother...how are you feeling?" I grabbed his hand and hugged him lightly, giving thanks to the Lord at the same time. "You look terrific. Tell me, what has the doctor said about your recovery?"

"Hi Pete, it's good to be seen! I didn't know if I'd make it there for awhile, but the doctors fixed me up and said to rest for about six weeks and I'll be good as new."

"We're blessed Pete," added Shirley. "They said he had major artery blockage, so bad that it should have killed him, but the angioplasty that they performed was a success. They think it should last for a while, but if it doesn't then he's going to need bypass surgery."

"Yeah, the leftover balloons are over there," Mac cracked, pointing to the get well balloons from well wishers.

"Whatever, Mac. What a scare you gave all of us... I'll tell you something; the day you were brought here we must have had over a hundred people come to the hospital to find out how you were doing. You must be doing something right my friend; you've had legions of people praying for you."

"Thanks Pete, that's probably what saved me. He must still have some things that He wants me to get done here before he calls me home.

But He sure knows how to get someone's attention doesn't He?"

Mac shifted in bed so that he could hang his legs over the side. Shirley grabbed both his hands and helped him up. "Doc says that I have to get up every hour and walk around...it's supposed to speed my recovery. Pete, how's it working out...partnering with Benson?"

I followed Shirley and Mac out into the hallway as they started their lap around the nurses' station.

"Just as you said it would Mac, she's a good cop—tough too! We had a chase last night. She did the driving and then ran down the guy on foot after they all bailed. I'm very pleased."

"That's great," he said. "Who's working the desk on mids?"

"They pulled in Sgt. Castro off the day shift. I'll tell you what...when I finally get off the graveyard shift, I want to work for him. He's a good guy."

Mac completed his lap and headed back into the room. Shirl gave him a hand so that he could sit in one of the chairs.

"Yep, Castro's a good man," Mac said. "He could probably be a lieutenant if he wanted to, but he's not all that interested in going any higher than sergeant. I think that he regrets leaving the street to ride a desk."

"I think that you're right Mac. He as much as said that to us after he told me and Benson what a good job we did last night."

"Hey, how is Rosato handling Castro so far...any battles yet?"

I grabbed a seat on the edge of the bed across from Mac. "Oh yeah, he's already tested the waters to see how far he can go with Castro. He didn't make it very far; Castro shut him up right away."

"Good," said Mac.

"Yeah, not only that, but Marilyn put him in his place when Rosato tried to bust my chops. I really like that gal."

"Pete I'm so glad to hear that. You know, I was worried about you. I didn't know how you would handle losing Joe. Some cops are never the same after they get involved in a shooting, especially one in which either they or their partner are hit. You seemed to have handled it well, but promise me son that you'll use the counseling program if you feel out of sorts."

"I will Mac, I promise."

"And remember...I'm always here for you also...day or night the door's always open."

"You're the best Mac."

We talked for another thirty minutes or so until it was meal time. I said my goodbyes and left to head over to see Father Mike. I told him that I needed to talk about me and Beth. I had been putting that on the back burner the past few days, but after seeing her at the hospital I definitely wanted to talk to someone to get me on the path to resolving the split. I got over to Queens just as he was pulling into his parking spot behind the rectory.

"Fr. Mike!"

"Hey Pete! I just got back from an interview with the Cardinal. The yearly obligatory meeting to let him know that I'm still alive and that Queen's is doing well as a parish. Of course the real reason that he pulls any of us down there is so that he can tell us that we need to increase the weekly offering total."

I followed him to the back door, "Are we still on for our meeting?"

"Of course," he said while opening the door. "I'll have the housekeeper put on a pot of coffee; the Cardinal almost put me to sleep."

"None for me, I still have to get in a quick nap before reporting for duty tonight."

We exchanged some small talk while the coffee was brewing, then retreated to Father Mike's office on the second floor. "So Pete, what brings you here today?"

"Beth. You know that we are separated; she's staying with her folks over in Beverly."

"No, I didn't know that. I have spoken with her though, and while I won't reveal anything she said in confidence, I will tell you that she has had a rough three years Pete. She poured her heart out to me for over two hours, explaining what happened on the trip to Boston, and the aftermath of it all. One thing I know...she has more than paid for her sins. Most importantly, she admitted to the Lord that she was wrong and asked for His forgiveness. Once she did that she could finally forgive herself. That has been one of the biggest hurdles that she has had to overcome."

"I saw her at the hospital while I was visiting our sergeant; she looked a little better physically," I said.

"That's all part of the healing process Pete. She was hiding behind alcohol and just trying to get control of anything that she could. She couldn't face you...every time she looked into your eyes, she couldn't bring herself to tell you what she had done. She has been torturing herself over what happened."

I shifted in my chair, feeling a little embarrassed now for not really seeing things from her perspective, yet still feeling that I was the party that had been wronged. "Father, how can I ever trust her again not to do the same thing? How do I allow her back into my life and expect things to ever be the same?"

"The simple answer is that things won't be the same as they were before she was unfaithful. But what's also possible is that things might even be better. She has had a major upheaval in her whole belief system as a result of her actions. Her life is never going to be the same either. Her guilt still weighs heavily on her, and it will take a long time, if ever, until the burden is gone. Her misstep has caused her to really fully understand how important those marriage vows are. It's my guess that she will never allow herself to be tempted again."

"So you think that I should forgive her?"

"Pete, are you that conceited and arrogant that you cannot forgive someone for having hurt you? Have you ever done anything in your life that was wrong, or that you were embarrassed about? Did not our Savior forgive those who crucified Him, yet you purport to be more important than our Lord saying that you can't forgive your wife?"

I immediately saw his point. Who was I to think that I was better than anyone else? Isn't that a basic Christian tenant, to forgive? "You're right Father. I guess that I've been feeling sorry for myself. So much has happened recently…I feel as if the Lord has been testing me; He wants to see how much of a burden I can bear."

"Life is not without struggles Pete. Everyone has challenges and crosses to bear. The Lord wants you to succeed and lead a fulfilling life here on earth. But he also wants to see how you react to those obstacles that He places in your way. The road to Heaven is sometimes rocky. At times we lose our way, or maybe we just lose sight of the goal altogether. God knows that as humans we need to sometimes be taken by the scruff of the neck and shaken until we finally get our attention back to where it should be. You and Beth have had a good marriage for a long time. Now He has sent you both a test. Depending on how you handle it, will determine whether you have been listening to Him all this time or just pretending to listen."

He made a lot of sense. Beth and I really never had a crisis like this. Sure we went through my parents' death, but this incident was much different. When they were killed, we had each other to lean on. And Father Mike was right…how childish of me to act like a spoiled brat and not give Beth a second chance. After all, I'm not perfect. I've done things in the past for which I've been ashamed of. I'm certainly not better than our Lord…

"You're right Father; I haven't been a very good Christian through all of this. I need to give Beth a second chance. I know that if the shoe were on the other foot, she would probably forgive me."

Father Mike stood up, "I agree. Go to her. As hurt as you are Pete, I can assure you that she is suffering just as much."

"I will."

"And Pete, do me a favor?"

"Sure thing Father, what is it."

"I know that you are a busy guy with work and school, but promise me that you will just stop and listen...listen for His voice. He wants you to talk with Him every day, I don't mean saying prayers, just tell Him how you feel, how grateful you are, how much you love Him."

I shook his hand and said, "I'll do that. I do need to talk to Him more, need to put Him back on top of everything. Thanks Father."

I left there feeling better than I had in some time. I vowed to sit down with Beth tomorrow and get this over and done with. To be honest, I missed being with her—she was my better half in a lot of ways. I didn't realize it until she was gone, but I really didn't want to live my life without her.

Thank you Lord for opening my eyes.

<u>34</u>
Robbery In Progress

I woke up from my nap feeling great. My visit with Mac at the hospital, and then my meeting with Father Mike had given me a whole new perspective on things. I felt hopeful about the future, rather than feeling sorry for myself. I needed to get beyond disappointments and hurt, and make the best of the gifts that I had been blessed with.

It was too late to give Beth a call now, but I promised myself that I would call her in the morning and set up a dinner date. I wanted to let her know that I forgave her; wanted her to realize that I still thought we could make it through this test of faith and love. I actually felt a little giddy about it, like a schoolboy that has just passed his first "I love you" note to a girl in the fifth grade. I had truly missed "my Beth" and I wanted my best friend and lover back in my life.

In the meantime, I gathered my equipment and headed to the station. It was Sunday night—there shouldn't be too much going on. It would be a great opportunity to do some car stops with Bens. I got suited up in the locker room and headed to roll call where I took a seat next to my partner.

"Did you get any sleep Marilyn?"

"Enough...I was still kind of jacked up over the car chase. I couldn't get to sleep right away, so I wound up going out for a long run. How about you?"

"The same—I wasn't tired at all after the shift. I went to the hospital...Guess what? Mac is out of ICU and in a room. His doctor did an angio on him and he should be good to go in about six weeks."

"Oh man, that's great," she said. "He sure was lucky. The way he looked that first day..."

"Yeah, I know. I'm so thankful that we didn't lose him, so is Shirley and the grandbabies."

Sgt. Castro walked in the room..."Fall in!"

After inspection he read off the assignments. When he came to Rosato he said, "Rosato, you're going to work alone tonight on 895, the traffic car. You're partner called in sick...well I guess injured on duty is more like it. He was at an in-service a couple days ago at the Academy for a handcuffing and defensive tactics refresher. Seems he got a little over-aggressive with the instructor, John Lanata, and wound up getting his shoulder separated after Lanata took him down hard to the mat."

Rosato laughed and said, "He let that old guy throw him down? I would have kicked his ass."

Castro immediately took umbrage with that remark. "Listen Rosato, Lanata's got 30 years on the job—he was my PT and DT Instructor when I went through recruit training. He's as tough as he ever was, and would make you squeal like a pig if he wanted to. Come and see me when you're 60 years old, show me what kind of shape you're in, and then maybe you can make a disparaging remark like that. Until then you're only putting you enormous ignorance on display for all of us to enjoy."

That had Rosato squirming uncomfortably in his seat. "Well I don't plan on bein' here at 60, only idiots work that long."

The older guys in the room gave Rosato a hard look after he made that remark. He wasn't making any friends with this crowd.

"All right, enough with the chit-chat. It's Sunday night...should be quiet. It's a good night to get your Beat Books up to date, get all the Special Attentions taken care of and any other admin matters that you may be delinquent with. If there are no questions, hit the bricks."

Me and Bens located our squad in the lot and checked everything. We got into the car and headed out.

"Coffee Pete?"

"No," I said. "I'm okay, still pretty charged over last night's activity."

"Yeah, me too. I think that I can make it through tonight without it."

She was looking over the Beat Book while I drove. "Pete, you seem really happy about something...is it Mac?"

"Yes, it's Mac. I'm so grateful that he's going to be okay. But I also had a meeting with our pastor, and I think that I've finally worked out my problems with Beth. He showed me how childish I've been... I'm kind of excited about giving her a call after work."

"Pete, that's great!"

"I'm going to invite her out for dinner and then break the news to her that I want her to come back home. I was being selfish and uncharitable in my behavior. We've been together 15 years; that's not something you just arbitrarily throw away when you face a challenge."

"I think that you're doing the right thing, and the fact that you feel so good about it tells me that you know it's right too."

"Thanks," I said. "I was really getting tired of feeling sad and lonely, but things are looking up...Mac's better, Beth and I will be back together, and I've got a great partner!"

Marilyn turned and smiled at me, "So do I..."

We took a ride through all the alleys on both sides of 63rd St, looking for any activity of break- ins. I was just about to head down to the airport to check on the rental lots and hotels when the radio sprang to life.

"All units in the 8th District and on City-Wide, we've got a silent hold up alarm at Bill's Pizza and Tavern, 3147 W. 71st Street. Any units available?"

Marilyn grabbed the mic..."813's goin' squad."

"813—10-4"

"895 squad, I'm close by," said Rosato.

"895—10-4"

I punched it and flew up Pulaski to 71st Street, lights and siren goin' to beat the band, then made a left and barreled toward the address. "That's 71st and Kedzie Bens...should be a tavern right next to the gas station. I know that joint, been in there before. There's a front door and a side door that empties out to the gas station lot. I'm going to put us in the lot to cover the side..."

We flew over the railroad tracks, past the Park District building on the left. I saw 895 come to a halt right at the front door of the place. Rosato hopped out of his car and ran to the front door, gun in hand. At the same time, the robbery suspect came running out the door smack into Rosato, knocking them both to the ground. Rosato's gun went flying one way, while he went the other. We pulled into the gas station lot next door...

"Bens, stay down and cover me. Watch the side door too in case there's more than one offender!"

"Got it Pete!"

Rosato got up slowly and had to retrieve his pistol. That gave the bad guy an opportunity to try to make a run for it. As charged up as I was feeling, that wasn't going to happen. I bolted after him and caught him just as he went around the corner on Troy Street. Grabbing his arm and neck, I quickly threw him down. He tried to offer some resistance, but he was truly outmatched in this contest. I had the cuffs on him so fast that I even surprised myself.

"813, suspect in custody" I said as I hauled him to his feet. I was walking him back around the corner when I heard Bens shouting commands.

"Look away from me; get down on your knees and keep your hands up high in the air...don't move! Rosato, I'll keep him covered—cuff 'em."

Rosato moved in, put the cuffs on him, then smacked him in the back of the head and gave him a quick shot to the gut. "Are you stupid or what," he shouted at the guy. "Don't you know you can't get mess with The Hammer?" He dragged the guy to his cage car and threw him in the back.

I got on the air and had a wagon come by for our prisoner. Rosato could do what he wanted with his prisoner, but I didn't want him anywhere near our guy.

"Pete, did you see that idiot Rosato? He smacked the guy around after he had him cuffed."

"Yeah, that's his style. It's going to come back to bite him one of these days. We're going to bring this guy to a separate interview room once the wagon drops him off at the station. I don't want Rosato to interfere with this arrestee."

"Yeah, we'll have a beef on our hands if Rosato gets this guy alone in a room."

"Incidentally, good job on calling that second guy out."

"Thanks, but I could hardly control myself after I saw your guy knock Rosato on his butt!"

I laughed, "Yeah, The Hammer got hammered!"

We met the wagon at the station and unloaded our prisoner and then took care of the necessary paperwork. We avoided Rosato as much as we could, but he was going around the station boasting about how he tackled the guy coming out, and then took care of the second suspect. It was typical Hammer braggadocio...it was all bogus.

We finished up and went back out on patrol for a few hours, but found nothing much going on. When the shift was over, we went in for check off. Sgt. Morales was handling that tonight. We handed him our paperwork and were about to head to the parking area.

"Shannon,...Benson, hold up a minute," said Morales. "One of the two guys arrested tonight wants to make a beef about getting slapped around when he was arrested. Do you guys know anything about that?"

I looked at him, "He's saying we hit him?"

"No not you...Rosato. Sgt. Castro took the complaint and forwarded it on to OPR. They'll be contacting you both for a statement. He ordered the tape from your dash cam inventoried as evidence too; just wanted to give you guys a heads up."

"Okay Sarge, thanks," said Bens.

"Well, partner, welcome to 'Hammer's World' where everyone and everything around him becomes tainted."

"Pete, I'm not putting my job in jeopardy for that guy," said Marilyn.

"I know, neither am I. We're going to tell it like it is. Rosato is bad news. He keeps digging his own grave by doing this kind of garbage. Pretty soon it's going to be deep enough for him to fall in and be buried by it."

"I'm not going down with him Pete and neither are you. That guy really ticks me off."

We walked out to our cars together. We had the next two days off, and I was looking forward to calling Beth and setting up our dinner. I said good bye to Marilyn, hopped inside my truck, and said a quick prayer of thanksgiving to St.Michael for backing me up tonight. I wasn't going to let Rosato's stupid behavior ruin my reunion with my wife. I pointed the truck toward home and dialed Beth's cell...this was going to be a great day!

<u>35</u>
The Airport

"Beth, hi it's me babe!"

"Pete, what's wrong? Are you okay?"

"Whoa....I'm fine. Can't I call my wife and tell her good morning?"

"Yes, of course you can," she said. "I'm just surprised that you called me since we haven't exactly been experiencing the best of times lately. I was afraid that something was wrong with either you or Mac."

"No, nothing's wrong. In fact, Mac is getting out of the hospital probably today or tomorrow and will be back to work in about six weeks."

"Wow, that's great news hon. The Good Lord really answered our prayers," she said.

I expected her to be in her car driving to the airport parking lot. Instead, I heard what sounded like the airport terminal itself.

"Are you on your way to work Beth?"

"Actually, no I'm not. I'm at Midway about to catch a flight to Milwaukee; I have to attend a conference there this week."

"You didn't mention anything like that to me," I said.

"Pete, we don't live together anymore; we don't talk. My parents know about the trip, as do my friends and co-workers..."

"I'm sorry; I didn't mean anything by that remark. The reason I'm calling is because I wanted to ask you out to dinner tonight."

There was a brief silence on the other end of the line. "Pete...why?"

"I have something very important to tell you Beth."

I heard the trepidation and fear in her voice. "Don't hurt me anymore Pete, not when I'm about to leave on a trip," she said. "I can't take anymore heartache in my life…I'm trying to make amends with the Lord and with my ways. Please Pete, don't say we're through…"

This was not at all going the way that I had envisioned it in my mind. "Wait a second Beth, that's not why I'm calling." I could hear a muffled sob on the phone. "I wanted to tell you how much you mean to me; that I want us to be back together. Where are you?….What time does the flight leave?…I'm on my way to the airport."

"Oh Pete, I can't believe it! Thank you Lord, thank you Jesus… I'm at the ticket counter, waiting to check in at United."

"You wait there babe, I'll be at the airport in 15 minutes."

"I'll be here hon. Wild horses couldn't drag me away."

I headed toward Midway filled with anticipation and gratefulness. I was frankly surprised that she thought I was calling to tell her that we were finished. I guess that it helped me realize just how much pain and suffering this problem has caused us both. I was convinced that this was a test that the Father had orchestrated. In fact, I think it was a test for me to see if I could be a forgiving person, or was I just talking the talk, and not walking the walk. I almost failed, I thought. I was prepared to play the victim and tell the person that I loved the most in my life to take a walk, it was over. Some Christian I was.

I pulled into the day parking lot and ran toward United. I spotted Beth standing by the windows with her carry on. I ran to her, my whole being filled with love and longing, two emotions that had been lying dormant for too long in my soul.

I picked her up and gave her a kiss on those beautiful lips, "Beth, I'm sorry. I have been such a fool. I forgive you babe, and I want us to move on from this—together."

She held him tightly, sobbing gently. "Pete thank you so much. I've have been praying so hard for this day. I didn't know if it would come or not; I was preparing myself for the worst, thinking that I had hurt you so badly that you wouldn't want to be with me ever again."

"Let's not even talk about that Beth, let's move forward and focus on our future. I've been praying also, and talking with Father Mike. He helped me to realize how unfair I have been through this whole chain of events, how un-Christian I had been acting. I couldn't see it because I was feeling sorry for myself. But now I want to ensure that we focus on each other so that something like that never happens again. I think we both became apathetic in our marriage; we took each other for granted. I know that I did. I'm not going to let that happen again. You mean the world to me Beth, and I want you to be my wife forever."

"Oh babe, I'm so happy! What a surprise! I was prepared to spend a whole week in Milwaukee praying and agonizing over what you were going to decide about us. Now at least I can forget the agonizing part, but I'm still going to pray."

"Do you really have to go," I said.

She had a Kleenex out now trying to wipe away the mascara that had run down her face from her tears. "Yes, I'm making a couple of presentations during the conference. It's too late to back out now. But Pete I will call you every day, maybe twice a day! No, you'll be sleeping. I'll think of something. I feel like we just got married!"

"I know, so do I. Thank God it's over with!"

"I've got to get to the gate babe, the flight is boarding. Listen, I know that I probably don't even need to say this but I will. Don't worry about me being gone this week. Every waking thought of mine will be about you babe. I can't wait until Friday so that I can get 'home' to where I belong, and for that moment when I lay in your arms again."

I pulled her close and gave her another kiss. I trembled when my lips met hers. How could I have doubted her love? "You're right Beth; you don't have to say anything. I trust you...I love you...and I can't wait until Friday either. Have a safe trip. I'll be praying for you each day."

We let each other go and as she turned to make her way to the gate she said, "I never stopped loving you or praying for you Pete, and I never will. Bye hon...see you Friday."

I watched her walk to the screening area and felt so much joy in my heart that Father Mike's words came back to me..."Promise me that you will just stop and listen Pete, listen for His word, He wants to talk with you each day if you will just stop and listen."

Well, I was listening now, and I was thankful that both my heart and my ears were open.

<u>36</u>
Time For Celebration

Even though my dinner plans got scuttled, I felt like I was on top of the world. I needed to share my joy with someone. On the ride home I planned my day... First a workout and a run at St. Xav's, then over to Susan's to spend time with her and the boys, maybe even take the boys out to Dairy Queen for ice cream. I was much too giddy to eat by myself tonight, but who to call... Marilyn? Why not? We really had not had much opportunity to get to know very much about each other's lives. If we were going to be working together for awhile, it always helps to know what makes each other tick.

I dialed her number as I pulled into my driveway.

"Pete? What's up?"

"I just wanted to share some great news with you partner...Beth and I are back together!"

"Pete that's great! I thought that you were going to break the news to her over dinner tonight."

I got my gear from the trunk and went into the kitchen through the garage. "That was the plan but I called her and found out that she was at the airport about to board a flight to Milwaukee, so I beat feet over there and told her this morning. I'm glad that I did, I don't think that I could have held my feelings inside for a whole week while she was away."

"Well partner, all the prayers were answered," she said. "But I must admit, as much as I wanted you both to resolve your problems for the sake of your marriage, it was somewhat altruistic on my part."

"How so?

"You're a great cop Pete, but I need *all of you* working with me when we're on the street. There have been a couple of moments lately when your head wasn't completely in the game. That's dangerous for both of us," said Marilyn.

"Sorry Bens. Let me make it up to you by buying you dinner tonight. That way all my plans aren't ruined. Besides, we need to talk about this Rosato brutality beef."

"That sounds great...where and when?"

"How about Palermo's at 95th and Cicero around 6:30?"

"Okay, that's my favorite Italian joint for baked ziti, see you there partner."

"Bye Marilyn."

I hung up the phone and started a pot of coffee brewing, checked my email, then did a quick assessment of the house. Hmm...a little messy and dirty. Beth never let it get out of hand like this. I got busy straightening and cleaning, loaded up the dishwasher, took out the trash, and tidied up the bathrooms. An hour later I had it looking presentable again. Now the trick was to keep it that way while Beth was away; I didn't want to resume our relationship on the wrong foot.

Thirty minutes later I was walking through the front door of the gym at Xav's. I headed for the locker room and saw Father Mike getting ready to leave after his workout.

"Pete, what's up my friend?"

"I'm ready for a tough workout today Father, chest and tri's, then a timed three miler around the campus."

"You're an animal," said the priest. "Any progress on your plans to reconcile with Beth?"

"Tremendous progress! I met with her this morning at the airport and we made our amends. We're back together again. You were right about forgiving her. I had been wrong to allow things to go as far as they had. I feel like a kid waiting for Santa to arrive."

"Remember Pete, the Bible tells us to forgive and we will be forgiven. That means your loved ones and your enemies." Father Mike closed his locker and looked at me straight on... "When you forgive someone, it releases you from anger and allows you to receive the healing that you need. God does not want anything to stand between you and Him; His love is beyond our comprehension. Forgiving others spares us from the consequences of living out of an unforgiving heart. Don't you feel much better since you and Beth have forgiven each other?"

"Father, I feel fantastic!"

"Good, God's truth is at work. I'm off my friend; I have to prepare for Catechism classes tonight. Have a great workout, God bless you."

"Thanks Father."

A couple of hours later after the workout, I was over at Susan's playing soccer in the back yard. Joe's boys seemed a little lost without their Dad around. I sensed that they were clinging to me a bit more than usual. Later, Susan called us all inside for a great snack of watermelon and popsicles. The boys ate theirs quickly and ran back outside. I stayed inside to talk with Susan.

I told her about my meeting with Beth this morning and how much better I was feeling about things now. "I know this sounds crazy, but after all these years together I didn't think those butterflies in my stomach would ever return, but I felt them this morning. When I saw her at the airport, it was as if we had been apart for years."

Susan's eyes started to tear up... "I'm sorry Susan, how stupid of me to talk like this after what you've been through."

She wiped her eyes, "No Pete, these are tears of joy for you both. Beth has been here comforting me while she herself has been in turmoil. Her unselfishness and love for my family is one of the reasons that I've been able to carry on...I drew a lot of strength from that wife of yours. I've been praying for you both, that you would put your hurt feelings aside and just open your hearts to each other again. You are married to a remarkable woman Pete."

"I know that, and frankly I became a little too comfortable in my marriage and focused too much on what *I wanted and what I needed.* I'm afraid that I didn't place Beth above my own needs. I'm not going to allow that to happen again."

"Good. Making up is one of the best parts of a marriage. Joe and I didn't have many disagreements, but when it came to the making up part, we thoroughly enjoyed it."

I reached across the table and grabbed her hand... "Joe thought that you and the boys were the best thing that ever happened to him Susan. We'd talk for hours in that squad car we shared, and never once did an unkind word ever come out of his mouth about his family. He adored you. If I ever have children, my goal is to be just half as good at being a father to them as Joe was to your kids."

She wiped her tears again. "Thank you Pete. I know that I was blessed to have a husband like him, and I'm thankful for the time that we had. It will be hard, but we will move on and be happy because Joe would want us to."

I played a while longer with the kids before I had to leave to freshen up for my dinner with Marilyn. On my drive home I thought about Susan and remembered the verse from Jeremiah...

"For I know the plans I have for you," declared the Lord, "plans to prosper you and not to harm you, plans to give you hope and a future."

I was confident that our Savior was going to take care of her, and that Joe would be standing right by His side.

Palermo's was crowded as usual; it has always been one of the most popular Italian restaurants on the South side of Chicago, and I knew well enough to make a reservation. We placed our orders, and within a few minutes our salads arrived.

"Bens, would you mind if I blessed the meal?"

"Not at all Pete."

We bowed our heads and prayed..."Father, we thank you for this day and all of the blessings that you bring us each day. Thank you for our families and our health, thank you for your wisdom and guidance when we lose our way, and thank you for bringing the two of us together as partners. We pray that you will watch over us as we fight to keep Satan and his kind in check. Now we ask that you bless this meal so that it will make us stronger warriors. In Jesus' name we pray, Amen."

"Amen."

Marilyn dug into her salad. "Pete that was beautiful. I'm learning so many things from you, not only on the street, but how to conduct my private life as well."

I snagged a piece of French bread, and offered the bowl to her.

"Oh no thanks, I'll be eating enough carbs already once the ziti comes, I don't want to make it worse by adding bread to it."

"Wow, you're much more disciplined than I am. And by the way, I'm learning from you as well Marilyn; thank you for the compliment though."

"You're welcome. I guess what I mean to say is that I admire the way that you don't hide the fact that you're a Christian. Blessing the meal...most guys would be too embarrassed to do that, especially with another cop. But to you it comes naturally; it's all part of your character. I'm trying to get where you're at Pete. I've had some rough times in the past, some due to my own reckless lifestyle. I don't want to go back to those times, I want to move forward. I can do that so much easier by following your lead."

I took a drink of water. "I'm humbled that you think so much of me. But know that I struggle too Marilyn, and I've made some bad choices as well. But I recognize that if I walk with Him each day, He'll get me back on the path that leads to eternal salvation. The other 'ace in the hole' that I play, is my other partner—St. Michael."

"The Archangel," she said.

"Yes, I pray my prayer to him each night that he will be my back up when Satan tries his best to be victorious over me."

We finished our salads just as the main course arrived.

Digging into her pasta dish, Marilyn said, "Pete, I hadn't thought much about him, but he is after all the patron saint for us cops. I think I'll start saying a prayer to him before each shift as well. It couldn't hurt could it?"

We finished our meal amidst some small talk and then walked out to the lot where our vehicles were parked. "Pete, this Rosato beef has got me worried. Not from the standpoint of me being involved, but other than the video from my dash cam, I'm the best witness to The Hammer roughing that guy up."

"I know, but don't let it worry you," I said. "The mere fact that you are working with me, automatically makes you a target in Rosato's book. We'll just have to watch our backs even more until the complaint gets resolved. But something tells me that Sgt. Castro is going to watch this one closely. He's not a member of the 'Hammer Fan Club,' if you know what I mean. We should get a quick investigation and disposition."

We walked to her car and she opened the door. "Well I wish either we were on another shift, or that he was, but with both of us in school that's not even an option. Working together is going to get more uncomfortable than it already is."

"I know, but given his record down at Internal Affairs, I don't think that they'll cut him any slack on this one. He could be on the way out."

"I hope so," she said.

"Listen, I'll see you Thursday night Marilyn. Get some rest and don't worry about Rosato. We'll watch our backs and let St. Michael handle the rest."

"Okay partner, goodnight."

"Goodnight Bens."

<u>37</u>
The Hammer's Gun

I woke up the next day feeling rested and prepared to enjoy my day off. As I started to prepare a pot of coffee the phone rang.

"Pete, Sgt. Castro here. I hope that I didn't wake you, I intended on leaving a message on your machine but you picked up."

"No sarge," I said. "I'm up and fixing coffee."

"Good. I'm calling to tell you to report in plain clothes Thursday, you're back on Tac."

"Man, that's great news, thanks. Wait a minute...who will my partner be?"

"Well, Capt Steele and I discussed that last night. The complaint against Rosato helped us make what was already a fairly easy decision—you'll be partnered with Marilyn. She's a good cop; based on her record and what I've seen thus far, she is deserving of this assignment. Plus, getting you both out of uniform and not attending roll call with Rosato, will hopefully ease some probable tension between you guys."

I was elated. I wasn't losing Marilyn and I didn't have to break in a new partner. "Have you told Benson yet?"

"No. I was about to call her next, unless you care to do that for me."

"I sure will sarge," I said. "Thanks for everything. You know I was worried about who would be filling in for Mac during his recovery, but you have been a pleasure to work for."

"Thanks Pete. You and Marilyn are both on the same page as I am, not only with regard to police work, but life in general. I would go through any door with either of you—you're good cops."

"That means a lot," I said. "See you tomorrow Sarge."

"Okay Pete, don't' forget to call Benson"

"Roger that."

I waited till nine o'clock then dialed Marilyn's cell phone.

"Good morning Pete!"

"Morning Bens, you sound wide-awake..."

"I should be," she said. "I just finished a five mile run; I'm having a cup of coffee before I head over to the gym for a workout."

"Listen, I've got some great news for you...I spoke with Castro this morning—welcome to the Tac Team!"

There was a brief pause on the other end. "No...you're kidding me!"

"Nope, report to work Thursday in plain clothes."

"Man, that's super news, thanks Pete. I'm fired up now...think I'll do squats today—heavy!"

"Good for you partner. I've got to get my workout in, and then I've got an afternoon class."

"Well you have a great day partner. I can't wait to get back to work!"

"I know," I said, "me too."

"Pete..."

"What Bens?"

"God's been good to us hasn't He."

"He sure has partner; He loves us."

"Where the hell you at Frankie?" said Rosato into the phone. He was getting impatient with this punk now. He was to have met with him on Taylor Street in Little Italy twenty minutes ago with the gun.

"I'm comin' Hammer, I'm right around the corner," came the reply.

"Well hurry your ass up and get in my car when you get here."

"Still got that Hummer?"

"Yeah idiot, I'm in front of the tattoo joint."   Hammer was getting impatient.

Frankie was an ex-con that grew up with Rosato. They had spent lots of time together in the principal's office in school, sometimes for pranks, but most times for fighting. They teamed up to wreak havoc on many on their classmates, stealing lunch money and being typical bullies in school and afterward. Frankie never made it past the third year at Hubbard High School. He teamed up with several other neighborhood ne'r do wells, and they got involved with the drug trade. Frankie was no stranger to jail or the State Penitentiary, having done stints in both for drug and gun charges. He quickly gained a "rep" for being able to get just about any type of gun that one might need. That's why he was here to meet with Rosato today.

A minute later Frankie hopped in the front seat of the Hummer. "How you doin' man?" Ain't seen you for awhile..."

"I'm fine you idiot: got the piece?"

"Sure do...what's it for man?" Frankie pulled the .22 caliber Ruger from his waistband.

"None of your damn business you dumb wop, and nobody better ever know that you seen me today, capice?"

Frankie handed the revolver over to Rosato. "A wheel gun? I wanted a pistol man."

"Hey I got what I could on short notice. Anyway, there's no problems with this one—serial numbers have been all filed off—no way to trace it." Frankie crossed his arms and puffed his chest. "Nothing but the best for my bud... Got my dough?"

Rosato handed Frankie $300. "Hey man, I said five bills for this piece!"

"Shut up asshole unless you want cops all over your corner tonight. I can put the word out about your drug turf to my buddies in Vice."

Frankie grudgingly took the money Rosato handed him. "This ain't right man..."

"Don't worry about it, and keep your mouth shut. Now get outta here loser."

"Yeah, sure, have a nice fuckin' day." Frankie jumped out of the Hummer and watched as Rosato drove away. "That guy's gonna get his one of these days," thought Frankie. "I hope that I'm around to see him go down."

<u>38</u>
Sal...I'm Hit!

My biology class today left my head swimming, maybe because I just wasn't able to focus on the material. I was thinking about getting back on the Tac Team, and realizing how much more freedom that assignment offers cops like me that really love working the street. To be able to work the entire 8th District, rather than having to stay within the boundaries of one's beat is the best job ever. I was excited as well about Beth coming home tomorrow...we needed some time together to heal our wounds and repair our relationship. God had given me a gift when he brought her into my life, and I was going to be thankful each day from this moment forward.

I got home and had a quick snack of yogurt and a bran muffin, then headed for the bedroom to grab some sleep before it was time for work. Life was good...

Beth couldn't believe her good fortune. The group that she was to present to on Friday, had made another commitment for the same time slot, and therefore couldn't be there as agreed upon earlier. She called her supervisor in Chicago and got permission to leave early. She would be home tonight instead of Friday night. Her flight would get her back to Chicago around 7:30 pm, which meant that she could be home around eight. Hopefully Pete would be napping in preparation for work that night. If she played her cards right, Pete would be in for a big surprise.

Several hours later, Beth eased into their driveway. Not wanting to make any noise, she didn't pull into the garage. Pete liked sleeping with a "sound machine" on to drown out any distraction that would interrupt his sleep. But Beth wasn't taking any chances. She quietly entered through the front door, and went to the guest bedroom where she dropped her luggage. She used the bathroom in there to undress and freshen up, and then she crept into their bedroom.

Pete was sleeping like a baby, unaware that she was in the room. Gazing at her husband, she paused a moment to reflect on what God had given her. This man had devoted his life to her; she would never again hurt him. She pulled back the covers and slid into bed next to him.

"What...who?"

"It's me honey...surprise!"

Pete rubbed his eyes in disbelief. "I thought you weren't coming home until tomorrow."

"Me too," she said. "But they didn't need me at the conference today, so I got permission to leave early. Aren't' you happy?"

Pete wrapped his arms around his wife. "Happy *and* grateful babe-- welcome home!"

They shared a long passionate kiss. "Pete, I don't ever want to be away from you again," said Beth. "If you don't have any objections, I'd like to get busy on bringing a 'Pete junior' into this world."

"Are you serious? Objections...none whatsoever. You're sure about this...the baby part?"

"I've never been as sure of anything as I am of this right now."

The sound machine echoed the ocean's gentle waves lapping against the sandy beach, while Pete and Beth drifted away, buoyed by their rebirth of love and commitment.

A few hours later, Pete was walking into the back door of the 8th District. He went directly to the Tac room where Beth was already looking over the crime reports. "Looks like there's a burglary pattern Pete, warehouses being hit and office equipment being taken. What do you think? Want to focus on that tonight?"

"Well hello to you too," I said.

"Oh, sorry Pete," she said. "I'm just really excited about this new assignment. Hi."

"Sure, that's sounds like a good place to start," I said.

"Great! Let's get busy partner."

We located our unmarked car in the parking lot, and made our way out to the industrial area around Ford City. This area was prime for burglaries—lots of businesses, warehouses, and trucking companies, plus the mall occupied several square miles of this Chicago real estate. Midnights were the ideal time for thieves to work the area. We cruised around for a couple of hours, checked a few doors, but failed to find any suspicious activity.

"Pete, are you ready for a cup?"

Marilyn had been driving and was probably getting a little sleepy. "Sure," I said. "Dunkin Donuts sounds good."

Ten minutes later we were inside getting a couple of cups to go. As we made our way back to our vehicle, Rosato pulled in next to us.

"Well...look what we got here, Starsky and Hutch! More ass kissin' Shannon?"

"Take it easy brother, there's no need to get hostile," I said.

Rosato got out of his car and squared up to me and Marilyn. "Yeah, no need to get hostile, except I got two cops that turn out to be rats."

"What are you talking about Sal?"

"What am I talkin' about?" he said. "I'm talkin' about you two dimin' me out to Castro, saying I smacked that scumbag from the pizza joint robbery."

Marilyn bristled at that. "Hey, don't go blaming us for you stupid behavior. We didn't say anything to Castro about you; Sgt Morales told us at check off that the prisoner complained about getting roughed up. That's when Castro called OPR. We didn't know a thing about any of it until we came in at the end of the shift. Besides, the dash cam video was inventoried as evidence that will speak for itself."

Rosato didn't like that response. "You guys know that the bosses are lookin' for any excuse to fire me. It would help if when you gave your statements, that you just say that you didn't see anything."

Marilyn looked him straight in the eye and said, "Are you asking us to lie?"

"It's not lying man, besides haven't you smacked somebody around just to teach them a lesson?"

I was getting angry now, almost on the verge of saying something that I would probably regret later. "No Sal, I've never hit anyone unless it was in self defense. I don't treat people like that, and neither should you. Whatever you do on the street, you'll have to live with, right or wrong. You may get away with it once in a while, but eventually you're going to pay the price, either here on earth or on judgment day."

"You know what Shannon, I'm sick of your holier than thou attitude. You think you're so pure, that you're some kind of 'White Knight' or something? Now you got 'Wonder Woman' working with you and you both think your shit don't stink. Well if you were such a great cop, how come O'Hara got killed? Yeah Benson, watch your back, this guy's dangerous."

I started to move toward Rosato, but Marilyn quickly stepped in between us. "Pete, let's get away from this creep, he's polluting the air that I breathe."

We got into our car while Rosato was still running his mouth... "Yeah, run away Shannon you coward. Maybe if you were more of a man your old partner would still be alive."

Marilyn headed back toward the Ford City area. "I can't believe that guy," she said. "Pete, don't let that idiot get to you. And for God's sake, don't take what he said about Joe to heart. We all know what went down that night...you both did a great job. What happened was neither your fault nor Joe's."

"You're right," I said. "I guess I let him get my goat there. It ticks me off because I had such a great day, and I let him ruin it."

"Care to expound on that," she said.

"Beth came home early and surprised me while I was napping."

"Whoa, that's enough partner," she said. "I get the picture."

She turned down 72nd Street, "All kidding aside though, that's great Pete. You two are well on your way to making up for lost time."

"Yes we are, and it's such a relief..."

"I'm glad for you both," said Marilyn. "I hope that I'm where you're at some day. I was almost there at one point, and then it all fell apart."

"Want to talk about it?" I said.

She pulled over and explained while we drank our coffee. "A few years ago I was living with a guy, and yes, I know it was wrong, but I thought that he was 'the one.' Anyway, I got wind that he was seeing other women and...I'm not proud of this, but I followed him one night and caught him meeting another gal downtown. I confronted him when he came home, and he lied about everything until I told him that I had followed him and I that I had seen him with her. He moved out the next day, and for about a year I lived recklessly trying to blot out any memories of him."

"What do you mean, recklessly?"

Sipping her coffee she said, "I dated a bunch of guys and, regretfully, had a few one night stands. The last guy I dated turned out to be the stalker type...wouldn't leave me alone. He called my home and would leave dozens of messages on the machine. I finally got fed up and ran a criminal history on him—he had served time for rape. That scared me; it made me re-evaluate who I was and where I was going. I sat down with a girlfriend of mine, one who is very spiritual and has a great relationship with Christ. She told me that I had looked for comfort in every place except the right place. I decided to turn all my problems over to God, and surrender to His will. My life improved after that, I still had problems mind you, but I no longer had to hide from them. I just brought them to Him. I'm still working on the spiritual part of things, but life is getting better."

"That's a powerful story Bens, thanks for sharing that with me."

"You're welcome," she said. "I just hope that someday I'll have a relationship like you and Beth, until then I'm going to concentrate on being the best person and the best cop that I can be."

"Amen Marilyn."

"Beat 833, we've got a report of a possible break in at the warehouse, 4500 block on 72nd Street."

We heard the simulcast and headed in that direction. "I wonder if that's bogus, we just checked that area," Marilyn said.

"Yeah, I know, but we could have missed something, let's give 833 a hand checking it out."

A couple of minutes later we killed our lights and eased into a cul-de-sac on the side of a five story building. "Got your light partner?"

"Got it", she said.

Beat 833, Officer Herm Groman, was a one man unit, we decided to team up with him to do a search of the building. Groman went in first, followed by Marilyn. As I was about to enter, Rosato pulled up in his one man unit.

"I'll check the perimeter and doors," he said.

As much as I hated to do it, I couldn't let him do that alone. "Bens, go with Groman. I've got to help Sal with the outside search."

"Pete, be careful," she said.

"Will do partner."

We checked the West side of the building which had multiple doorways and a couple of outside stairwells. We made our way around the back of the structure. Not much light; some of the outside fixtures had either burnt out or been busted by vandals. From the corner of my eye, I spotted some movement by an alcove on the side of the building.

"Sal, I've got movement over there," I whispered. I directed the beam from my flashlight directly on the wall's indentation, "Police! Come out, do it now!"

I moved to a position to my right, and took cover behind a utility pole. Rosato did the same to my left. As I got into position, I yelled once more—"Police, I see you, come out now with your hands in the air, do it now!"

A figure slowly emerged from the shadows...

"Gun!" I shouted as I saw the subject holding a weapon in one hand.

"Put the gun on the ground, now!"

He bent over slowly and put the gun down. He stood back up, blinded by the beams of light from both our flashlights.

"Now turn around," I said. "Move slowly backward toward the sound of my voice."

What looked to be a Hispanic male in his 20's, followed my commands until I told him to stop.

"Now, slowly get down on your knees, keep your hands in the air, and don't move."

"You got 'em covered Sal?" I was about to holster my weapon and move forward to cuff this guy when my whole world exploded! I heard the loud report of a weapon firing and felt a sledgehammer-like force strike me in the chest.

How could he have shot me? We had him triangulated, the bad guy at the apex, Sal and me at the base. After all, this guy had already dropped his weapon and was complying with my commands.

I'm hit, I thought..."Sal, Sal, I'm hit!"

But how? I saw this guy drop his gun. Did he pull another one that I missed?

Just then another shot, but I'm positive that it's not coming my way. What's happening...?

My vest saved me from serious injury; the kinetic energy of the round knocked the wind out of me and bruised my chest. *But I'm alive....*

Recovering some of my senses I see Sal standing over me.

"Help me up buddy."

Sal's not moving—something's wrong here. Sal has something in his hand—a gun, but it's not his police pistol.

"Sal, what's going on? Sal..."

Then the most intense pain that I have ever felt as I feel a bullet smash into my skull. The last thing that I remember is the smell of gunpowder, and then looking into Sal's eyes and feeling like I am staring directly at Satan himself.

<u>39</u>
Shots Fired—Officer Involved!

Marilyn and Groman made their way down the stairway. As they exited the building they heard the shots.

"Oh my God—Pete!" shouted Marilyn.

They ran around the corner of the building, weapons drawn, and coming around the corner they saw two bodies lying on the ground...one of the bodies was Pete. Marilyn ran to the motionless form of her partner and immediately knelt down beside her fallen comrade.

"Pete! Pete!" She immediately got on the radio, "10-1, Officer down, send an ambulance, 4500 on 72nd Street...10-1!"

Looking to Rosato she asked, "What happened here?"

Rosato looked at her and shrugged, "The guy pulled a gun and shot; I returned fire and killed him. I was so busy and so focused on the bad guy, that I didn't even know Shannon was hit."

Marilyn quickly assessed Pete's wound—*shot in the head she thought, he needs medical care now!* She noticed a bullet hole in Pete's shirt also, must've got hit in the vest too she thought. *But then how did he get hit in the head?* And though he was bleeding heavily, her military and police experience led her to believe that it was a survivable wound. *Something's not right here, but first things first; I've got to get him to the ER.*

Seconds later the ambulance arrived on the scene. They did a quick medical eval, and then loaded him into the back.

"Groman, I'm going with him," Marilyn told him. "Stay here and protect the crime scene, there's something wrong here—keep your eye on Rosato, I think he's up to something."

"Sure thing," he said. "I hope Pete's okay."

"Say a prayer," she said.

They sped off into the city night, blue lights flashing and siren wailing like a ship rocketing through space. Inside the back of the ambulance, amidst all the noise and confusion, Marilyn willed her spirit to be transported to a place in time where she used to talk comfortably with her Lord. She was on her knees in church, staring at the Crucifix...

Dear Jesus, my Lord and Savior, I pray that if it be Thy will, that you lay your healing hands on your servant, Pete, and heal him of his wounds. I pray that you forgive him his sins, and ask that you allow him to continue to fight evil here on earth. Lord, I see you working through him in many ways to benefit myself and others. I pray that you will give him the strength that he needs to recover...Amen.

The ambulance pulled into the ER at Little Company, and thankfully Dr Grossman and the ER staff were waiting to take Pete from the ambulance. Marilyn had heard of Pete's friendship with the doctor, and the fact that he felt that Dr. Grossman was a miracle man when it came to saving the lives of gunshot victims. He would have his chance to live up to that reputation now, thought Marilyn. I hope that Pete was right...

They quickly unloaded Pete and brought him into the ER. There was a flurry of activity, that to the untrained eye seemed disjointed, but in fact, this ER team was well choreographed and knew exactly what to do. After some quick preliminary assessment, starting of fluids, and stoppage of bleeding, they wheeled him into x-ray within minutes. There's always been what's referred to as the "Golden Hour" when it comes to serious injuries. It is widely believed that the victim's chances of survival are greatest if they receive definitive care in the operating room within the first hour after a severe injury. Pete had made it here within twenty minutes; if that rule was indeed a valid one, then Pete would have a chance.

St. Michael the Archangel hovered over Pete's wounded body...Peter; you have been a faithful servant to Our Lord, Jesus Christ. You have done well in your battles against Satan and his evil followers. You have listened to His words and lived them. The Lord has looked with favor upon you; He has deemed that Satan will not win this battle. This day you will live to fight again in His name. Well done good and faithful servant, receive the blessings of the Lord; receive life...

Beth had fallen asleep in the arms of the man that she had loved forever. Their reconciliation had been nothing short of what fairy tales are made of. Making love with a divine purpose made their coupling all the more sacred. Her last thoughts were those of thankfulness and gratitude that they had been given a second chance at a life together. Her peaceful sleep was now interrupted by something...was that the doorbell she thought? She got up from bed and made her way to the front door. Looking out through the curtains she saw an unmarked police car; she looked through the peephole and saw two official looking types.

Opening the door a crack using the safety lock, Beth said, "Who are you and what do you want?"

"Mrs. Shannon, I'm Sgt. Tim Bollig, and this is Reverend Dean, we're with the Chicago Police Department. There's been an accident...."

<u>40</u>
Facing The Fear

The ride in the back of the police car to the hospital seemed to take forever. Beth tried to get information from Rev. Dean and Sgt. Bollig, but they would only say that Pete had been involved in an incident with a burglary suspect. Although she was still upset, her uneasiness was tempered by the fact that this had happened with Pete in the past. There were several occasions where he wound up in the ER for stitches or fractures after having been involved in a tussle with an arrestee.

As they pulled into the hospital though, Beth's heart stopped. There were dozens of police cars and news media trucks parked all over the property. ***Pete's dead, she thought...*** She ran out of the car and into the ER. She spotted Marilyn immediately and ran to her... "What happened...is Pete alright...tell me he's okay...please, tell me he's not dead!"

Marilyn wrapped her arms around Beth and held her close as Beth broke down. "He's not dead Beth. Dr. Grossman is working on him right now; they sent him to x-ray to see exactly where the bullet is at."

"Where is he shot?" Beth asked.

Marilyn grabbed her by the shoulders and looked her straight in the eye. "Beth, listen to me, I've seen dozens of gunshot wounds in my career. I know that I'm not a doctor, but from what I saw of Pete's wound, it was likely a survivable one. Not only that, but Pete has an incredibly strong will to survive. If anyone can get through this, it's Pete."

"Where is he shot?"

"In the head," Marilyn replied.

"Oh...Lord no..." Beth wailed and collapsed in Marilyn's arms. Rev. Dean assisted her in getting Beth into one of the chairs that lined the halls of the ER. The news cameras started to close in on them until Sgt. Bollig threatened them with arrest. Just then the Police Superintendent walked through the ER doors and into a phalanx of reporters.

"Chief, tell us what happened."

"Is the officer dead?"

"Who shot your officer, Chief? Is it gang related?"

A barrage of questions rained down upon him as he was quickly enveloped in a fog of reporters. Having only a few answers himself, he deferred to his Media Relations Specialist, Sgt. Amy Grey.

"Sgt, what's the officer's name, how many years has he been on the force?

Sgt. Grey was adept at manipulating the press. She had been befuddling even the most extreme left wingers that wanted to blame the cops anytime a shooting occurred in the city. This night she would lead them down the same path again without them even realizing it. She steered them outside to the entrance doors and effortlessly dodged many of the questions that would identify Pete as the wounded officer. It was Department policy not to release any personal information until such time as all family members were notified. Pete's sister had yet to be contacted, therefore the press would just have to wait until that occurred. In the meantime, Amy would run interference for both her boss and the family. It was an assignment that she relished.

Beth's head felt like it was about to explode. The scene at the hospital was surreal...this couldn't be happening to them now—not after they had just reconciled and spent such a beautiful night together. *Lord, I beg you, please don't take him from me. Not now. Not after what we've been through already. Have we not suffered enough?* She lifted her silent prayers to God as the reality of what happened began to sink in.

As she regained some composure, Rev. Dean moved her into the Chaplain's office. "Beth, I know that you and Pete are Catholics. May I call your pastor and advise him of what has happened?"

"Yes reverend, please do. I need Pete to receive the Sacrament of the Anointing of the Sick," Beth answered.

"Fine, I'll do that right now. In the meantime, use this phone to contact any family members or friends that you need to. And if I may, let me tell you this—your husband is no stranger to me. I've known Pete for some time, and I know that he is a fine Christian man in every sense of the word. He has been living a blessed life, and he serves as an example to his colleagues and friends. I am confident that our Lord will be with both of you through all of this. He won't turn a deaf ear to your prayers. The Bible tells us in Luke 11:9, ***Ask and it will be given to you...*** Pray Beth.

I will pray, she thought. I know that He listens to his children. Just as He rescued me from my infidelity and alcohol abuse, so also will He hear my prayers for Pete. I know that He has plans for us, just as He told us in Jeremiah, ***"plans to prosper you and not to harm you, plans to give you hope and a future."*** My dear Lord and Savior please let there be a future for us...

41
Look In The Dumpster

The Major Case Squad and Crime Lab personnel had arrived at the shooting scene. Before their arrival however, Officer Groman had preserved the scene by marking off the area with bright yellow crime scene tape. Remembering Benson's words before she left for the hospital with Pete, he kept his eyes on Rosato. During the time that he was cordoning off the area, he noticed Rosato walk to the far end of the lot in the area reserved for the garbage dumpsters. Rather than ask him about it, Groman decided that he would advise the crime scene investigators of the unusual behavior.

The detectives took a preliminary statement from Rosato, trying to piece together what had occurred. "So you're telling me that the subject fired at Shannon as he came out from behind cover," asked Det. Latarski. She had been with the Major Case Squad for several years and had a bright analytical mind. She already had an idea as to what may have happened here tonight, and it was not good.

"Yeah, that's what I said," Rosato replied. "I don't know why Shannon broke cover, we didn't have the guy controlled yet, didn't even know if he had a gun or not. I think he's just the 'Cowboy' type, likes to take chances. You know his partner was killed a while back?"

"Yes, I know that," Latarski said. "But tell me...how is it that Shannon has been shot twice, once in the head, and once in the chest?"

"Uh...I don't know. I guess the guy could have fired twice... You know how it is in shootings, stuff happens so fast that you don't really know for sure what went on."

"You're right Rosato, I don't know for sure what happened here. But here's what I do know...the perp's gun is a six shot revolver, one round's been fired. Shannon's got two bullet holes. There's two .40 caliber spent casings lying in some tall weeds near the fence line. It seems logical to me that there may have been more than one shooter. Does that make sense to you?"

The Hammer began to get a little nervous and started to stammer. He had looked for those empty casings but wasn't able to locate them before Benson and Groman came on the scene. "Listen, I don't know what you trying to say here, but I don't like the sound of it. You tryin' to accuse me of somethin'?"

Latarski kept her cool and said, "I'm not accusing you of anything Officer Rosato. All I'm saying is the bad guy's got one hole, Shannon's got two holes. That adds up to three shots where I come from. You say you fired one time after the bad guy shot Pete. It's my job to investigate the circumstances surrounding this shooting, and to do it impartially. I intend to gather all of the facts through interviews and evidence collection. That being said, I need you to surrender your weapon to me for ballistic testing at the Crime Lab."

"That's bullshit! You're tryin' to frame me...hey, I tried to save Shannon's life here!"

By now Rosato's protestations had drawn the attention of the WC, Capt. Steele. He quickly came over to exert control over the situation. "Rosato, it's standard procedure for all weapons to be inventoried and sent to the Crime Lab for testing. That includes yours, Shannon's, and the offender's weapon. You need to cooperate with the investigation or be subject to disciplinary action."

The Hammer reluctantly drew his weapon and handed it over to Capt. Steele. "This ain't right boss, I'm in pain here. I just saw my partner get shot, and I was forced to shoot an individual. I need some down time here."

Steele looked at Latarski. "Do you have enough information from him at this point? If so, I'd like to release him to a representative from the Employee Assistance Program. As you know, when any of our people are involved in a critical incident they have the right to be counseled by the EAP Unit."

"I think that I've got exactly what I need Captain," she said. "He's free to go."

Steele led Rosato over to his command vehicle. They both left for the station where EAP would meet with him for counseling. As soon as they pulled away, Groman approached Latarski.

"Detective, can I have a word with you?"

"What is it?" Latarski asked.

"Before your team arrived, I noticed that Officer Rosato walked over to that set of dumpsters at the far end of the lot," Groman said as he pointed in the direction of the dumpsters. "I'm not sure, but I think that he may have put something in one of them."

"Really...?"

"Yeah, and while Benson and I were inside the building, we came across a security room with monitors. If you check it out there's probably some surveillance cameras somewhere on the property that may shed even more light on what went down here tonight."

"Thanks for that information Officer. I'll have the crime scene team include that in their search. That and the cameras may provide the missing piece of the puzzle that I need to validate my hypothesis."

"You're welcome," Groman said. "It just seems fishy to me...Shannon's a good cop. He wouldn't break cover unless he knew the guy was either unarmed, or that his partner was covering him."

"We'll check it out, believe me. Something's not right with this one..."

<u>42</u>
St. Michael

It was now two hours since Pete had been shot, and the hospital looked like a media event at some Hollywood movie premier. Television and other news outlets had their trucks and lighting set up for their reporters to go "live" from the hospital. The influx of family, friends, and colleagues swelled the hospital's ER area until it looked like some type of government giveaway program was underway.

Beth was still tucked safely away in the Chaplains' office. By now she had been joined by Father Mike, Pete's sister, Lisa, Beth's parents, Mac and his wife Shirley, and Susan O'Hara. Still no word from Dr. Grossman... The last information Beth had was that Pete was on his way to the x-ray department.

The TV was on and tuned to the local ABC news station, where it was being reported that a police shooting had occurred on Chicago's Southwest Side. A suspected burglar was shot to death, and a police officer seriously wounded and in life-threatening condition at Little Company of Mary Hospital. The local reporter was interviewing the detectives on the scene...

"We're told by Det. Sanela Latarski of the Major Case Squad that this is an open investigation..."

Turning to Latarski, the reporter asked, "Detective, why is this case still open? Wasn't the offender shot and killed?"

Latarski looked up from her notes, "We believe that there were two shooters involved, one is deceased, and the other is at large. Until we can get our physical evidence to the Crime Lab, I can't give any more information other than what I've already told you. Thank you."

Latarski walked away and conferred with the other members of the team, then quickly got into her car to head toward the hospital. She needed to talk with the doctor on duty before she was fully confident that her hunch about what happened tonight was right.

Finally making her way to the ER and fighting her way through the gaggle of reporters, she spotted Marilyn pacing the hallway. She and Benson had known each other for a few years, after having met at a Law Enforcement Torch Run. They kept in touch through phone calls and emails, each of them sharing an interest in police work and fitness.

"Marilyn, how are you? I'm so sorry about Pete; I know that you both had only just started working together...this is so terrible."

Fighting back the tears, Marilyn hugged Latarski. "Sanela, I'm crushed...I feel like I let him down. I should have stayed with him instead of going with Groman..."

"Nonsense," said Latarski. "I talked with Groman at the scene. He said Pete made the decision to go with Rosato and help him with the perimeter search. It's nobody's fault."

"Maybe so, but how could it have happened? Pete's a great cop— he's tactically sound and super cautious. He doesn't take chances."

"I know that Marilyn," Latarski answered, "That's why I need to speak with whoever is handling Pete's treatment here. If my hunch is correct about what went down out there, we've got a huge problem on our hands."

Marilyn was puzzled now, *what could she mean by that?* "Dr. Grossman is the ER doc on duty. In fact, see if you can't get an update for us—he hasn't been out in over an hour, and we're all going nutty worrying. I'll be in the Chaplain's office with the family."

"Okay," said Latarski as she made her way to the nurses' station.

Ten minutes later Latarski and Grossman walked into the Chaplain's office. Beth held her mother tightly, "Doctor, is Pete okay? Is he going to live?"

Grossman closed the door and addressed Beth directly, "Your husband is a strong man, in both body and spirit. In the last few years I've come to know Pete as someone who cares very much about his family, his job, and the community that he serves. Mrs. Shannon, I will share this with you...there hasn't been one time that Pete and I have talked about anything, whether here at the hospital, or on a Department ride a long that he occasionally takes me on, that he hasn't talked about you and how much he loves you. He worships the ground that you walk on. Not only that, but Pete walks with Christ each day. So much so, that he even convinced me to renew my faith in the Lord. Pete Shannon is truly a disciple of Christ."

Beth was appreciative of the doctor's words, but she feared that he was softening the harsh reality that he was about to share with her. She felt herself ready to collapse at any moment...

"Something miraculous happened out there tonight," Grossman said. "Pete was shot in the head. An injury like that is normally either fatal or leaves the patient with permanent brain damage. Neither of those two things happened to Pete."

"Thank you Lord...thank you Jesus," Beth burst out in tears of joy that her prayers of healing had been answered, which led to everyone else in the room sobbing and giving thanks as well.

"Pete's prognosis is good. He was shot with what looks to be a .22 caliber bullet. Those can be extremely damaging once they enter the brain or the body cavity. Their high velocity causes them to bounce around inside, cutting and nicking veins and arteries, and damaging organs. In Pete's case, either due to the angle of the gunshot itself, or possibly a round that wasn't fully charged, this bullet struck his skull and travelled around it, just under the skin, and stopped behind his right ear. He has a slight skull fracture, and a concussion, but absolutely no brain damage. I had him undergo an MRI, which is noninvasive; to verify that there was indeed no damage. I'll double check with our Chief Neurologist, Dr. Kearney, but I'm almost positive that he's fine. Barring any complications, he should be able to be back at work in about six weeks. Anyway, that's why I'm so tardy in coming out to give you an update. Can you forgive me?"

Beth jumped up out of her chair and hugged Grossman. "Yes doctor, you are forgiven. Thank you so much... Can I see him now?"

"I had him moved to ICU. He's still unconscious," said Grossman, "but that doesn't concern me; it's the body's way of shutting down until the trauma passes. The fact that Pete survived this ordeal tonight was in large measure due to his physical fitness. It's been my experience, in both the military and civilian worlds, that most people die from the trauma associated with being shot, rather than the actual injury. He should regain consciousness anytime. Your husband's fitness, among other things, saved his life."

Beth was so relieved. She believed what the doctor said about Pete's fitness, but knowing her Lord and Savior as she and Pete both did, she knew that His hand was involved.

Grossman took her by the arm, "C'mon, I'll bring you to see him."

They walked to the South Pavilion ICU where Pete was laying amidst a plethora of machines and tubes. His head was bandaged and his face still carried some of the dried blood from the wound and was a bit swollen, but through it all Beth thought that he looked as handsome as ever.

"When he wakes up he'll be sore and groggy. I've got him on a saline drip and some pain killer also. Don't be surprised if he says something wacky at first until he gets his bearings. I've got to update his chart and see some other patients, but the nurses are close by if you need anything."

Beth gave him another hug and said, "Dr. Grossman, you are an angel, and words can't express how grateful I am to you for saving my husband's life."

"Mrs. Shannon, I did what I was trained to do. But frankly I think that Pete's life was saved more through divine intervention than medicine. Did he ever tell you that he prayed to St. Michael the Archangel before his shift each day?"

"Yes, he told me," said Beth.

"Well just between you and me, I think that St. Michael came to his aid tonight. I think that when the angel saw that Pete was in trouble, he made sure that his fellow warrior would pull through. Sometimes things happen that are inexplicable—this is one of them. I'll see you in a bit..."

Grossman walked out of the ICU and Beth bent over her wounded husband. "Pete, honey can you hear me? It's Beth. You're going to be fine babe. You rest as long as you need to, and when you feel strong enough to awaken I'll be right here waiting for you. I'll never leave you honey...ever."

She pulled a chair close to the bed, grabbed Pete's hand and lay her head down on his hospital bed and began to pray..."Lord, you are the light that shines bright in times of darkness. You have the power to give, and the power to take away. I bless you for hearing my prayers for your servant Pete. Your light shines bright in my soul. I praise you in good times and in bad, and know that it is your will and not mine that will be done. Open my heart even more, that I might stop and hear your word always. Lord I pray that I will remember that you are by my side and that I can do all things through you."

I almost lost him, she thought. I've been so wrapped up in what I wanted and who I was, that I almost failed my devoted husband. How blessed am I? God put us together for a reason, He does want us to have a future, and I focused too much on things that really have no meaning, instead of focusing on being the family that He wants us to be and praising Him. *Father forgive me...*

She felt Pete squeeze her hand...

"Beth?"

"Yes, I'm here babe, I'm here. Welcome back; I've missed you!"

She stood and gently kissed his lips, lingering momentarily to gaze into his beautiful blue eyes. "Pete, I thought that I had lost you. I've been praying that He wouldn't take you home just yet, until I can show you how sorry I am, and how much I love you."

"Honey, I already know that. Why do you think I fought so hard to stay alive?"

Beth sat on the bed next to Pete. "Can you remember what

happened tonight? I'm still not clear on how you were shot."

"I'm really not sure myself," he said. "I don't want you to think that I'm crazy, but I think that maybe Sal shot me."

"What?"

"I know, I know. I told you it might sound crazy, but the last thing that I remember is Sal standing over me with a gun. I remember it well because it wasn't our department weapon; it was like a smaller revolver type gun."

Beth couldn't believe what she was hearing. "Pete, Dr. Grossman said that you might be a little groggy when you wake up and may not be thinking clearly. Why don't you just think things over a little more while the medication wears off?"

Pete shifted around in the bed..."It's not that Beth, I'm serious—I think Sal may have shot me."

"Honey I think that you should save it until the department wants you to give a statement."

"I'm not crazy babe...there's something else."

"What," she said.

"After I felt the pain of being shot, St. Michael appeared to me. He told me that Satan wouldn't win this battle, that I would live."

Beth didn't know what to think at this point. Pete seemed to be rational, but did the apparition really happen? God works in mysterious ways she thought. If my husband said that it happened, then I have to believe that it did. After all, faith is believing without being able to see Him. And if indeed the Archangel saved Pete's life, then God is working through him. Miracles happen. Even Dr. Grossman believes that there was some divine intervention involved in Pete's survival.

Miraculous or not, Pete was alive and talking with her. Grateful hardly described how Beth felt at this moment.

<u>43</u>
Detective Sanela Latarski

"Marilyn, come out here for a minute," said Latarski as she popped her head in the office and motioned for her to join her in the hall. They stepped outside the Chaplain's Office and began to walk down the hall leading away from all the confusion that still existed around the ER.

"What is it Sanela?"

"I told you that I had pretty much figured out what happened out there at the shooting scene, but that I needed the doctor to tell me what type of rounds Pete was hit with. Before I tell you what my conclusions are, I'd like to tape your preliminary statement concerning your actions at the scene. In a couple of weeks we'll have you give a more comprehensive statement. Are you okay with that, or do you want time to reflect or to see a counselor?"

"No," said Marilyn, "I'm fine...still a little upset about letting Pete go with Rosato, but now that I know that he's going to be okay, let's do it."

Marilyn gave her a brief statement as to her and Groman's activities, the gunshots they heard, and then going to Pete's side as he lay on the ground.

"What about Rosato? Did he seem to be acting normally, given that he was just involved in a shooting?"

Marilyn cupped her chin in thought. "You know, he was acting strangely."

"How so?" asked Latarski.

"Well, it seemed that he was preoccupied...he was looking around the area for something."

"Was he looking downward perhaps?" asked the detective.

"Yes, as if he was searching the ground for something that he missed.”

“Anything else Marilyn?”

“Just that he didn’t seem very upset that Pete had just been shot, his focus was somewhere else.”

“Okay, that’s all I need right now. We’ll probably contact you in the next couple of weeks to come in and give us a signed statement and add anything that you may have forgotten. In the meantime, I’m going to call my partner with this and the info from the doctor.”

They walked back toward the office and then saw Beth coming down the hall. She came up to Marilyn and took both her hands into her own.

“I have to apologize to you Marilyn.”

“Why?” She said

“That day I saw you with Pete when you came to visit Mac here at the hospital, I thought that maybe you and Pete were dating. I immediately thought ill of you, and I now want to apologize.”

Marilyn hugged her and said, “Beth, there’s no need for that. I respect you and Pete too much for that to ever be a consideration. Your husband is one of a kind. In the short time that we’ve been partners I’ve learned so much from him...about police work and life itself.”

“Thanks Marilyn. He’s taught me a lot about life too, just in the last couple of days.”

“So how is he,” asked Marilyn.

“Well he fell asleep while we were talking, and he seems to be ‘my old Pete’. But he said something weird.”

“What.”

Beth leaned in a little closer to Marilyn as if to whisper, “He said he thinks that Sal shot him.”

Marilyn leaned back, “No...you are kidding me!”

“I’m not. He said that he remembers Rosato standing over him with a revolver."

"Holy cow," said Marilyn. "I'll be back in a minute. I have to see Det. Latarski."

Marilyn rushed down the hall and out the ER doors. Dawn was breaking over the city. It would be a glorious day, she thought...Pete's okay, and God is good. Looking around the parking area she spotted Latarski on her cell phone. She jogged over to where she was involved in a conversation on her phone.

Latarski finished her conversation and turned to Benson. "What's up Marilyn?"

"I don't know what you and your team concluded happened, but I just spoke with Beth. She had just finished her visit with Pete in ICU; she told me that Pete thinks that Sal shot him... Well...aren't you a little shocked?"

"Not shocked," said the detective, "just more convinced."

"What? You thought all along that Sal was the shooter?"

"Yeah, the evidence all pointed toward it. Rosato had a motive, an opportunity, and a means to do it. The problem is that he was rushed, and there were too many witnesses—one in particular that saw the entire incident unfold."

"You're kidding, someone eyeballed the whole thing?"

"Not someone, some thing," said Latarski. "Groman told me that you two came across a security room inside the building that had a wall of monitors, which means that there had to be surveillance cameras somewhere. We located one on the corner of the building and had the Security Chief come in and play it back for us. It captured everything. Sal shot Pete with his service weapon, then he the burglar. Then he pulled a small gun out of his pocket, stood over Pete while he was lying on the ground, and shot him in the head. He then threw the burglar's gun in a dumpster and replaced it with a drop gun that he shot Pete in the head with."

Marilyn shook her head in disbelief. "I knew that he was evil, but I didn't think he would resort to anything like that."

"Unfortunately the bad guy is dead, but with all of the physical evidence and Pete's testimony, Rosato's future with the department is non-existent, and his freedom is about to come to an end."

Latarski got in her car to head back to the scene to help her colleagues finish processing the area. It's the strangest thing; she thought to herself, you would think that when bad cops wanted to break the law they would come up with a perfect plan—one that would be unsolvable. But more often than not they leave more clues than most street thugs do...go figure. Oh well, it makes my job easier. Officer Rosato, you're next on my list of things to do.

<u>44</u>
Getting Back To Normal

The next week saw an uptick in the wave of excitement and news interest surrounding Pete's shooting. Pete himself was up and walking around the hospital, and beginning to get cabin fever.

"Beth, I'm ready to get out of here," he said as he made another lap around the hospital floor. He had been transferred to a private room two days ago. "I'm feeling fine and I've got a lot of things to do around the house, and my finals are coming up at school."

"I know honey, I know.   Dr. Grossman said that he would see us today and make a determination about your condition and whether you could go home or not."

"You know, I'd be getting a lot more sleep and be more rested if I could go home. It's impossible to get a full night's sleep around here. Nurses are coming and going all through the night."

I switched on the TV to the White Sox game. They were playing the Tigers in Detroit at Comerica Park. I settled in and resigned myself to idling away the hours watching the game, while I waited for my doctors to give me the verdict on my release.

I fell asleep around the third inning, right after Beth had dozed off, but was awakened a short time later by a nurse.

"Mr. Shannon, I'm here to get one last draw of blood and take your vitals. Dr. Grossman just came in and will visit you momentarily."

"That's great," I said. "That means that I could get out of here today."

"I can't make that determination sir; you'll have to wait for the doctor for that answer."   She finished taking my blood pressure, temperature, and a vial of blood. "Ninety eight point six, and 120/72, everything looks normal sir." She gathered up her instruments and made her way out of the room. "Stay awake, he's on his way."

Good, I thought. I'd heard that hospitals were the worst places to be when one is sick or injured. I never understood that until now.

About ten minutes later, Dr. Grossman walked in.

"Jeff, how are you my friend? God been good to you today," I asked.

Beth was now awake and greeted the doctor as well.

"Yes he has Pete. So, how's the patient today...and the patient's wife?"

"Jeff, we're both well and ready to leave as soon as you say the word."

Grossman examined the now smaller bandages that protected Pete's wounds, and then looked at the bruising on his chest that had occurred when the first round struck his vest.

"Everything looks good Pete; I think we can let you go home. I spoke with Dr. Kearney again; he has no concerns."

"Wow, that's great news Jeff, thank you."

Beth let out a sigh of relief, and privately thanked the Lord.

"Before I release you, we need to set a few guidelines. No working out! That means running and pumping iron. You can walk if you want, but no hard, physical exertion. That fracture needs to heal completely, and the concussion needs to be re-evaluated in a few weeks to ensure that there are no lasting effects."

"Can I go to classes," I asked.

"Sure, "said Jeff, "that won't be a problem. But I want you to get plenty of rest and a full night's sleep each day. I want to see you again in three weeks before I fully release you to return to duty. Agreed?"

"Yes sir! You know Jeff, this whole incident has been one that's been life-changing. I don't know if Beth told you, but I'm certain that St. Michael was sent by God to save my life. I know that some people will think that I imagined that, but it was clear to me that He decided that He had more for me to do on this earth before He called me home. I firmly believe that Michael backed me up that night."

Grossman looked at them both and said, "I don't doubt you at all my friend. Knowing you as I do, I think that's a perfectly logical explanation. Everything came together for you at the right time—your faith, your fitness, and your commitment to fight those that are evil in our society."

"Thanks for believing in me Jeff."

"You're welcome Pete, though I must admit when I saw you in the back of the ambulance that night, and we had heard from the EMTs on the way in that the patient had been shot in the head, I lifted up a prayer that He would guide my hand to save your life."

"You turned out to be an angel too doctor," Beth said. "Pete always talked about your ability to save those that should have died from stabbings and shootings. When I saw that you were tending to my husband, I must admit to feeling relieved."

Grossman finished Pete's chart. "Thanks Beth, I'll see you in a few weeks Pete, enjoy your recovery time at home."

"Thanks brother."

Less than an hour later we were on our way home. Beth pulled the car into the garage, and as we walked into the kitchen I was overcome with tears of joy. To actually be home again, when there was a time that I wasn't sure if I would even live, was overwhelming.

Beth held me and both of us wept.

"I know babe. I've been praying for this moment too," she said, "and I'm so thankful that we're finally home...together. I know it sounds clichéd to say, but this is the first day of the rest of our lives together. We've been given a second chance at our marriage, and to praise Him for His love and compassion. I'm not going to let Him down again, or you. Pete, you're my whole world, you're all that I've ever wanted. I love you so much..."

We stood there holding onto each other, afraid to let go, thankful for the blessings that had come our way. Life was good once again. It was a new day for us...

<u>45</u>
More Evidence

"Sanela!" Lt. Borelli stuck his head around the door of his office and shouted for Latarski to join him.

"What's up Frank?"

"The Shannon shooting, that's what's up," he said. "This guy Rosato is dirty, more dirty than we thought if that's even possible. Don't wrap up that investigative summary just yet; we've got more fuel for the fire."

"Now what?" Latarski wondered. She had almost finished with her report. The Crime Lab had fired the gun that Rosato alleged the burglar shot Shannon with. Ballistics matched; however, a review of the surveillance video showed Rosato taking the weapon from his own pocket and standing over Shannon, shooting him in the head. The video also showed Rosato firing his own service weapon at Shannon as Pete left cover to handcuff the suspect, then shooting the suspect. The bullet that she retrieved from Pete's vest matched ballistically with Rosato's service weapon, as did the round retrieved from the deceased's body.

The camera also captured Rosato going over and replacing the bad guy's gun with the drop gun. He then walked around the area, apparently looking to collect the spent casings from his own pistol, but was interrupted by Officers Benson and Groman. A short while later, the tape shows Rosato walking off camera. Luckily Groman saw him at this point, as he went to the dumpster in an effort to hide the bad guy's gun. A subsequent search produced the gun in the trash.

The Crime Lab guys had done a good job, finding and preserving Rosato's fingerprints on the bad guy's gun and the drop gun. They also used a relatively new technique developed in the State Police Crime Lab to raise the serial number that had been filed down. It came back to a robbery two years ago at a gun shop on the West Side in which the proprietor was seriously wounded. All of the video, physical evidence at the scene, and Pete's subsequent memory of what happened, seemed to make for an air-tight case against The Hammer.

Borelli sat down at his desk and motioned for Lararski to sit. "Gang Crimes busted a guy last night in 'Little Italy'. The guy's name is Frank Folanozzo, a punk that's been arrested numerous times for drugs and guns. Seems he got caught holdin' dope and a gun last night in a buy-bust that Gang Crimes was working with ATF. He's looking at going back to the joint for a long time, based on this bust and his criminal history. He wants to make a deal...says he knows a cop that's dirty...one that bought drugs from him in the past and a gun. The Gangs guy asked for a name so they could verify the info—Sal Rosato was the name he gave up."

"Holy cow, lew, what else is this guy into? He's on admin leave with pay right now, but I think we need to talk with legal and have this guy suspended. We need to get his Star and gun taken away."

"I agree," said the lieutenant. "He's milking this EAP thing for all its worth. We need to get him indicted as soon as possible. I'll call legal and get the ball rolling, and have the Gang Unit fax Folanozzo's statement over here. This case will never go to trial; Rosato's going to deal on this one if he's smart."

Latarski got up to leave the office. "One other thing lew...this thing is going to be all over the papers and TV. I think that we owe it to Pete and Beth to fill them in on what's going on, before they see it on the news."

"Yeah, good idea Sanela. Do that at your earliest convenience, and remind them that it's an open investigation—everything's confidential until I say otherwise."

"Will do boss."

"Sanela..."

"Yes sir?"

"I'm really happy with the job that you're doing. Your investigative skills and your professional demeanor are admirable. I know that you're on the sergeant's promotional list. I'd hope that if you have the chance to come back to the unit, you'll give it strong consideration."

Turning a little red, Latarski responded. "That's means a lot Frank, thank you."

"My pleasure; I think that a leader is obligated to give praise when it's deserved and correction when it's needed. I wish that all of my detectives were like you."

Sanela walked out feeling good about a lot of things—the job, her boss, Pete's recovery, and the fact that she was about to get a bad cop off the street. Life was good.

<u>46</u>
On The Mend

It was great to be home. Beth and I spent more time together than we ever had in the past. She took vacation time from work while I was recovering. Our relationship seemed almost brand new—different in a way—almost like we were newlyweds. We recognized that we came very close to losing the bond that He had blessed when we got married.

The last two weeks of the summer semester came to an end. I had no trouble in maintaining the course work and taking the finals. My life was getting back on track in the face of what could have easily been a disaster. Although I had never doubted my faith in the past, this incident had reinforced everything that I believed in. My love for the Lord grew even stronger, as was my dedication to serve Him in every way.

I had my final evaluation scheduled with Dr. Grossman in two days. My strength had returned, and although I had adhered to what he told me to do as far as not working out and running, I was out walking every day—three to four miles.

My friend Mac had gone back to work, another miracle. They offered him the day shift, but Mac turned them down, wanting to be back with his old crew. I was looking forward to tomorrow; Beth had arranged to have Mac, Shirley, and Marilyn come over for a barbeque. It would be good to see all of my old friends again.

"Beth, what's on the menu for tomorrow," I asked.

She was busy preparing things already. "All-American babe—hot dogs and hamburgers, baked beans, cole slaw, and for your partner, turkey burgers."

I gave her a big hug. "Did I ever tell you how glad I am that I married you?"

"Yes Pete, so many times that I've lost count."

"Well, I'm telling you again—I love you!"

Planting a big kiss on me, she said "I love you too honey."

The doorbell rang. "Who could that be," I wondered out loud.   I took a look out the front window and saw Det. Latarski on the front porch.

I opened the door, "Sanela, how are you?"

"I'm fine Pete. I hope that I'm not interrupting, but I wanted to fill you in on a few things that you need to know about before you read it in the papers."

"Come in... Beth, its Sanela Latarski."

Beth came in to welcome her. "How are you today detective, and to what do we owe this honor?"

We made our way into the kitchen; Beth prepared coffee for all of us.

"Our investigation is almost complete. Officer Rosato is about to be suspended and indicted, so it's only right that you hear it from me before it's all over the news."

"Well, I kind of figured that would be the case," I said, "but it's nice of you to inform us before the fact."

"Neither my lieutenant, nor myself think that it will go to trial based on the watershed of evidence that we have against him, but if we do go you know that you'll have to testify."

"I know that, and as much as I dislike having to testify against a fellow police officer, when I put it in the context of what he's done it leaves me no choice."

Sanela nodded, "You're absolutely right Pete. I must tell you though that I find it very admirable that you have never made any disparaging remarks about Rosato, even though he tried to kill you. Most other guys would be out for revenge, or at least be cussing him up one side and down the other."

"I'm not like that," I said. "I'm not the one that will judge Sal, either here on earth or in the next life."

"Amen Pete. Thanks for the coffee Beth, and Pete, thank you for being the type of cop that you are. You're truly an inspiration for many of us on the department. When are you going back to work? You look fit and ready for duty to me."

"Hopefully in a couple of days," I replied. "Just between us, I can't wait. I've missed the job."

She made her way to the front door. "Well good luck on getting released. Incidentally, Marilyn and I are good friends; I know that she wouldn't mind me telling you this, but she is really pleased about the two of you working on the Tac Team together—she can't wait for your return either."

"Thanks Sanela, the feeling is mutual. She's a good cop."

Latarski waved good-bye, got into her department vehicle and drove off.

Beth turned to me and said, "Pete, we are truly blessed, we have so much...our marriage, families, friends, and good jobs. I need to do something to give back. Tomorrow I'm going over to Queen's to talk with Father Mike and see if I can help out with the Catechism classes. It would probably involve one night per week, plus a couple of hours on Sunday mornings. Do you mind?"

I gave her a hug, "How can I mind? You're doing the Lord's work. He's been good to us babe, and we need to return the favor."

"Thanks hon. Now I've got to go out to the store and pick up a couple more items for the barbeque tomorrow."

"Not without me you're not...I need to spend as much time with you as I can. I'll never take you for granted again."

<u>47</u>
Under The Bridge

The first week back at work was taxing on me. I guess that I wasn't as physically prepared as I thought, and the midnight shift was tough to get used to again. Not only that, but I had several court appearances, traffic and criminal, to attend. It seemed like my days and nights were full. I was cleared to resume my normal workouts—wow, I had lost my edge there as well. After the first couple of weight sessions at Xav's, I cut it back to every other day, until my strength returned. I felt like the skinny kid you see on his first day at the gym.

Marilyn was considerate; she barely talked about her workouts even though it was evident by looking at her that she was doing some serious heavy lifting. If I had to guess, she was close to being ready for another bodybuilding competition. We eased back into our routine on the Tac Team as we rolled into late summer. The 8th District was a busy place and provided us with plenty of opportunities to hone our skills.

It was the last week in August. Kids were bored by now with vacation and most were ready for the return to school. Just before they go back, there always seems to be an uptick in juvenile activity on the street—burglaries, vehicle break-ins and joy rides. Marilyn and I had reviewed the crime reports at the station and noticed that there seemed to be a pattern developing at Marquette Park. It showed that juvies were congregating there around midnight and beyond to sell and smoke dope. We thought that it would be a good idea to work that problem to see if we couldn't grab a couple of sellers at least. If not, we would at least let them know that the cops knew what was going on.

"So, what's our game plan here Pete," asked Marilyn as we turned into the east side of the park.

"The reports said that on at least two occasions these kids were hanging out under the bridge on Kedzie. I think that we'll park the car over by the running track and then go on foot. When we get close, I'll cross over on top of Kedzie to the west side while you stay on the east—they'll all be boxed in on the foot bridge."

Marilyn looked at me and said, "Pete you need to heading up a squad of soldiers. That was a brilliant plan of attack."

"Whatever," I said. "But we may get over there and find that no one's around too."

I parked the car and we left on foot toward the bridge that passes underneath Kedzie Avenue. As we got closer, we turned off our radios so that we wouldn't alert anyone that may be there.

Marilyn stopped just shy of the turn to go underneath. "Pete, I hear voices..." she whispered.

"Give me a minute to get over to the other end of the path. When you hear me yell, 'Police' make your move."

"Okay Pete."

I hurried over to the other side, took a peek down the path, then turned on my flashlight and made my move... "Police!"

A flurry of activity ensued as Marilyn and I converged toward the middle, corralling seven young boys and girls.

"Everybody face the wall and put your hands on it," I barked. There were two females in the group; we had them move toward Marilyn's side."

"Cover me Pete."

Marilyn started to go through the two girls while I kept watch on the others.

"They're clean partner," she said

She placed them both back on the wall and we switched duties. My first kid was young, maybe 14, he was shaking with fear but other than the smell of marijuana on him he was clean. The next two kids each had joints in their pockets; they were each 15 and 16. The last two looked older, maybe 17 or 19. The 19 year old was definitely giving attitude;

maybe he had been through this before and was probably showing off for the younger ones.

"What's this?" I asked as I pulled a wad of cash from his pants pocket.

"I just got paid man," he said.

I leaned in close to him and said, "Let's start this out right my friend. You will refer to me as either 'sir' or 'officer,' not man. Understood?"

"Yes sir," he replied.

"Now what about the roll of money?"

"Sir it's not mine," he said. "I have to give it to someone in the morning..."

He went on to tell me that he was working for an older guy in the neighborhood. The boy's friend next to him was holding the marijuana stash; the "coke" was up under the bridge.

We called a wagon and brought them all into the station to sort everything out. A couple of hours later, we had the dicks in the Juvenile Division handling those under 16, and our guy with the wad of money turned out to be the only adult—17 years of age.

"So Matthew," started Marilyn, "What you don't realize is that you aren't going home tonight. You are considered an adult now, which means that you are going to be held in the lockup unless you can post bond. Can your folks come up with a thousand dollars by morning?"

The kid looked scared. He obviously hadn't played this game before. His rap sheet only showed a couple curfew violations and a shoplifting charge during his juvenile days. He had no idea what he had gotten himself involved in.

"My mom works midnights cleaning office buildings," he said. "She barely has enough money to pay the rent and food bill. My dad's an alcoholic; he's hardly ever home, and when he is he hits mom up for money so's he can go get drunk again."

Marilyn and I looked at each other...

"Pete, come out in the hall for a minute."

We kept the boy handcuffed to the wall in the interrogation room while we talked.

"What do you think Pete, should we go to bat for this kid?"

"Marilyn I think that we should. This kid's at a critical juncture in his life. He's just turned legal as far as the criminal justice system is concerned. If we can get him to change now, we may save him from a lifetime of heartache for himself and his mom."

"Tell you what," she said. "I don't have class tomorrow. He's definitely going to sit tonight and go to court in the morning. I'll go to the prelim and talk with the State's Attorney about a deal if this kid gives up the information on who he's selling the dope for."

"That's a great idea Marilyn. See if you can't get the kid an "I" bond as well, since his mother doesn't have the means to bail him out. If he sits in the County Jail for any length of time, he's dead meat."

"You're right about," she said. "They'll tear a young kid like Matthew apart in there. I think it's the right thing to do."

"Okay," I said. "Let's go back in there and tell Matthew the facts of life."

That morning Marilyn arrived at 26th & California, the largest Criminal Court Building in the country. A person could easily become lost in this huge, cavernous structure with its high ceilings and floor to ceiling windows, and its judges' benches on raised platforms. It truly sends a message to all defendants that they are but mere specs under the judicial magnifying glass. Over the years the expansive halls and wide stairwells have seen their share of escape attempts by prisoners gasping for freedom's fresh air.

Marilyn was to meet with Cook County Assistant State's Attorney Al Malinchak to discuss Matthew's case. As she walked through the marble tiled hallway, a woman was waiting by the courtroom door, "Officer, may I speak with you?"

She was short and skinny, with a worn look that didn't quite fit with a 30 something woman. Marilyn thought to herself that this woman has seen much sorrow and hardship.

"How can I help you ma'am?"

"Are you Officer Benson?" she asked.

"Yes I am."

"I'm here for my son Matthew. I'm Kathy Roberts; when can I see him?" she asked.

"Nice to meet you ma'am: Matthew is being held in the lockup until his case is called. At that time the judge will determine his bond."

The woman looked tired and dejected. "There's no way that I can bail him out," she said. "I have absolutely no money saved. My paycheck is spent before I even get it, and what little I try to save my husband takes to spend on booze. I've told him that I don't love him anymore, but he forces himself on me and then I don't see him for days."

Marilyn took her by the hand and led her to a bench along the wall. "I'm sorry about your predicament. Matthew has serious problems here; he was caught with marijuana and there was also cocaine involved, although not technically in his possession, it was in the area where he was arrested."

"Oh God," the woman sighed.

"Before you lose hope," said Marilyn, "let me explain something. "Matthew is basically a good kid. We checked his juvenile record and he has only a couple of minor arrests—nothing very serious. I think that we can make this incident a pivotal point in his life. I'm here to tell the court that your son has agreed to work with us to get the people that got him involved in selling drugs. His cooperation, along with this being his first arrest as an adult, I hope will allow the judge to look favorably upon Matthew's rehabilitation. I believe in your son Mrs. Roberts, and I'm confident that we can get him back on track."

Looking somewhat relieved, the boy's mother asked, "But what about the bond? Where will I get the money?"

"I hope that the prosecutor can convince the judge that your son is not a flight risk, nor a danger to the community—we'll ask for an 'I Bond,' one that requires only a signature. But you will also have to testify that you are willing to ensure that Matthew will show up for his next court date. And at any time after his release should he get into trouble, he will go right back to jail until the court date."

"Thank you Officer for your help, and I hope that your faith in my boy is not misplaced."

Marilyn got up from the bench. "My partner will make sure that Matthew understands the chance that he is being given. He intends to keep a close eye on your son; in fact he has a plan to put him to work so that he doesn't have the time to get in trouble."

"That would be the answer to my prayers" she said. "I work all night and can't keep track of him. You and your partner are Heaven sent..."

"Maybe not sent from Heaven, but we certainly keep in touch," said Marilyn. "I'll see you inside in a little while."

As she walked to State's Attorney Malinchak's office she said a silent prayer. "Dear Father, one of your flock was lost, but now is found. Help us to rejoice, fill his soul with your love and presence. Help us to bring Matthew back into your light."

<u>48</u>
Tommy and Lisa

"So how did it go this morning," I asked Marilyn as we loaded our gear into the unmarked squad car.

"It went well Pete. ASA Malinchak was on board with what we talked about and gave Matthew a personal recognizance bond; his mom was thrilled."

"That's great; I gave my buddy Andy a call at Marathon Sports. He runs a tee shirt business and produces shirts for all of the big sporting events in the Chicago area. He's agreed to hire Matthew on a part-time basis; he can work after school and on weekends. It's hard work, but Andy is a good Christian family man and will keep an eye on Matthew while he perhaps teaches him a trade.

"Pete, I feel good about this whole thing, especially after meeting Matthew's mom. She is really down on her luck. She works all night, and then comes home to feed her kids and then get them off to school on time. Her drunken husband comes and goes, sometimes forcing himself on her...what a terrible life. If we can get her son back on track, I think that it will really ease some of her anxiety."

"I agree. I don't think that it was merely a coincidence that we arrested him last night," I said. "I think the Lord put us in Matthew's life to help straighten him out before he got too far off the beaten path."

We climbed into the car, ready to begin our shift. "Well, one thing's for sure—Matthew's not going to be under the bridge tonight!"

We laughed as I pulled out into traffic. "Pete..."

"What?

"Do me a favor?"

"Sure Marilyn, what is it?"

"I believe you when you say that you saw St. Michael after you were shot. Can you teach me that prayer? I think that I want to include that as part of my prayer routine each day."

"I'd be happy to partner..." I taught her the prayer and then we said it together. Afterward we rolled west on 63rd Street.

The serenity of the moment was interrupted by the radio, "All units in the 8th District, we have a robbery in progress, a robbery in progress at the donut shop at 65th & Pulaski."

"Pete, that's Tommy's store!"

"You're right Bens..." I switched on the emergency equipment and siren and pointed our squad in that direction.

"Units heading to the robbery on Pulaski," barked the radio, "use caution, shots fired, shots fired. An eyewitness advises one male, Hispanic, early 20s, white tee shirt, blue jeans, and baseball cap."

I was within a block of the location in less than a minute. Cars were streaming into Tommy's shop, hoping to catch the bad guy before he escaped.

"Pete, across the street, white shirt and jeans running east!"

Marilyn prepared to bail as I turned in that direction.

"We don't split up partner!"

"Right she yelled."

I braked and slammed the car in park just short of the mouth of the alley on the East side of Pulaski—we jumped out in tandem as we saw our suspect running South thru the alley.

Marilyn got on the air, "860 Emergency—we have a robbery suspect running southbound in the East alley of Pulaski...my partner and I are in pursuit in plain clothes...need a car to block the South exit on 66th Street!"

"Roger that 860. All units, 860 on foot pursuit, east alley of Pulaski, southbound toward 66th Street, any unit available to come in from the south end...please respond."

As we closed ground on our guy he turned right and into a gangway out of our sight. Within a couple of seconds we were there at the narrow opening between two garages. I put my light down on the ground to shine in his direction, did a quick peek, and spotted our guy trapped against a locked chain link gate. Marilyn quickly did a limited pen to cover him and blind him with her light.

"Police; Don't Move!"

Without anywhere to go, our guy had a decision to make. Try to climb the eight foot gate topped with barbed wire, shoot it out with us, or surrender.

I gave the command again..."Police; Don't Move!"

He turned to face us. This was the critical time in police work that the civilian population will never understand; facing down a gunman in a dark alley and trying to interpret his actions...are they threatening or are they those of a scared human being trying to cooperate? Cops have to make that split second decision over and over again, never with the benefit of hindsight that jurors and judges have.

Thank God for whoever owned the property that we ended up at, because without that security fence and wire, our subject's decision may not have been as easy to make. Faced with blinding lights in his face, and unable to see anything except two Glock .40 caliber pistols pointed in his direction, he made the right decision.

"Slowly, place your weapon on the ground," I commanded him. "Now, turn around and slowly walk back toward the sound of my voice."

I got him into the prone position for Marilyn to cuff him, retrieved his weapon, and we started to head back toward our vehicle. Bens got on the radio...

"860, suspect in custody. Can you send us a wagon to transport?"

A wagon was already waiting at the mouth of the alley for us. We searched our guy, put him inside, and then jumped back into our car to see what had happened at the donut shop.

It didn't look good as we pulled into the lot at Dunkin. A wagon was loading a victim on a stretcher, it was a female...I hoped that it wasn't Tommy's wife Lisa.

Bens ran to the back of the wagon, and my worst fear was realized. "Lisa, what happened?"

In obvious pain she explained, "A guy came in and ordered a small coffee. When I turned around to pour it, he yells at me—*Robbery! Give me the money!*—I'm scared and confused. I froze up Bens; I guess that I wasn't acting quickly enough for him and he shot me. I never had a chance to give him any money."

Marilyn got into the back of the wagon with her. "Pete, I hate to do this to you, but can you process our shooter? I need to go to the hospital with her, at least until Tommy can get there."

"Absolutely," I said. "Give me a call when you're ready to be picked up. In the meantime, don't worry about a thing. Tell Lisa that I will be praying for her."

"I will Pete. You're the best!"

I closed up the back door of the paddy wagon and said a quick prayer that Lisa would be okay. And while I was at it, I thanked our backup, St. Michael, for the assist. I did a quick assessment of what had just happened...Bens and I worked well together. Our tactics were seamless and sound, our fitness level was more than adequate, and our ultimate backup, St. Michael, was unquestionably Heaven sent. Life was good...again!

A few hours later I was driving to Little Company Hospital to pick up Marilyn. I pulled into the ER and found her outside talking with Tommy, Lisa's husband. I hopped out of the car and went up to them both.

"How is she doing," I asked. Tommy looked stressed out, almost shell shocked if you will, but he was holding up.

"The docs say that she'll be okay," he said. "The bullet went right through her shoulder without hitting any bone or arteries; she was really lucky. She's just about to be moved into a private room, so I wanted to come out and tell you both how much I appreciate that you caught the guy that shot her."

Marilyn turned to him, took his hands in hers and said, "Tommy, no thanks necessary. Besides, that's our job. Anyway, we would have felt terrible if this guy was able to get away. What did you find out about the shooter Pete?"

"I started processing him as soon as I got in the station, and sent his prints off right away since he didn't have any ID on him. The robbery dicks showed up about an hour later; they knew who the guy was. Seems they busted him twice before. He's an illegal who's been deported twice, but somehow keeps slipping back into the country."

"No thanks to our politicians," added Tommy.

"Right," I said. "You wouldn't believe how many illegals we arrest every week. His gun comes back stolen. It's on the way to the Crime Lab for ballistics, maybe we can clear up some other shootings if we're lucky."

"You know, it's not like the old days when it was really a pleasure to have your own business," Tommy reflected. "We used to know most of our customers, many of them by name, now the area is changing. The night shift is scary; all kinds of creepy people out on the street at night. I don't know that I want to put my family at risk anymore; maybe it's time to move on."

"I can't blame you if you did," said Marilyn. "But I for one would certainly miss your smiling faces. I look forward to seeing you guys every day." Marilyn leaned into Tommy and gave him a big hug.

"We'll see," he said. I'll talk it over with Lisa; she may be too afraid to work nights again."

"I know that you'll make the right decision for your family," said Marilyn. "I'll pray for Lisa's quick recovery, and I'll be by to see her tomorrow. Good night Tommy."

"Good night you two, and thanks again."

The sun was peeking out over the tops of the buildings, and cars and people rushing to work began to fill the city streets. Rush hour was about to begin in the Windy City as our shift drew to a close.

"So Marilyn, what's on your schedule today, we're looking at two days off?"

"Actually, I have a full day planned" I'm going to grab a couple hours sleep, then meet my workout partner for a super workout with legs and shoulders; then I need to study for a statistics exam."

"Whew, I'm tired just thinking about it! I meant to ask you...are you training for a contest or just trying to make your partner look bad?"

"Pete...you were shot remember? You were off for six weeks recuperating," she said. "But yes, I am entered in the Miss Illinois contest. In fact, this week I start my diet so don't be surprised if I get a little cranky. I'll be cutting out carbs and not taking in as much water."

"Wow! That's super...mind if me and Beth show up to watch you compete?"

"Not at all, I'd be honored Pete. In fact, I have five tickets up front; great seats. If you think that you will definitely attend then I'll give you two."

"It's a deal. I'll run it by Beth tonight, but I'm almost certain that we'll both attend. Hey...I could be partnered with 'Miss Illinois,' what an honor."

"Don't jinx me...I'm training to win, but I at least want to place higher than fourth like I did at last year's contest."

"Okay, okay. But seriously, knowing you and how you are so focused on your goals, I'm sure that you will place well."

"Marilyn..."

"Yes Pete?"

"You said that you had five tickets, are the others for your family?"

"No...two for you and Beth, two for my workout partner, and one for the guy that I'm seeing."

"Whoa," I said. "You never told me about him. Care to explain?"

"Not much to explain Pete. I met him...where else but at the gym? His name is Gary; we've been kind of seeing each other for about eight months. Right now I'm not really sure where I'm going with it. Since I started working with you a lot has changed. I'm really into the job, school, and competing. On top of that, I really am excited about my spiritual life again and I don't know that something like that will go over real well with my boyfriend."

We arrived back at the station and I pulled the squad car over by our personal vehicles so that we could unload our gear.

"I'm no counselor or therapist Marilyn, but I know that you've been hurt in the past. I'm here if you need to talk things out or ask for an opinion. Just take your time and put your trust in Him."

"That's what I intend to do partner, and being able to talk about it with someone that I can trust will be a big help," she said.

"Good. Let's get our equipment returned and get our butts in gear. In fact, I better head straight to Xav's for a workout. I'm started to look like a 98 pound weakling compared to you!"

"No comment Pete; have a great day partner, and say hello to Beth for me."

"Will do; God bless you partner."

<u>49</u>
The Dinner Date

"One more heavy set of squats and we'll be finished with legs today," said Marilyn's workout partner Kim. "You are awesome today girl! What did you do last night with that man while you were on duty?"

"Knock it off Kim, Pete and I aren't like that, it's strictly police work with us. Besides, I told you that he's married. I've met his wife—she's a great gal and they're perfect together."

Marilyn situated herself directly underneath the bar on the Smith Machine, adjusted where it would lay across her shoulders, then started repetitions with 275 pounds. She gutted out another ten, and then let Kim take her turn.

"Well, married or not this guy has really made you into a different person since you teamed up with him...ugh, this is heavy," she commented on her sixth rep. "You used to have your down days every now and again, but the last few months you've been full of energy and enthusiasm. What's your secret?"

Kim knocked out her ten reps and they walked over to grab a drink at the water fountain.

"There's no secret," said Marilyn. "I enjoy working with him; the chemistry is great. He's a super cop, and I love the fact that he is an unabashed Christian. He's not afraid to wear his faith on his sleeve for everyone to see."

"Yeah, that is unusual," said Kim.

"It sure is," Marilyn replied. "I'll tell you what else is refreshing about Pete...he doesn't use all the harsh language that lots of cops use. I've worked with cops that use the F-word in every sentence. That gets old."

"I hear ya girl. You should hear some of my guys talk down at the fire station... I thought that I'd heard it all until I became a firefighter."

Marilyn finished up another set of squats. "I still can't believe that you sleep with all those guys in the same room."

"I know," said Kim. "At first I was kind of shy and self conscious about showering and going to bed. But after a while, after the newness of being the only woman in the house wore off, they all started treating me like a sister. Besides, none of them have anything that I haven't seen before."

"Let's not go there," said Marilyn. "I've heard enough of your adventures with men to last a lifetime."

"Okay, okay," she said, "as if you haven't had your share... Let's get these last sets in the bank so we can bust out of here and get something to eat. I'm starving."

"Sorry Kim, not me. I start my pre-contest diet today—no grand slam breakfasts for me until after the show. It will be chicken breasts and tuna, plenty of veggies, and cardio each day."

"Glad I'm not entered in this one," said Kim. "But I'll be honest with you Marilyn, you're already close to being where you need to be. You don't need to do very much cutting; it looks like your body fat is around 10 or 12 per cent right now. You cut much too more and you might lose some size."

"I know. Last contest the judges told me that I wasn't big enough, so I've got to really watch the diet this time."

"Well, I'm with you all the way girl; I'll be that critical eye that you hate to hear from. In fact, let's go in the posing room now so that we can assess where you're at, I'll do a body fat caliper test on you."

Afterward, Marilyn finished up at the gym and made her way home to feast on some protein. She was halfway through her lunch when the phone rang.

"Hello Marilyn, this is Gary."

"Hi Gar, what's up?"

"Hey, I missed you at the gym this morning...came in a little later since I worked until two in the morning last night."

"That's okay, Kim and I had a killer leg work out; I wouldn't have been much company for you."

"Are you up for lunch," he asked.

"No, I'm just finishing up. But you can take me to dinner if you want."

"Dinner and what else?" came the answer.

Marilyn didn't really want anything else other than dinner. She'd been thinking hard about this relationship lately, and she wasn't really sure that there was a future with Gary. The last several dates had been uncomfortable. He'd been secretive about his past all along, saying only that he was former Special Forces. His job as a bouncer at a club on 111th Street couldn't possibly have supported his lifestyle. And his size seemed a bit too big to be natural.

He also had been pressuring her for sex, his hands going places where she didn't really want them to go. Those days of hopping into bed with someone were over for her. Her new relationship with Christ had opened her eyes to the importance of love and commitment.

"Just dinner," she said. "I've had a long day and I really don't want to stay out late."

A pause on the other end..."Okay, dinner it is. I'll be over to pick you up around seven."

"Okay Gary, but no big Italian meals. I started my pre-contest diet today."

"Oh man...okay we'll grab something healthy. See you at seven."

Marilyn finished with her lunch, cleaned the few dishes, and headed toward the bathroom to shower from her workout. She undressed in the bedroom in front of the full length mirror and took inventory of her physique. This was going to be the contest where she could finally compete against other women that were serious about bodybuilding. If she could win or place second, it would give her national recognition. Winning the Miss Illinois title would open other doors.

She surveyed everything from her shoulders to her calves. It all looked good; big, without being masculine, and symmetrical—no one body part developed more than another. If she could just time this diet right so that she peaked at contest time, she felt confident that she could win.

Stepping into the shower immediately relaxed her. The hot water and accompanying steam soothed her muscles and gave her skin a healthy, clean feel. Luxuriating in the gentle spray, she thought that maybe tonight would be a good time to tell Gary that she didn't see much of a future with him. She wasn't really into him that much, although at first it was exciting to have a big hunk of a guy chasing after you. But as the months passed by, she saw that there wasn't much to Gary once you got past the exterior. She needed someone with depth and passion, someone with goals and a spiritual thirst.

She had enough on her plate now anyway. Her professional life was progressing nicely, but more importantly, she loved working with Pete and locking up people that preyed on the weak and helpless. School was also coming along; she should get her MBA in less than a year. Her fitness and bodybuilding passion were on fire. It was almost like an addiction...if she didn't do something each day she felt guilty.

But the most important part of her life now was rediscovering her faith. It was exciting in a way that she had never known before. She actually looked forward to praying and just talking with God each day. Sometimes it may just be thanking Him for a beautiful sunrise or sunset, or being grateful to Him after a long, satisfying run. She couldn't remember ever having been so taken with something. She felt like she was on the right road...

She spent a couple of hours studying her coursework then began to get dressed for her dinner date with Gary. She fixed her hair and makeup and was about to slip into a pair of slacks and a blouse when the doorbell rang. Wouldn't you know he'd be punctual, she thought as she opened the door for him.

"Hi Mar, guess I'm a little early."

"Just a little," she replied. "What's in the bag?"

"I thought that we'd have a glass of wine before we left. I brought a great red wine, which as you know, is an antioxidant, so it's healthy!"

"Okay. You go in the kitchen and pour while I get dressed. I can only have one glass; I told you that I'm on the diet."

"I know," he said. "This is good stuff, you'll love it."

Marilyn went into the bedroom and started dressing. A minute or so later, Gary walked in with two glasses of wine.

"Here you go sweetheart, nectar of the gods... Mind if I watch you get dressed?"

"Kind of... Tell you what," she said. "I'll drink this while I'm dressing; you go turn on the TV. I'll be done in a few minutes."

"What are you afraid of," he pouted. "Hell, I see you in your workout clothes at the gym all the time and you're just as unclothed. Besides, we've been going together for a long time now...I have needs."

She took a long drink of the wine. "Gary, we talked about this before. I'm not going to just hop into bed with anyone; that's not me. I'm looking for something more than just sex with a guy. That will come down the road, hopefully after marriage, but right now I've got too much going on in my life."

"Man..." he said in disgust. "This is how you treat me after all the time and money I've spent on you?" He walked defiantly out of the bedroom and into the front room.

She took another drink and thought to herself that this was definitely the night that she would tell him they were finished. In fact, why even go through the motions of dinner? Why not just tell him now?

She took one more sip, set the glass down on her dresser and put her robe on. She started to walk toward the bedroom door, but became suddenly dizzy and disoriented and fell down. ***What's happening?*** As she tried to pick herself up near the bed, the room started spinning. Just before she blacked out she was in Gary's arms being placed on the bed...

<u>50</u>
"I Feel Sick"

"The boys are really doing well aren't they Susan?" Beth had stopped over at Susan O'Hara's house for a quick visit before her appointment at the beauty parlor.

Susan was finishing up with the breakfast dishes at the sink while they talked. "They are now," she replied. "The first couple of weeks we were all like zombies, none of us able to tell up from down, just going through each day praying and crying. They've adjusted to the fact that their Daddy is gone; my parents have helped us immeasurably also. Mac and Shirley have taken them a couple of times for overnights, which has allowed me to have some time for myself. I am just so thankful to be blessed with family and friends that love us so much..."

Beth got up from the table and poured herself another cup of coffee. "That's great Susan. Remember that Pete and I are always here for you too—that will never change."

"Thanks, that means a lot. Hey, you are really looking healthy Beth. You and Pete must have resolved all of your problems."

Beth sipped her coffee, "We have made great strides, it's almost like we're dating again. There's this feeling of newness that surrounds our relationship."

"God has really blessed you both," said Susan.

"Amen. Anyway... ugh, excuse me for a minute."

Beth rushed to the bathroom barely making it in time before she lost her breakfast. Susan heard what happened and yelled through the closed door... "Beth, are you okay?"

"Yes...be out in a minute." She finished rinsing her mouth and washing her hands then walked out of the bathroom.

"Sorry Sue, this past week I've been feeling nauseous...must be coming down with something."

"Can I ask you something," said Susan.

"Sure."

"Have you considered the fact that you may be pregnant?"

"What?" said Beth? "No, it never entered my mind! Oh my gosh...that would be such a gift from God if I am. I need to find out; Susan forgive me but I'm going to Walgreens to buy a home pregnancy test."

She gathered her purse and headed toward the front door. "Am I an idiot or what?" she asked Susan. That should have been the first thing that I thought about but I didn't."

Opening the front door to leave, she said, "Sue, please don't say anything about this to anyone, especially Pete. If I am pregnant, it will be the answer to so many prayers..."

"Don't worry honey, I won't. But you have to call me when you know—agreed?"

"I will. God bless you for your wisdom, love, and friendship."

"You're welcome; good luck with the test and thanks for the visit. The children love when you stop over." "Bye."

Susan shut the door and made her way back to the kitchen to finish with the cleaning. She said a silent prayer for Beth and Pete. *Dear Father, I pray that you will bless them with a child, a gift that they both deserve. Please be with my dear friend Beth, guide her through a healthy pregnancy and fill her with a spirit of your love and wisdom so that she can instill that same love and faith in their little baby. In Jesus' name I pray...Amen.*

Still deep in thought, she said another prayer for her own children, and then as she had done each day since his death, she spent some time talking with her husband Joe. The pain and longing was still there...

<u>51</u>
"Roofies"

Marilyn woke up and immediately felt confused and "hung over." *What happened to me?* she thought. She glanced over at the clock on the nightstand—one in the morning. *What's going on?* She wondered. She sat up in bed, needing to relieve herself. That only caused her to become dizzy, so she sat for a while with her legs hanging over the side of the bed.

Looking around her bedroom, things didn't look right. Her undergarments and robe were on the floor as if they had been flung across the room. Her bed covers were a mess, something that never happens...what went on here? Trying to get her thoughts together, she remembered that she was going out to dinner with Gary, but did they even go? *What's wrong with me, why can't I remember last night?*

Struggling to get up, she put her hand on the bed for support and into something moist on the sheet. What...? *Did I have an accident?* Forcing herself to concentrate, and putting together what few facts that she could remember from Gary's visit, she came to a bitter conclusion. Her date must have forced himself on her!

Collapsing back on the bed the full realization struck her—she had allowed herself to be taken advantage of by someone who was only after one thing—sex. Since she was unwillingly to give it to him, he instead had taken what he wanted. *Oh Lord what do I do now?* She thought? But how... how did he do it? He's a strong guy, but not strong enough to do that...

Forcing herself to get out of bed, she carefully made her way to the bathroom. She relieved herself and turned on the shower, wanting to rid herself of the disgust and shame that she felt was covering her inside and out, smothering her self-respect. But suddenly remembering her police training, she thought better of that idea. And as much as she wanted to scrub herself clean of the filth that had invaded her body, she reluctantly shut off the water.

Pull yourself together girl, think...think!   Again her balance wavered so she decided to crawl back to the bed. I need help she thought; I need to call Pete. Making her way on her hands and knees, she picked up the phone and dialed Pete's number.

Attuned to most things even while sleeping, Pete picked up the receiver on the first ring. Beth continued to sleep peacefully by his side.

"Hello."

"Pete it's me, Marilyn. I need your help. I'm home but something happened and I can't think clearly...please come."

"Okay Marilyn, I'll be there shortly."

I threw on my clothes trying not to disturb Beth, and stopped on the way out the kitchen door to the garage to write a quick note on the board to let her know where I was. No sense getting her too worried about anything until I find out what's going on.

Within ten minutes I was at Marilyn's place and began to ring the bell. After what seemed like an inordinate amount of time, she finally opened the door.

"Pete! Thank goodness you're here."

I walked inside, grabbing her by an arm as she lost her balance, and led her to the sofa. She looked terrible, as if she was drunk, but she didn't reek of alcohol like most drunks do.

"Marilyn, what happened?" I said. "Have you been drinking?"

"Pete I don't know what happened; I'm confused. I was supposed to go out last night with Gary, but I can't remember if I did or not."

"Was he here...at the apartment?"

"Yes, and that's about all that I can remember. But Pete, I think that he may have raped me..."

Oh dear Jesus no, not Marilyn, I thought.

"Why do you say that Marilyn?"

"Pete, it's too embarrassing, but believe me when I tell you that I think he forced himself on me, even though I don't remember a thing happening."

Wait a minute I thought. ***Roofies--the date rape drug.*** I had a case involving this drug a couple of years back at the ER when a woman showed up with the same signs—physical evidence of rape, but no memory of anything happening. Amnesia is typical in these cases, and without the actual drug residue in the drink, urine samples have to be taken quickly to detect its presence. We finally determined that a guy that she had met at the club that night had slipped it into her drink. That must be what happened here.

I took her face into my hands and forced her to look at me. "Marilyn, listen closely. I think that your friend may have slipped something in your drink before giving it to you. Were you drinking with him last night?"

"Yes," she answered. "I do remember that he brought a bottle of wine with him, and I told him that I could only have one glass."

"Okay, that must be it. I need to find the glass that you drank from. Hopefully there is still some of the drink left so that we can get it analyzed."

"Pete, I'm not drunk," she said.

"I know Bens. Listen, we have to get to the ER and have a rape swab taken. We're going to have to report this and gather as much evidence as we can. He's not going to get away with this partner."

She collapsed forward against me and I held her so that she wouldn't fall off the sofa.

"Pete...I let you down. I couldn't take care of myself...let some scumbag hurt me... I'm sorry."

Stroking her hair I tried to soothe her feelings.

"Marilyn you didn't let me down. He slipped something in your drink; you had no clue and were defenseless. Get dressed now and put on fresh clothes. We'll bring the dicks back later to gather up the clothes that you were wearing and the sheets from the bed so that we can inventory them as evidence. We'll make sure this guy pays for what he did to you."

"Pete, thank you for helping me; you are the best backup a cop could have...you and St. Michael."

I did a mental inventory of what might be evidence, including her glass with two fingers of wine remaining, so that I could alert the evidence technicians. I got her down to my car giving her a little help so that she wouldn't fall, and we headed toward Little Company. I called the desk on the way, thankfully Mac was the desk sergeant, and I let him know what was going on. He said that he would send a beat car to meet us at the ER.

Marilyn fell asleep on the way to the hospital. I thought about what I wanted to do to this Gary guy, but realized that it's not my purview to judge. Only God does that. I quickly said a prayer for Marilyn...*Father, please be with your child Marilyn. Comfort her physically and emotionally in this time of trouble. Let there be no long lasting ill effects from this experience, and may your light shine upon her...*

Thankfully there seemed to be little action this night in the ER. It was close to three in the morning and the staff was trying to take advantage and catch a nap. But once they found out that Marilyn had been raped, they came alive and quickly sprang into action. The beat car arrived and began taking the initial report, and no sooner was that completed than the detectives showed up at the hospital.

"Sanela, good to see you!" I gave her a big hug. "Thank goodness you caught this case tonight, now I'm positive things will be handled properly."

"Thanks Pete and it's good to see you as well," she said. "What in the world happened tonight? How did our girl get assaulted?"

I told her as much as I had gleaned from Marilyn—the wine and the drug—and let her know that there was a lot of physical evidence still at the scene.

"Tell you what…I've got a team from the mobile crime lab enroute to the apartment," she said. "In order to expedite getting this stuff to the lab for analysis, can you get the key from Marilyn and meet them there? I trust your judgment as to what's evidence in this matter. Between your knowledge of what happened, and the technicians' expertise, we should have plenty to make this case stick."

"Of course," I said. "I'll get the key and be on my way. I can't tell you how glad I am to see that you are the investigator on this one. Marilyn is so embarrassed about what happened; it will be good for her to have a true friend here to help."

"Thanks Pete. Having investigated hundreds of rapes, I know what's going through her mind right now. She'll be blaming herself, thinking that it was her fault and beating herself up over it. My biggest challenge won't be to make the case; it will be getting her head back on straight. I may need your help with that."

"Anything…she's a fantastic woman and partner, one with unlimited potential. I don't want anything to prevent her from reaching that potential."

"You're a good man Pete Shannon. I can see why she enjoys being your partner."

I grabbed the keys from Marilyn and headed out to the parking lot deep in thought…

The evil one had won another battle but not the war. This will only strengthen my resolve to fight him with all my might. St. Michael I pray that you'll be with me and Marilyn every step of the way as we do battle with Satan in the person of Gary. Help us bring him to justice.

<u>52</u>
The "ER"

The mobile crime lab personnel were waiting for me as I pulled up to Marilyn's place. They gathered their equipment from the trunks of their cars and followed me inside, I briefed them in the hall, not wanting to go inside and further contaminate the crime scene. As I waited out there my cell phone rang.

"Hello..."

"Pete, where are you; what happened to Marilyn?"

Beth sounded like she had just awakened and had an anxious tone to her voice.

"Marilyn's boyfriend raped her last night by slipping a drug into her drink. She's at the hospital being examined and interviewed; I'm at her house with the guys from the Crime Lab."

"Oh, how terrible," she said. "Pete is she hurt, will she be alright?"

"She's not physically hurt," I said, "but I can't say for certain that emotionally she won't be damaged. She's a strong woman, but something like this can really damage one's self-esteem. If there is anything good about this, it's that Sanela caught the case and is interviewing her."

"Pete, will you be home in time today for us to go to mass together?"

"I'm not sure yet," I replied. "Let me see how it goes at the hospital and I will call you to let you know. Regardless, please pray for her and tell Father Mike what happened as well, and that we need prayers for her."

"For sure babe. Where's the guy that did this to her?"

That's a good question I thought, and with all of my concern being for Marilyn's welfare I'd completely forgotten about the guy. "I don't know," I said, "but it's not like he's some stranger. We'll get this guy today or whenever—he's not going anywhere."

"Okay hon keep me informed, and if there's anything that I can do give me a call.   Maybe I can sit with her for awhile or pray with her...let me know."

"I will Beth. Sorry about ruining our day off I'll make it up to you babe."

"Nothing to apologize for Pete, she's your partner and our friend as well. She needs you, and she needs prayer. Do your best and come home when you can. I love you."

"I love you too," I said and hung up. *How lucky am I to have a woman like Beth as my wife? God has truly blessed me.* Now I need to tend to Marilyn and let her know that she is loved and cared about by more people than she can imagine.

A couple hours later the guys from the lab finished up at Marilyn's. I phoned Sanela at the hospital and told her that I was going to clean the apartment before Marilyn came home. I didn't want her coming back to any more reminders than necessary from what had happened at her home. I got fresh sheets and made the bed, straightened up whatever mess the lab guys had made while they were doing their job, then headed back to the hospital.

Marilyn had finished with her exam and interviews, and was waiting in the Chaplain's Office with Sanela and Rev. Dean. I walked in not really sure what to expect and sat down without saying anything.

Sanela turned to me and said, "Pete we're all finished here with the interviews and medical care. We've contacted the Employee Assistance Unit for Marilyn to help her get through this, but she says that she doesn't think that it's necessary."

"I'm fine," she said. "The drug has just about worn off now, and I'm feeling much, much better. In fact, I'm ready to go kick Gary's door in and throw the cuffs on him."

"Whoa, partner... I feel the same way, but let Sanela handle the arrest so that everything is done according to the book. We don't want to screw this thing up."

Sanela chimed in, "Pete's right Marilyn, the worst thing that you can do is even contact this guy. As hard as it is to accept, you're a victim here not a cop."

Everyone stood up to leave, and Reverand Dean turned to Marilyn. "Remember that the EAP folks understand what rape victims have to deal with emotionally. You may not feel that you need their help right now, but in the next several days or weeks you may feel differently about it. Please keep that in mind."

"I will," she said, "and thanks for all your help Dean, it means a lot."

"You're welcome. There are a lot of people that want to help you Marilyn, my advice to you is to allow that to happen. You've been hurt, but God won't give you more than you can handle. Remember that."

"Shall we get you home now partner?" I asked.

"Yes. I'm exhausted and just want to fall into a deep sleep."

"Well, you've earned it," I told her. "I spoke with Mac...you're to take as much time off as you need."

"Thanks, but a day or so should do it. If I start feeling sorry for myself, then I let that scumbag Gary do even more damage to me. I'm not going to give him that satisfaction."

We drove to her house in silence. She seemed to be nodding off, or at the very least deep in thought. I parked the car and walked her to the apartment.

"Bens, I took the liberty of cleaning the place up after the Crime Lab guys; I put fresh sheets on the bed and did the dishes."

As we walked through her apartment door, she turned and said, "Pete, I am so blessed to have you in my life. You have made this ordeal much easier to endure because of your concern and your faith in me."

"The feeling is mutual partner. Anyway you're like family...like another sister."

"I feel like this has been a watershed moment in my life...like He has thrown this challenge at me to test me to see if I am really committed to His word."

I looked at her and asked, "Are you?"

"Now more than ever," she said. "Reverand Dean told me that God wouldn't give me more than I could handle...I believe that. This whole experience has invigorated my faith. And as much as I hate the fact that Gary did this to me, I see now that He used Satan to challenge my faith."

"Amen Marilyn."

We said our good-byes and I made my way back to the house. There was still plenty of time to salvage my day off with Beth. I called and told her that I was on the way....

<u>53</u>
Eating For Two

After finishing her conversation with Pete, Beth got up to make herself breakfast; after all she was now eating for two. After she left Susan's house, she had gone straight to the drug store and purchased a home pregnancy test. Much to her delight, the test had come back positive. *Praise Jesus, she was pregnant!* She couldn't wait to tell Pete about the miracle, but after what he told her about what had happened to Marilyn, this was not going to be the time. But being so filled with excitement, and with an overwhelming need to share her good news with someone, she decided to call Susan.

Susan answered after a couple of rings. "Hello..."

"Sue, this is Beth, can you talk?"

"Yes, we're all up and out in the backyard already. I'll be rounding them up in a bit to get them ready for mass."

"Good," said Beth. "Sue, remember what you told me yesterday when I was sick at your house?"

"Yes," she said. "I told you that you may not be sick, that you might be pregnant."

"Sue...you were right!"

"Woo Hoo!" came the response from Sue."

"God is good, isn't he," said Beth.

"Yes He is. He has blessed you both with a gift that you will cherish forever. What was Pete's reaction?"

"I haven't told him yet," she said. "He left in the middle of the night after getting a call from Marilyn at the hospital."

"Oh no, what's wrong?"

"It's terrible Sue; Marilyn's boyfriend apparently drugged her somehow and then raped her."

"Is she hurt?"

"Pete said that physically she's okay, but I guess that we won't know for a while how she's doing emotionally."

"That's a good point," said Susan. "Tell her she's on my prayer list...I pray that God will cleanse her body and soul of all evil associated with that despicable act."

"I'll tell her Susan. Pete told me that she's Catholic but has kind of fallen away until now. He said that her faith is strong though, that's she's seemed to have rediscovered the Lord."

"Good Beth, she sounds delightful. I just hope that this incident doesn't destroy her new found relationship with Him."

"I hear you, that's why she needs our prayers now," said Beth.

"If you don't mind, please keep the news about my pregnancy to yourself. I don't want the word getting out before I get a chance to tell my husband."

"I promise that I won't tell a soul Beth. God bless you and the baby."

"Thank you. I will talk with you later" said Beth.

"Bye...."

Susan thought to herself...*I promised not to say anything, but Joe, guess what...Beth and Pete are finally pregnant! Isn't that great honey?*

Her husband was still her best friend and confidant, even though he was no longer present—*Joe I miss you so....*

<u>54</u>
The DEA

"Hello?"

"Pete, this is Sanela. I know it's your day off, but can we talk?"

"Sure, what's up?" I sat down at the kitchen table with a cup of coffee and listened to what Sanela had to say.

"Pete I know that you and Marilyn are partners," she said. "I've known her for several years now on a casual basis, but you know her better than I do since you work with her."

"Sure," I said. "But what's this all about?"

"Well, I got together with my boss about the guy that raped Marilyn. He told me that the DEA has been working a case on him. They've got several buys into him with their own CI (confidential informant), as well as one of their own agents working undercover. They've been working him for about six months, buying dope and steroids, and they're about to make a major buy from him that will really cement their case."

"That's great," I said. "But what does this mean exactly?"

"It means that rather than go out and put the cuffs on Walker for the rape, the DEA would like us to hold off until they can seal their deal." Sanela paused briefly, "We're still going to indict him, but we'll seal the indictment so that he doesn't get wind of what's going on. We don't want him to know that Marilyn even reported what happened."

I pondered what Marilyn might think about this. She may be outraged that he's still walking around after what he did to her.

"So anyway Pete, I thought that I'd run it by you before we gave DEA an answer. My supervisor, Frank Borelli, said that if Marilyn has a problem with the deal we'll go out and bust Walker right away and the hell with DEA."

"That's good," I said. "I like the way this Borelli guy thinks."

"The next step is this...I can meet with her and tell her what's going on, or if you think that she would take the news a little better if it came from you, then you can explain things to her."

"I can do that if you'd like."

"I would like that," she said. "Marilyn is a tough woman, but her world has been rocked and who knows how she'll react to this news. Just tell her that if she's not comfortable with what we're doing, we'll just tell DEA to forget about it. Oh, and Pete..."

"What?"

"Let her know that since the rape occurred, DEA has had him under constant surveillance. He's not going anywhere or doing anything that they don't know about. The last thing that they want to have happen is for this scumbag to get away, especially if he gets wind that he's wanted for raping Marilyn."

"Well that's good to know, and that will go a long way with her if she knows that we can grab him at any time. I'll give Marilyn a call and set up a meeting to run this by her."

"Thanks Pete, tell her that it's her call either way—no pressure."

"Will do Sanela; I'll get back to you after we meet."

We hung up and I thought about the proposal. I really didn't see too much harm in it since it would guarantee that this guy would be getting hard time for both drugs and the rape. And, since DEA had him under 24/7 surveillance, we could snatch him at any time. Marilyn may go along with this, unless she was bent on seeing him behind bars as quickly as possible. I dialed her number...

"Marilyn...this is Pete. How are you?"

"Hi Pete; I'm doing okay. I slept most of the day yesterday. I guess that the drug more than anything else had me groggy. But I got up early, made some coffee and went out for a three mile run."

"God bless you girl, I am so proud of you," I said.

"Pete, there's nothing to be proud about. I'm still peeved about that guy doing what he did to me. I feel used and dirty, but I'm not letting this thing change my plans. I'm still a cop..."

"And a darned good one!" I added.

"Thanks," she said. "And I still have the contest coming up, and there's school, hey, I've got a life!"

"There you go, I love your attitude."

"Well I'll tell you...I thought about what Reverand Dean said—that God gives you challenges some times. I'm okay Pete. I was down on my knees last night and we talked. It was probably one of the most sincere conversations that I've had with Him in ages. I know that God wants me to be strong during this matter. He tested my faith and thankfully I didn't fail—my love for the Father is stronger than ever."

"Amen Marilyn. I need to talk with you about the case, and I'd rather do it in person. Can I come over, or can we meet for coffee?"

"Sure, I'm ready for some fresh air anyway. Let's meet at the Starbucks at the mall."

"10-4 partner, half hour from now?"

"Okay," she said.

I let Beth know what was going on then headed out to the mall. As I drove I thought about how badly this whole incident could have ended for Marilyn. She could have physically been hurt, either from Walker himself or the drug. Emotionally, she could have been tremendously scarred to the point where she'd be in denial about the whole thing. And while we still didn't know for certain about her emotional health, physically she's a fighter and appears to be doing just fine. Her time spent with the Father apparently buoyed her spirit. She's a remarkable woman, I thought. The Lord truly blessed me when He made us partners. Now it's time to see how she'll react to Sanela's proposal...

Ten minutes later I was at the coffee shop. I walked inside to find her seated comfortably at a booth in the corner, sipping on some foofoo drink. "What's that? " I asked.

"Before you start to preach about my contest diet...it's a non-fat, sugar-free latte," she said. "It's less than 100 calories, besides it's too darn hot to have coffee."

"Good, I want to see you win that contest so that I can say that my partner is Miss Illinois!"

I walked up to the counter and ordered a small coffee, and then went back over to where Marilyn was seated. She was looking good, not like someone who had just undergone a traumatic event. She wore a pair of cargo shorts, belted, and a form fitting, blue Nike top. Her arms and legs looked muscular and cut. I imagine that she must have drawn tons of stares when she walked through the mall.

"So what's up Pete; why the meeting?"

I sat down and took a drink of the always too hot coffee, then set it down. "Sanela gave me a call and ran something by me that you need to make a decision about."

She looked puzzled and asked, "What do you mean? What kind of decision do I have to make, I'm the victim?"

"That's right. But there's a twist to the case that we just found out about." I explained about the DEA angle and their request to hold off on making the arrest.

"Wow Pete, I had no idea that he was into those types of things. How naïve can a girl be?"

"It's not that you're naïve Marilyn. You just had so much going on in your life that he wasn't that much of a priority so you didn't care to delve into his history."

"Thanks," she said. "That's a nice way of telling me that I missed some pretty big clues."

"No...you didn't miss anything. This guy's a pretty good actor, and he never came on to you with any drug activity so how would you know?"

"You're right about that," she said. "Our relationship was really kind of shallow—dinners and movies once in a while. Once he found out that I wasn't going to jump into bed with him, our relationship began to fade."

I took another drink of the still too hot coffee of the day. "So what do think about holding off on the arrest? Can you live with that, especially since you may have to see him at the gym?"

"Yeah, that's going to be tough," she said. "I've got to really steel myself so that I don't let on about what's happening. What do I say if he asks about that night?"

"I don't know Bens. I guess if it was me, I'd just play dumb, like I didn't even know what happened."

She seemed to ponder that for a moment and then said, "I think that I can do it. As long as he's under a sealed indictment and DEA has him in pocket 24-7... I can live with that."

"Good. The more charges that we can pile on this guy, the less inclined the judge will be to plea bargain down the rape to assault."

She finished up her drink and moved to leave. I followed her cue and we walked out through the mall to our cars.

"I'll call Sanela and tell her we're on," I said.

"Good Pete. And I'll call Mac and tell him to put me back on duty tomorrow. I don't want you working with someone that I can't trust to have your back."

"That's your call," I said. "I don't want you coming back sooner than you should. But given a choice of partners, there's no one else that even comes close to you."

She gave me a hug and said, "You sure know how to make a girl feel good Officer Shannon. Now get home to that wonderful wife of yours and tell her how much you love her."

"I'll do that. We went our separate ways, and as I drove back home I thought about the strength of character that Marilyn must have. She is truly one of God's Warriors.

<u>55</u>
Leslie Lends A Hand

Marilyn got home and parked her car in the lot. As she approached the stairs to her apartment, she saw a woman walking her dog. Wanting to be neighborly, Marilyn looked at her and said hello.

"Hi," the woman replied. "I hope that I'm not being rude, but I couldn't help but notice that the police were at your apartment the other night. Is everything okay?"

Wondering how much she should tell this woman, but still wanting to be a good neighbor, Marilyn answered, "Everything is fine ma'am. I had a little trouble with a boyfriend but it's all resolved now. Thank you for asking."

"I'm glad to hear that," the woman said. "As soon as I saw that it was your apartment I began to pray that you would be safe. It seems that my prayers were answered."

Feeling a bit more comfortable speaking with her, Marilyn said, "Thank you so much for your concern. I am blessed to have such a caring neighbor. What's your name? Mine's Marilyn."

"Marilyn, that's a pretty name. You know that your name is a blend of two names: Mary and Lyn; Mary of course is in honor of Christ's mother."

"I never knew that," replied Marilyn. She was really beginning to take a liking to this woman. She seemed so sincere, so inviting, like someone that you could share your deepest secrets with. She must be a great mother to someone, and probably a wife to one lucky man. She appeared to be around 35 or 40 years old, but she had style and grace beyond her years.

"What's your name," asked Marilyn.

"Leslie."

"Well Leslie, I am very glad to meet you, and so touched that you would pray for me."

Leslie's dog was becoming somewhat rambunctious and was straining at the leash. "I pray for all God's children when they are in trouble. I know that you're a police officer; I've seen you come and go in your uniform. The fact that you live close to me has given me a sense of security. But even though you are an officer and are obviously extremely fit, sometimes He will test you and give you a challenge that may be overwhelming. That's where prayer comes in. How can I pray for you today Marilyn?"

She was feeling very touched by this woman. She could see God at work here, bringing this Christian woman into her life just when she needed spiritual support. It was as if He was bringing Christ's disciples into her life, rewarding her for her new found faith. First Pete... now this woman. She could almost feel the Holy Spirit filling her soul and transforming her so that she was no longer comfortable with her old life. Marilyn felt tears beginning to run down her cheeks; she was overcome with gratitude and thanksgiving. "Leslie, I need to talk. Can you spare some time for me?"

"Of course I can. Give me five minutes to put the dog away and I'll be right over."

Marilyn walked up to her apartment and closed the door behind her. She got on her knees immediately..."Dear Father God, I just thank you for your love. I know that Leslie has been sent by you and I thank you. Help me unburden my heart from those ugly things that have caused me to ignore you for so many years. I pray that this day I surrender to your will, knowing that only you know what is good for me and what will lead to my salvation. Help me to listen Father, open my ears and close my mouth, that I may hear your voice. In Jesus' name I pray, Amen.

Leslie returned in minutes and Marilyn talked for hours while Leslie listened. It was the most cathartic experience that she had had for as long as she could remember. By the end of their time together they were both exhausted.

"Marilyn, thank you for sharing with me, I know that was difficult for you."

"Actually it wasn't Leslie, I prayed for strength to chase some demons from my soul and He gave it to me. I guess that you were the instrument that He chose."

Leslie got up to leave and gave her a hug. "To be able to minister to someone in need is a gift. I don't know which one of us has been more blessed—you or me."

"I don't know either," said Marilyn. "But I know that I need you in my life. I truly believe that you were sent from above. I've never had a woman that was a spiritual mentor in my life. I've had plenty of bad role models, but none like you. Thank you for giving of yourself."

"You are so welcome...let's exchange phone numbers. I may need to call upon you sometime as well. Besides, you seem to have God's ear."

"I don't know about that," said Marilyn, "but I know that I have his attention."

"Yes you do my friend, yes you do. Good night Marilyn."

"Good night Leslie, and thank you again. God bless you."

God's been good to me, Marilyn thought. She felt excited about her new relationship with God, wanting to dedicate her whole life to Him. Despite the recent events, she vowed to be the best Christian woman that she could be, and she made a promise to walk with Him each day. Almost too excited to sleep, she lay awake glowing in the light of her Creator.

<u>56</u>
Officer Meyers

I walked into the station and Mac signaled me to come over to the desk. "Hi Pete, how's everything going?"

"Hi Mac, God's been good to me as usual," I said. "What's up?"

"With Marilyn off, and it being the middle of summer, lots of guys are taking vacation time. I don't have a partner for you tonight on tac. Do you mind working a beat car in uniform?"

"No, that would be fine. I keep a fresh uniform in my locker all the time; I'll go down and change."

"Thanks Pete. I'll see you at roll call."

A short time later I was sitting down listening to Mac hand out assignments.

"Shannon and Meyers, Beat 850, traffic car, and pay special attention to Ford City Drive. The drag racers are back and they're making all kinds of racket. The neighbors are complaining about noise and safety concerns. Let's make sure nobody gets killed."

A few minutes later Mac had finished with assignments and some admin matters from Headquarters. I made my way out to the lot with my radio and shotgun and began to look for our car. I spotted it parked by the fence, my partner already sitting in the driver's seat waiting.

I opened the passenger's door, "Hi partner, boy you're raring to go!"

"Yeah," he replied. "I need to get over to a liquor store on 59th Street. I know the owner; he likes me to park out front while he closes shop."

"Was he robbed recently?"

"Nah...he just wants to make sure that nobody tries anything. I've been doing it for about a year now; the guy really appreciates it if you know what I mean..."

I thought about that for a minute and hoped that it didn't mean that the guy was paying a cop to babysit his store. Situations like that are not uncommon in police work. Store owners are not shy about offering cops an incentive for a little extra protection. I never understood how a cop could put his whole career in jeopardy by taking money from someone for just doing their job.

Meyers put the car in gear and we headed toward the store. Eddie was a middle aged cop with a lot of time on the job. He had long ago abandoned any regard for his personal appearance; his uniform seemed to always look wrinkled and dirty. Coffee and condiment stains were a common sight on his shirt. His pants were so worn that they were paper thin and you could almost see your reflection in them. His leather gear was probably original, the black worn off in so many spots as to give it a speckled appearance. He still carried a .38 revolver even though our department had transitioned to semi automatic pistols years ago. He looked to be probably 80 or 90 pounds overweight, and his balding head and coke bottle glasses gave him the appearance of a shopkeeper rather than a cop. Eddie was anything but an authority figure.

As we drove through the now quiet streets, I began to feel a little uneasy. "Eddie, did you go through the car?"

He drove through a red light for no apparent reason. "What do ya mean?"

"Did you check under the seats and all—making sure no one stashed anything?"

"Naw, I usually don't do that, unless I see something sticking out somewhere..."

"How about the emergency equipment, did you check it?"

"What do ya mean?" he said again.

"The lights and siren, medical gear...did you make sure everything is working?"

"Naw, I don't really do that. If the 4-12 guys have a problem with it, they'll get it fixed or tell me about it."

I wasn't at all comfortable with the way the night was starting out. "Eddie, when we're done with your friend, pull over in a parking lot somewhere so that I can do a quick search. I don't want to arrest someone and put them in the back where there might be some type of weapon hidden."

"Yeah, whatever... I don't usually worry about that stuff. I try not to arrest anybody cuz then I have to go to court. I work a second job during the day; I don't have time for court. Well, except for traffic court. I go there once a month. That's all I do—write tickets, keeps the bosses off my back."

Eddie drove through another red light and then pulled up to a liquor store. He opened the door to get out and said, "Wait here, I'll be back in a couple of minutes."

Before I could answer he was out of the car and into the store. I thought about going inside, but I was probably better off not getting involved in anything having to do with Eddie's business. I decided to spend the time going through our car and checking out the equipment. A short time later Eddie emerged with the store owner, each man was carrying a bag. Eddie walked him to his car and stood there until his guy drove off, then made his way back to our unit. Eddie got back in the driver's seat and put the bag in the backseat. It looked to be a six pack of beer.

"Eddie, you can't have booze in the squad car," I said.

"I know, we'll just run back to the station and I'll throw it in my car."

"You know you're taking a big chance doing this. What if the sergeant finds out?"

"He won't. All he cares about is tickets, and I'm good with that."

We drove back to the station and Eddie deposited his package in his own vehicle, a beat up rusty dodge van. It had numerous dents all over, paint peeling off the hood, and a broken tail light. He got back in our unit and we resumed patrol.

"Hey Eddie, do you ever get stopped driving that van of yours? The thing looks dangerous."

"Sometimes...mostly from rookies. Once I flash my star and they know I'm on the job, I'm on my way. You know...professional courtesy and all..."

Man I thought, this guy is taking total advantage of being a cop. Every opportunity that he has to use the system, he does. We spent the next couple of hours stopping cars for traffic violations, Eddie writing four moving violations, two of which in my judgment were questionable. Each time he wrote one, he finished with, "It's all about the numbers." He never once ran a tag to see if the car was hot, nor did he run the drivers. As long as they had a drivers license, Eddie was good with that. He didn't want to bring them into the station for anymore paperwork than was necessary.

"Eddie," I asked, "What about the drag racers over on Ford City Drive?"

"What about 'em?" he replied.

"Mac told us to give that area special attention tonight because the neighbors were complaining."

"Yeah well if they are racing over there that's the last place that I want to be."

I couldn't believe this guy. He acted as if he was his own little police force.

I looked at him and said, "Eddie, I want you to head over that way right now. We're going to see if anything is going on over there, and if there is we're going to take care of it."

Eddie looked over at me. "You ever try to stop kids drag racing? You can't do it—too dangerous."

"No Eddie, I never have, but tonight if they're over there I will try to stop them."

He gave me kind of a disgusted look and said, "I think you're nuts, but if it makes you happy we'll go see if they're racing."

"Thanks brother. Doesn't it feel good when you do your job?"

No answer from him, but we started in that direction.

We turned off Pulaski Road onto Ford City Drive and saw a car parked on the side of the road. Inside were a teenage boy and girl. As Eddie continued westbound, we saw several cars begin to leave the side of the road where they had been parked.

Eddie immediately deduced that nothing was going on, he said "See, things are quiet."

I thought differently; that car we passed as we made our turn onto the street was obviously the lookout. He either phoned or had a walkie-talkie to let the others know that the cops were here. "Eddie, make a u-turn and go back to where that car was parked on the side of the road. I want to check them out."

"Sure partner...you gonna write them for obstructing traffic or what?"

"No," I said. "I just want to see if my suspicions are correct."

"Whatever," he said as he made the u-turn.

As we approached the vehicle from the opposite direction, Eddie crossed over the center line and parked our unit facing theirs. "What are you doing?" I asked.

"You said you wanted to talk to them," he said.

"Back up and come behind them like you're supposed to do on a traffic stop. We're vulnerable here; they can see everything we do!"

"Whatever...it's just a couple a kids."

Eddie pulled behind them, but really not to my liking. He aligned our car with theirs, not placing our unit slightly to the left to give me protection from traffic. I got out and cautiously made my way to the driver's window. I waited for a moment to see if my backup was positioned on the passenger's side, but Eddie had not even exited the car.

I was on my own, so I said a quick prayer that St. Michael would have my back.

I shined my light quickly at and around the occupants, locating their hands, and then asked for the driver's license and registration. As I waited for compliance, the odor of marijuana wafted out from the inside of the vehicle. Handing me his license but no registration, I noticed that the driver seemed very nervous. I decided that this needed further investigation, so I ordered the driver out of the vehicle.

"Stay put passenger, until I tell you to move." I took the driver by the arm and led him to the rear of the vehicle. I looked incredulously at Eddie; he had yet to get out of our unit. I signaled and yelled at the same time, "Eddie, come here!"

He reluctantly got out and made his way between the two vehicles. "What do ya need?"

"I want you to watch this kid...I need to check the vehicle." I turned to the boy and asked, "Have you been smoking marijuana tonight?"

"No officer, why?"

"Because as soon as you rolled down your window I could smell it."

"Oh," he said. "That's not my car, it belongs to a friend. Maybe he was smoking it."

"Is that your friend in the passenger seat?" I asked.

"She's a friend, but not the one that owns the car," he replied.

"Okay, wait here with this officer." I went over to the passenger side, opened the door, and told the other teenager to get out.

"What have I done officer?"

"Nothing that I'm aware of I said, but I need to take a quick look at this car so I need you to join your friend who is with my partner. Understood?"

"Yes sir." She walked back to where Eddie was standing.

I did a quick visual inside. The ashtray held two roaches, and there was a pack of rolling papers on the seat. That was enough for me to make the arrest and search the vehicle. I went to the rear of the car and placed handcuffs on the driver. "Eddie, cuff the passenger."

"Why?" he asked.

"She's under arrest," I said.

Eddie looked at me in amazement, "I don't carry handcuffs—they bother me when I'm driving."

This was all just too much for me. I grabbed a pair of flex cuffs from the pouch on my belt and handcuffed the passenger. After they were both searched and placed in the rear of our squad car, I did a quick search of their car and found a couple of baggies of marijuana and other drug paraphernalia. I ordered a tow for the car and we made our way into the station.

I was fuming at Eddie. He had no business being a cop, and had put my safety in jeopardy by his poor police work. I silently said the Serenity Prayer and tried to calm down on the drive in. Once inside the station, I had to do most of the paperwork since Eddie said that he never makes drug arrests and therefore doesn't know the procedures. By the time we finished with the paper and booking, it was close to six o'clock. I dreaded having to go out again with Eddie, so I went to see Mac.

"Got a second Mac?"

"Sure Pete, what's up?"

"I'd like to take leave for the rest of the shift," I said. "Meyers has been too much of a challenge; he's dangerous and his ethics are questionable."

"Anything specific that you want to tell me," Mac asked.

"Well...the ethics thing is only my own opinion based on a couple of things that I saw tonight. I don't have any evidence. But his lack of procedure and tactics is going to get someone killed."

Mac scratched his head. "You're not the first to complain about Meyers; I have a difficult time finding anyone that will work with him. I promise you that I'll never put you with him again Pete...sorry."

"That's okay Mac, working with Meyers tonight made me appreciate working with Marilyn."

"Speaking about her, she's back on shift tomorrow night."

"Great," I said. "I'll be looking forward to it."

"Okay," said Mac. "Give me a leave slip for an hour and go home. I'll see you tomorrow."

"Thanks Mac, God bless you."

<u>57</u>
Beth Shares The News

I thought about Eddie on my drive home. He seemed to be an anachronism, for he was living thirty years in the past—still carrying his revolver and practicing tactics that had proven to be fatal to cops over the years. I prayed that God would keep him safe, but if he ever made the mistake of pulling someone over that was bent on violence, Eddie would be in trouble.

Getting off shift early would give me an opportunity to be with Beth while she got ready for work. I pulled into the garage and entered through the kitchen door. Beth was standing at the sink filling the coffee pot.

"Good morning babe!"

"Pete! What are you doing home, are you okay?"

"I'm fine," I said. "I just took a couple of hours leave. I was working with a guy tonight that made me uneasy, so after we made an arrest I thought that I'd quit while I was ahead."

She poured the water into the coffee maker. "Good...it's nice to have you here with me in the morning. Let me make breakfast for us, how about a nice egg white omelet and turkey sausage?"

"That would be super Beth, thanks."

Beth busied herself with fixing breakfast and I sat down at the table with a cup of coffee to watch, thinking about how blessed I was to have her as my wife. She broke some eggs into a pan and dropped a couple of sausage patties onto the skillet.

"So what are your plans for today Pete? You've got an early start to your day."

"Yeah, I could get used to this; I'm going to get a workout in, maybe a run with Father Mike. Then I think that I'll stop over at Susan's to visit her and the boys. I kind of miss those little guys; I haven't seen them in over two weeks."

"I know what you mean," she said. "I was over there last week visiting, they're just adorable."

"Yes they are and Susan is a super parent. Those boys are lucky, and even though they've lost their Dad, Susan will make sure that their grief won't be long term. You know if we ever have kids…" I quickly stopped in mid-sentence.

Beth turned around quickly from the stove to look at me. "What were you saying Pete, something about us having children?"

"I'm sorry honey. I said that I wouldn't bring that topic up again."

She made her way over to me and took my face into her hands. "Pete look at me—what were you about to say?"

"I didn't mean to cause trouble babe. I was just kind of thinking out loud that if we ever had children, I would like them to be like their kids."

"Pete remember how we talked about trying to have children? We had some problems, well, mostly I had problems. I didn't want to compound those problems by bringing children into a marriage that wasn't suitable for kids. That was then…this is now."

She continued to hold me as she stood next to my chair. "What are you saying Beth? Do you want us to have children?"

Her eyes began to tear up and she said, "Yes honey, I want us to have children."

I stood up and gave her a big strong hug and a kiss.

"Careful…be careful," she said.

"Why, what's wrong?"

"I don't want you to hurt the baby," she said.

"What? What are you talking about? Are you…"

"Yes, I'm pregnant—we're going to have a baby!"

"Thank you Lord, thank you Jesus!" I danced up and down like a silly teenager and cried like a baby. "How...when...I mean I know how it happened, but how did you know?"

Beth was crying now too, but through her tears she explained. "Actually, I was at Susan's. I got sick and thought that I was coming down with something, but Susan was the one that suggested that I might be pregnant. I took the pregnancy test and it came back positive. I have an appointment with the doctor next week to confirm it, but I'm positive that I'm carrying our baby."

"Oh Beth, this is the greatest news... I have wanted this for us for so long. I can only imagine how beautiful you will look pregnant."

"I don't know about beautiful," she said. "But I'm no longer fearful about having children. God intended for us to bring children into the world. I've been ignoring that for too long. And besides, I can't wait to see you with a little blond haired boy or girl up on your shoulders, walking around the park."

I took her into my arms again and just held her, knowing that our new baby was between us. "Beth I love you so much..."

"I know honey. And I love you too. Now we can share some of that love with a miracle from the Lord. We are truly blessed. One thing though..."

"What?" I asked.

"Not a word of this to anyone until the doctor confirms it, okay?"

"Okay," I said. "But it's going to be difficult because I'm bursting with pride!"

"I know babe. I'm excited too, but I just want that confirmation before we spread the news."

"My lips are sealed."

"Good. Now let's eat and then I've got to get ready to go to work."

Ninety minutes later, Beth was on her way to work and I was out the door on my way to St. Xav's. I was hoping to see Father Mike there so that I could get in a run with him, but maybe it would be better if he weren't so that I wouldn't be tempted to tell him about the baby. One thing I did know—this was going to be one of the happiest days of our lives. Our marriage would now be complete in the eyes of the God.

Once the doctor told Beth for sure that she was pregnant, I wanted to have a little party to make the announcement. I thought that a nice barbeque at our house would be suitable. I felt like a little kid entrusted with a secret from his best friend who was just aching to share it with everyone. But I promised Beth that I wouldn't say a word.

Beth's news caused me to completely forget about my night with Eddie. I was looking forward to Marilyn coming back on duty tonight. Things had progressed to the point of being so comfortable working with her, that when she was off it was difficult to work with anyone else. That synergy that develops between partners is special. Sometimes communication consists of only a look; you automatically know what they are going to do or say. You come to take it for granted, so that when you have to work with a different person for whatever reason, it's like working with a complete stranger. I wasn't sure how long our partnership would last. Each of us had our own lives and goals, but for the present life was good. After Joe's death I didn't think that I could ever have that kind of relationship with another partner, but Marilyn proved me wrong.

I was anxious to get back to work tonight and hoped that Marilyn's incident didn't affect her work. Hopefully she had been praying for His help; I know that Beth and I were. But knowing that our God is a merciful God, He will be with her guiding her path as always. In any case, I'd find out tonight.

Beth is pregnant! Thank you so much Lord...

<u>58</u>
Matthew At Marathon Sports

The week progressed slowly, nothing really significant happening at work. We made several gun arrests and caught a couple of armed robbery suspects. Marilyn displayed no ill effects from her incident. Beth and I planned a barbeque for Sunday, inviting family and friends. We didn't let on about the pregnancy, which was confirmed by her doctor, but that was going to be the purpose—to make the formal announcement.

I had finished up my workout for the day and wanted to check on Matthew, the kid that we had arrested for drugs in Marquette Park. I got in my truck and headed over to Marathon Sports. I found a parking spot right out front and walked in the front door. I heard all of the machinery at work in the back, so I took the liberty of going behind the counter to see what was going on. I spotted Andy right away; he was in the middle of two silkscreen machines, barking orders to the guys working on a job for the White Sox. Next to him was Matthew, who was working on one of the screening stations and was so engrossed in his job that he didn't even see me.

Andy looked over and spotted me. "Pete, how are you?"

He walked over to me. "I'm great Andy, God been good to you today brother?"

"Of course. What brings you here?"

"Well, I wanted to check on Matthew...how's he doing"

Andy looked over in Matthew's direction. "He's doing fine Pete. He's really a good kid and a hard worker. I almost have to kick him out of here at night. If I didn't tell him to leave he'd be here all night. The kid takes the bus here after school and jumps right into whatever job we've got going. Heck, I've already given him a raise—he's one of the best workers I have!"

"I'm so glad to hear that," I said. "I'm sure that his mother is relieved to see what's happening with him. I tell you Andy, he was in the devil's clutches. Without that arrest I think we would have lost the battle."

"I agree," Andy replied. "You know I sometimes drive him home if it gets too late. I worry about him getting on the bus at night. I spoke with his mom once when I dropped him off. She didn't say a whole lot, but I could tell that she's been through some tough times."

"Yes she has, but with Matthew back on track and bringing in some money, her burden has gotten somewhat lighter. God bless you Andy for what you've done."

"No problem, I'm blessed to be able to help him and his family," he said.

"Andy, we're having a barbeque at the house Sunday afternoon. We'd love to have you and Nano be a part of it."

"Great Pete, we'll be there. Can I bring anything?"

"No brother, we're good to go. Hey, where's Joe?" I asked. Joe was Joe Murphy, a former Chicago cop. He lived in the neighborhood and had been a detective on the force. A couple of years ago his wife was killed in an auto accident with a drunk driver. After that Joe had lost his desire to do the job anymore and had joined Andy in his business, just wanting to get away from it all. He had been a rising star in the department, having both a Masters and a Law Degree. But for the last couple of years he had thrown himself into this new endeavor to the point of working 12-15 hours a day, six days a week. He was a member of our church; Beth and I would see him there on some Sundays.

"Joe's out delivering an order in Oak Lawn," said Andy.

"Well if you wouldn't mind, would you please tell him that we would love for him to come to the barbeque?'

"I'll be sure to tell him," said Andy. "He definitely needs some R and R, he works too much."

"Great! I'm going to go over and say Hi to Matthew before I go. Thanks again for bringing him on board Andy."

"I should be thanking you Pete, he has been a definite asset to me."

I walked over to where Matthew was working and put my hand on his shoulder. "Matthew, hi what's up?"

Matthew turned around. "Officer Shannon, how are you?"

"I'm great. Are you enjoying the job?"

"I sure am," he said. "Andy and Joe are great guys to work for."

"Andy says that you are doing a wonderful job here and that he is really pleased with your hard work and dedication. I'm very proud of you Matthew, you recognized what a great opportunity was being offered to you and you seized it. That's a mark of maturity and responsibility. I expect that this is a sign of many good things to come your way."

"I know that I have you to thank for giving me a chance, when you could have just arrested me and allowed things to continue to go downhill. Thanks Officer Shannon."

"You're welcome Matthew, and from now on please just call me Pete."

"Okay Pete, thanks again."

I walked out and waved goodbye to Andy and Matthew. I couldn't help but feel really good about the outcome for Matthew. Marilyn and I came into his life at just the right time. God had put us all in the same place in time where He could have us do His work. *Thank you Father for working through me.*

<u>59</u>
Workout With Kim

"Man, this early morning stuff is killing me," said Kim. "How long before we can get back to normal workout hours Marilyn?"

"Shortly." Marilyn had asked her workout partner to change their workout times to as soon as they got off shift. She didn't want to chance seeing Gary Walker at the gym. The fact that he worked as a bouncer meant that he slept in most days, since he didn't get home until three or four in the morning. She was thankful that she hadn't had any contact with him since the night that he raped her—no phone calls, and she hadn't seen him around the gym. That was fine with her. She was still angry about being taken advantage of, and wasn't quite sure that she could hold back without smacking him. Hopefully DEA would make their case soon and put this creep behind bars where he belonged.

Kim finished her warm up on the elliptical machine. "What are we working today partner?"

"Chest and tri's baby, let's hit them hard. Only a few more weeks until contest time and I don't want to lose any size."

"Girlfriend you are lean and mean!" Kim looked her up and down. Marilyn wore a tank top and short lycra tights so that she could evaluate herself in the mirrors while she exercised.

"Thanks," said Marilyn. "I just worry about this show—there's such a fine line between being too big and not big enough. Hopefully the judges are looking for more feminine types this time around. The first time that I competed all they were looking for was size. Some of the gals could have placed in the 'Mr. Illinois' contest."

"I know," said Kim. "A couple times while I was backstage I overheard a couple competitors talking to each other. I swear that it sounded like a couple of guys talking."

Marilyn was at the Smith Machine loading a couple of 45s on the bar. "Well this one is supposed to be drug tested for the first time. Hopefully that will at least knock someone out that's been juicing."

"Good," Kim replied. "It's bad enough that steroids have taken over the pro ranks in bodybuilding, but I never thought that I'd see it in the amateurs."

"Believe me; it's all over the place," said Marilyn. "I've got a friend in the FBI that worked undercover for a couple of years buying steroids from guys at gyms all over the country. He told me that even high school kids were using them, boys and girls. He was shocked at the numbers himself, and when he told me about some of the side effects... It's crazy Kim; I can't understand kids wanting to put their health in jeopardy."

The bar was loaded and Kim laid down on the bench. "Okay, enough small talk, let's get busy and pump some iron."

They spent a couple of hours working out, Marilyn finished off the session with a half an hour of cardio. She wanted to get in a good one today because tomorrow was Pete's barbeque. Afterward she went home and had an egg white omelet and a chicken breast, then hopped into bed for a nap. She woke up around 5:30 feeling a little tired, but good overall. She put on a pot of coffee, and went out to the mailbox to get her mail. She retrieved a stack of bills and junk mail, and as she turned to go back to her place Leslie appeared.

"Marilyn, how are you? I haven't seen you in several days, are you doing okay?"

"I'm doing well Les. Listen, I just put a pot of coffee on. Do you have time for a cup?"

"Yes, thank you for asking," she said.

They walked inside to Marilyn's apartment where she poured them both a cup, and they sat at the kitchen table.

"You know Leslie, that first night that we talked was so cathartic and healing for me that it changed the way that I look at things. My spiritual life was on hold in a way. The only time that I prayed was when I was in some kind of trouble, or was asking God for something. Now since our talk, I'm just so grateful about so many things that I spend half my day just thanking Him."

"Praise God," said Leslie.

"Oh yeah. I'm reading my Bible again, and I went out and bought a daily devotional—I'm excited about the Lord and I'm committed to Him."

Leslie just sipped her coffee and listened. She was pleased to hear her friend's rebirth and joy, even in the face of a humiliating experience. But she knew that sometimes people had to hit bottom before they would pay attention to the Word. She was confident that Marilyn was right where she needed to be now.

They enjoyed their coffee and talked for about an hour when Leslie said that she had to leave to make dinner for her family. As she walked out the door Marilyn gave her a big hug. "I may call you when I need to talk, or need an answer to something that I've read. Is that okay?"

"Yes it is," said Leslie. "I get so much joy from speaking with you. You're excitement with the Lord is infectious and comforting. I feel close to Him when I'm with you."

"Oh my," exclaimed Marilyn. "Thank you, I guess."

"Don't be ashamed, I can see Him working in you—it's beautiful..."

"Good night Leslie and thanks."

<u>60</u>
The Barbeque

Sunday arrived sunny and warm, a perfect day for a barbeque. Work had been challenging last night. We caught one of two robbery suspects that had just held up a gas station. Once we got our guy into the station we convinced him to give up his partner, so we spent the rest of the night sitting on what was his home address. Even though you're sitting in a car and not doing anything it wears you out. Just having to focus on one house, as well as keeping your eyes peeled for anything happening around you, drains your strength. One of the ways that I've always been able to keep myself awake on midnights has been to keep moving. Surveillance lends itself to daydreaming and naps. Marilyn and I had to take turns keeping the eye for fear that both of us would fall asleep. I was glad when the shift ended.

I got home and walked into the kitchen to find Beth busy with preparing for the afternoon barbeque. "Hi babe, did you sleep well?"

Beth put a hand on her stomach and said, "Like a baby!"

I took her into my arms and gave her a big hug and kiss. "Thank you Lord for blessing us..."

"Amen," said Beth. "Pete I'm going to need a couple of things that I forgot to get last time that I was at the grocery store. Do you think that you can pick them up for me?"

"Of course, what mass are we going to this morning?"

"I'd like to go to 10:30, is that okay?"

"That's fine," I said.

"Are you working out today Pete?"

"I don't think so babe. I want to help you get everything ready, besides I don't want you to over exert yourself and hurt the baby."

"Pete, you're crazy," she said. "There's no chance of that happening at this early stage. Don't get into the habit of doing things for me unless I ask you. I don't want our way of life to change any more than is necessary. I'm sure that I'll probably appreciate your help in the last month, but until then I'll be fine."

"10-4 ma'am, I understand your orders," I replied sarcastically.

"Okay Pete, knock it off before you start to aggravate me."

"Sorry. Hey, how are we on the responses? Is everyone coming that was invited?"

Beth pulled out a head of lettuce and began making a salad. "The only one that hasn't responded is Joe Murphy. Have you heard from him?"

I hoped that Joe would show, he needs some time away from work. Andy told me that Joe's turned into a workaholic. "No I haven't, but he usually attends the 10:30 Mass. Let's look for him there."

"Okay, and if we do see him make sure you go up to him and ask whether he's coming or not."

"I will," I said. "It will do him good to get away from work. I worry about him; I don't know if he even sees any of his friends anymore."

"You know babe, with so much happening in our lives, I'm ashamed to say that I haven't given Joe much thought. Not very Christian of me, is it? Today at mass I'm going to offer up my Communion and ask the Lord to shine His light on Joe, that he'll give him comfort from the pain that he's been in."

"Beth that's a great idea," I said. "I'm just as guilty, let's pray for him now."

We put our hands together and bowed our heads while I lifted a prayer up for Joe...Dear Father in heaven; you are an awesome and loving God. We thank you and praise your name for the blessings that you bring us each day. Our brother Joe is in pain; we pray that you will comfort him and heal his heart. Help him to realize that his wife Pat is with you and would want him to be happy for her. Help him to resume a normal life and once again become one of your beloved children. In Jesus' name we pray...Amen."

We busied ourselves in the kitchen with further preparations until it was time to get ready for church. We arrived a little early and met with a couple of friends at the rear of the church, then went inside and found a seat on the side with the Blessed Mother. Beth had been praying to her, asking for her intercession that she would have her son bless our baby and keep him safe.

Father Mike was the celebrant for 10:30 mass, and as he began I saw Joe walk in the side door and take a seat. The gospel today was from Matthew, Chapter 18—The Parable of the Lost Sheep. I couldn't help but think how appropriate it was for us to hear that today. We had just prayed this morning for Joe, and now here he was.

"Pete, there's Joe," said Beth.

"I know honey."

"Make sure you talk with him afterward, okay?"

"I will."

After the final blessing I made my way to the section where Joe was seated and blended into the crowd behind him as everyone began to exit the church. Once outside I tapped him on the shoulder. "Joe..."

He turned around and saw me. "Hi Pete, I didn't see you inside. I guess I'm in my own little world these days."

We shook hands. "Did Andy tell you about the barbeque at my house today?"

"Oh yeah," he said. "He told me that you were having a bunch of people over."

"I asked him to tell you that you're invited...can you make it?"

Joe hesitated for a moment, "I uh...I haven't really given it much thought..."

"Joe c'mon, I know Andy has closed the shop today. He and Nano are coming, and we would love to have you join us. It's been ages since we've talked with you. Beth and I have been praying for you."

His eyes looked sad and his posture indicated that he was feeling depressed. *Please Lord, have him come...*

"Well, I guess that I can stop over. What time?"

I grabbed his hand again and shook it, "Two o'clock is fine," I said. "And bring your appetite."

"Okay Pete, I'll be there. Can I bring anything?"

"Yes, bring the old Joe with you—I miss him."

He turned and walked away and I thought to myself that he was really down in the dumps. I hoped that our get together today might be able to re-invigorate him into once again being part of the "old crowd." One thing that I knew for sure...I needed to keep Joe on my prayer list. He was in a bad place right now. This was the perfect opportunity for the *Evil One* to do his dirty work.

I walked back to the parking lot where Beth was talking with Father Mike.

"Pete, did you speak with Joe?"

"Yes, boy he is really feeling low. Let's make sure that we keep him right in the middle of things today."

Father Mike added, "That would be great guys. You know I used to see him and his wife at 10:30 Mass every Sunday without fail. Since she died I rarely see him.

"Will you be coming over today Father?" I asked.

"Definitely," he said. "I rarely ever pass up free food, and Beth just told me what was on the menu so count me in."

"Great, we'll see you later Father."

A few hours later the grill was hot and guests started arriving. Our deck and yard that had once appeared to be much more than the two of us needed, was now straining with a crowd of people. The good weather had encouraged people to attend. Beth's parents, my sister, Mac and Shirley, Marilyn, two of Beth's co-workers, our neighbors on either side of us, Andy and Nano, Susan and the boys, and Father Mike, had all arrived. The only one missing was Joe Murphy; where could he be?

I was busy at the grill, preparing a steady supply of regular and turkey burgers, regular and turkey Italian sausage, hot dogs, corn on the cob, and skewered veggies. Beth had an array of salads—Greek, Caesar, three bean, potato, and her special cole slaw, all made from scratch, laid out on the kitchen counters. The party was in full swing.

As I took another batch of burgers off the grill, Beth came out on the deck to ask me a question. "When should we make the announcement, everyone but Joe is here?"

"I know, but I really want him to be a part of it. Let's give it a few more minutes. If he's not here by 3:00 we'll go ahead."

"Okay babe." She gave me a kiss then whispered, "I love you so much Pete Shannon..."

"I love you too."

Mac was playing kick ball with Susan's boys when one of them kicked the ball down the driveway. "I'll get it Mac," I shouted. I ran down the drive and stopped it before it got out onto the street, and as I stood back up I spotted Joe walking down the sidewalk.

"Joe, thanks for coming brother!" I grabbed him and gave him a warm hug.

"Sorry I'm late Pete. I laid down for what I thought was going to be a little nap and before I knew it I had slept for two and half hours."

"No problem—I'm just glad you're here. C'mon in the back and grab some chow; I've got a ton of food left that I don't want to go to waste."

We walked into the backyard and I introduced Joe to the few people that didn't know who he was, then steered him up on the deck to fill a plate.

"Wow Pete, you guys went all out or do you eat like this every day?"

"No way," I said.   "Today is special; Beth and I have an announcement to make. I was holding off making it until you arrived."

Joe had finished filling his plate and said, "You didn't have to wait Pete."

"I know...but I did because I wanted my friends to all be here when we made it. You're a long-time friend Joe, and whether you're a cop or not makes no difference, we love you as a person. We care about you and are praying for you."

Joe shook his head... "I guess that I haven't heard kind words like that in a long time. Or maybe someone has said them, but I haven't wanted to hear them. Thanks Pete, you're a true friend."

"You're welcome." I looked around for Beth; it was time. I took her by the hand and led her out to the deck.

I whistled as loud as I could to get everyone's attention. "Family and friends...Beth and I thank you for your company today. We feel blessed to have all of you at our house. The reason that we wanted all of you here is because we have an announcement to make. Beth...."

"Pete's right, we have good news to share; such good news that my heart is almost bursting with joy—we're going to have a baby!"

With that everyone cheered and surrounded Beth and me, showering us with hugs and kisses. Beth's parents were in tears, as was my sister Liz. Seeing everyone crying I guess was contagious because even I started it. Father Mike asked for quiet...

"Friends this is a moment that belongs to God, please bow your head and pray with me.

Dear Father we thank you for all that you've given us. Thank you for grandparents who prayed for us before we were born, for parents and family that bind us together. Thank you for teaching us to love by loving us. Thank you for surrounding us with the miracle of your creation, from the heavens to the tiniest sparrows. Thank you for laughter, health, sight, and hearing and for hands to work and to hold. Thank you for shining your light on your children Pete and Beth, and for allowing them to experience the joy of parenthood. But most all Father, thank you for watching, for caring, for helping and for being who you are—a kind and compassionate Father. In Jesus' name we pray...Amen."

I went up to Father Mike to thank him for that beautiful prayer. "Father, you made our day by saying that wonderful prayer."

"It was my pleasure Pete. I am overjoyed by your good news. Just a short while ago we were hard pressed to see the Lord's light in your marriage, now He has smiled upon you both in a way that you never dreamed possible."

"You're right; He does work in mysterious ways."

"Pete thanks for the invite and including me in your special day. I have business to tend to at the rectory. I'll say my good-byes and be on my way."

"Okay Father, see you at the gym."

Marilyn came up from behind and gave me a big hug. "Pete, I'm so happy for you and Beth—you're going to be a daddy!"

"Yes, and I can't wait."

She glanced over in the direction of Joe who was in a conversation with Mac. "What's the story with Joe? Someone said that he used to be a cop?"

I filled her in on Joe's story.

"Oh, how terrible, and here I am thinking my life sucks..."

"I know what you mean. Anytime that I start to feel sorry for myself, all I need do is look around and I'll find someone in trouble. If you don't mind Bens, could you put Joe on your prayer list? Beth and I are worried about him."

"No problem," she said. "I need to go over and talk with him, maybe even cheer him up."

"Good, anything you can do to get him back to normal would be super."

Marilyn walked over to where Joe was standing with Mac. "Isn't it great news about Pete and Beth?"

"Fantastic," said Mac. "Those two will make great parents; I don't know what took them so long."

She looked at Joe's glass which was empty and said, "Joe, looks like you're ready for a refill. Can I get you anything, a glass of wine perhaps?"

"No thanks Marilyn. I don't drink anymore."

"Good for you," she said.

"Well I do, and since Shirley's driving us home I think that I'll have one more." Mac made his way to the kitchen, leaving Joe and Marilyn alone.

"Pete tells me that you used to be on the job...a homicide dick."

"Yeah, I left a couple of years ago. I guess that I lost my enthusiasm for the job."

Marilyn put her hand on Joe's arm and said, "He told me that you lost your wife Joe, I'm so sorry for you loss."

"Thanks," he said. "I know that it's been two years now, but I've just been feeling blah for so long...you know the feeling? You can't really get excited about anything so you try to lose yourself in anything that will keep you busy."

"Is that why you're working at the shirt shop twelve hours a day?"

"To tell you the truth, I don't even know how long I work each day. I just keep going until Andy sends me home. I hate going home—there's nothing there for me."

Marilyn understood what Pete meant now when he said Joe was seriously depressed. She was already feeling his pain.

"Hey, what am I doing," said Joe. "I'm ruining Pete's happy day here with my sob story. I'm sorry for crying on your shoulder..."

Marilyn quickly responded, "Sorry for what? There's no need to apologize Joe, I want to hear what you have to say. Besides, I know what it means to be lost...I've been there and I wish that someone would have allowed me the opportunity to talk about it. I'll tell you what...we'll suspend this conversation for now so that we can help Beth and Pete celebrate, but promise me that you and I can sit down over coffee and just talk. Can you pull yourself away from work long enough to do that Joe?"

A little smile began to form on Joe's face. "Are you sure about this Marilyn; I mean you hardly know me?"

"I'm positive."

"Okay then," he said. "It's a date."

Marilyn took his hand and shook it with both of hers..."Tomorrow okay for you?"

"Yes; let's meet at the Starbucks on Western around three," he said.

"I'll be there."

On the ride home Joe began to have second thoughts about what he had agreed to, thinking that in some way he was dishonoring the memory of his late wife Pat. But as he laid in bed that night thinking more about it, he made a decision that it was time... He needed his broken heart to mend for he was slowly dying inside. *Pat if you're there please don't be mad; I need to move on...I love you.*

61
Past Curfew

Right out of the chute while driving north down St. Louis Avenue, we spotted a couple of teens on the street. It was past curfew and they both looked younger than seventeen, so we decided to pull over and try to watch them for a while to see what they were up to. A short time later we were rewarded for our patience when they stopped by a fancy import car; one of the two smashed the driver's side window with a hammer. The kid with the hammer quickly got into the car, while his buddy served as a lookout.

"Our best chance is to stick with the kid in the car Bens, agreed?"

"Gotcha, the lookout's going to bolt. I'll try to put out a message on him if I can—let's go!"

I floored our car and made the half a block in time to watch the lookout take off down the street. The kid inside the car had been under the dash disconnecting something and had more of a delayed reaction to what was happening. That was all we needed to grab him as he tried to escape.

"Police! You're under arrest!" Marilyn let the kid know what was happening, as if he didn't already know. We put him spread eagle on the car; I searched him while Marilyn let the other units in the area know what had happened and gave a description of the other culprit on the run. The kid was clean; we cuffed him and had another unit transport him to the station for us while we got the info on the car and its owner. It seems that they had gone after the GPS unit and a CD player, things easily moved on the street. We notified the owner, who wasn't too pleased about the damage, and then went in to process our arrestee.

The kid turned out to be sixteen; we found out later that his accomplice was none other than his fifteen year old little brother. Although our guy was playing the tough guy role and wouldn't give up the information on why they were busting into cars, an hour later we called the boy's father and had him come in to pick him up. When the father came to the station, he told us that he had witnessed his other boy come home in a rush, sweating profusely. A couple key questions and a smack from the father quickly produced the story of what the duo had been involved in. It appeared that the boys feared their father's justice, more than the courts. Hopefully we wouldn't see these two kids out there again.

We decided to head over for some coffee at Tommy's donut shop. As we pulled in I could see Tommy behind the counter.

"Hi Tommy," said Marilyn. "How's Lisa doing; when is she coming back?"

"Hi guys. Physically she's fine, but I don't think Lisa's coming back to work. That whole incident with the shooting has changed her. She doesn't even want me to work here anymore. I think that we're going to sell our business."

"Oh, that's too bad," said Marilyn, "but I can't blame her for being afraid. She was very fortunate to have survived that gunshot wound."

"Yeah," replied Tommy, "she doesn't even want to get behind the counter anymore, even if it's on the day shift. That's why I'm working midnights. I hired my nephew to work days for me."

We got our coffees from him. "So Tommy, what will you do? Are you going to start at a different location?"

"No Pete, I think this whole robbery thing has been a sign that we need to count our blessings and retire. Both Lisa and I have been working hard all of our lives. We've been successful and made good money and good investments. It's time to quit while we're still healthy and put ourselves first for a change."

"Now you're talkin' Tommy," said Marilyn. "I think that's a great plan, you've earned it and made plenty of sacrifices over the years. God bless you and Lisa."

"Thank you both," he said. "You know I won't miss the business as much as I'll miss folks like the two of you. Lisa and I have been fortunate to have met some very wonderful people through the years..."

"The feeling is mutual Tommy; we'll miss seeing you guys. Good night..."

We rolled out of the lot and cruised the airport for awhile sipping our coffees.

"I really enjoyed myself at your party Pete; you have great friends and family."

"Thanks Marilyn. I saw you and Joe talking... What did you think?"

Marilyn took a drink, "I think that you're right—he's definitely still hurting. But I think that all he needs is a friend to talk to get it all out and put him back on track. He seems like a great guy with a lot going for him. It's sad that he's kind of put his life on hold for two years. I'm having coffee with him today."

"Really....that's great. He is a good guy with a wealth of knowledge about the job that he should be putting to good use. Not that the tee shirt job isn't worthwhile, but that's just not Joe."

"I don't know if he'll go back to the job," she said. "But I'd just like to see him move forward. I don't know how to explain it, but I feel a pull toward him...like God is telling me to minister to him to help get him through this crisis."

"You could be right," I said. "He does work in mysterious ways..."

As we finished out the night I thought about what Marilyn had said. Had the Father brought them together while both were in the midst of a storm that could destroy their lives? Marilyn's rape and Joe's loss— could these two tragedies be the catalyst that changes their lives for the better?

Lord, I pray that you have chosen to work through Marilyn. May you give her the tools that she needs to mend both of their hearts and give them rest.

<u>62</u>
Joe and Marilyn

Joe was already there when Marilyn walked into Starbucks. She spotted him sitting in the corner that looked cozy and inviting—three easy chairs and a coffee table. When Joe saw her he stood and signaled for her to join him.

"Hi Marilyn, how are you? Did you at least get in a nap today?"

"Got in a nap and a workout," she replied. "I see that you already have a cup of coffee, can I get you a refill?"

"No...I'll get yours, what'll you have?"

"Just a black coffee of the day is good for me Joe."

He nodded, "You definitely are a cop, drinking your cup o' joe black. No foofoo drink or latte, or maybe something exotic?"

"No, I'm watching my diet. I've got a contest in a couple of weeks."

"Right...black coffee it is; I'll be right back."

Joe went to get the coffee while Marilyn picked one of the chairs. They're all a little too soft for me she thought, but for the time being it will have to do. He came back with her coffee and a refill for himself, and then picked the chair farthest from her.

"Hey, I thought that we were going to talk. Do I look that intimidating that you have to sit so far away?"

"No...I just didn't want to seem too familiar. And no, you don't look intimidating—you look awesome."

She should she thought—her diet was right on schedule cutting excess fat and bringing her muscles out in bold definition. Once she cut her liquid intake the last week and a half, her skin would be paper thin for the day of the competition. Although the last few weeks before a contest were always the worst in terms of the strict diet, she enjoyed wearing clothes that showed off her physique to the fullest. For today she had chosen her light pink tank and navy blue shorts that rode mi-thigh. "Thanks for noticing Joe."

"You're welcome, but it wasn't only me...everyone in here stopped to look when you walked in—including the women. I'm sitting with a celebrity!"

"Thanks, but I'm not there yet. Maybe if I win the Miss Illinois I'll be on that path, but right now I'm just a simple street cop by night and student by day."

They drank from their cups and sat in momentary silence until Joe spoke. "So...tell me why you wanted to meet for coffee. Did Pete put you up to it?"

"Nobody put me up to anything Joe. I think that you're a great guy and I just wanted to get to know you better. I don't often get to meet single guys, especially as busy as I am. Most of the ones that I do meet aren't exactly looking for the same kind of companionship that I am, if you know what I mean."

"I can just imagine," he said. "But as great as you look, you must have guys after you all the time."

"Not at all; I haven't had many relationships, and the last one ended in disaster."

"Couldn't make a commitment?" Joe asked.

Marilyn paused for a moment, and then decided that if she expected him to be honest with her she would have to be honest as well. "Not exactly...he raped me."

"Oh no; Marilyn I'm sorry. I didn't mean to bring up anything like that, forgive me for even asking."

"It's alright Joe, I'm working through it. Frankly as bad as it was there's been a lot of good come from it. I re-discovered my faith and I met a woman that has been very inspirational to me. It's like that silver lining in the proverbial dark cloud."

"I'm glad to hear that it hasn't changed you except for the better. You're obviously as strong on the inside as you are on the outside." He paused for a few seconds before saying, "I wish that I could say the same."

Marilyn looked at him..."You don't look like a weak person to me Joe. But you may look like a person that could benefit from a friend that cares about you and wants to help heal your heart."

He had that look again she thought—that beaten down, depressed body language that she saw at Pete's. "Joe, can you bring yourself to just talk to me and tell me what you're feeling? I'd like to help you get past the pain that you're obviously still experiencing. I know that pain; I've been there too many times. But I know that it's also possible to get beyond it—if you want to."

Joe looked up, "How Marilyn...how do I forget about her?"

"You don't Joe; you will never forget her. What you have to do is let go of any guilt that you feel."

He sat back in his chair and began to share. "It was so quick...one day she was there, and then in an instant she was gone. No chance to say goodbye; no chance to tell her that I was sorry."

"Sorry about what Joe?"

"Sorry for causing her to put her dreams on hold for me. She had wanted to get her advanced degree in nursing to further her career. I told her that we couldn't afford it yet—I wanted us to buy a bigger house. Even though I had two Masters Degrees, I selfishly convinced her that she didn't need hers. I never realized how little attention I paid to what she really wanted until she was gone. And the killer is...she never complained."

"She sounds like a beautiful woman Joe, but it's not like you mistreated her. Maybe you should have been more receptive to her, but your marriage was solid wasn't it?"

"Yes, we were married for twelve years, all of them good years—lots of joy and happiness."

"Then there's the answer Joe. You had a great marriage, one that you both obviously embraced and loved. No relationship is perfect. It requires that both people work hard on it each day. What you have to remember is all of those happy times—the love, the laughter, the sharing. To constantly think of the one negative obfuscates all of the joy that you both derived from what sounds like a fantastic marriage. Joe, you have to get beyond it before it becomes so big that it destroys you."

"We did have a great marriage," he said. "We loved each other so much, and I think that's why it's been so difficult. We knew what the other person was about to do or say before they even did it. It was easy, so simple and comfortable to live with her. I looked forward to being with her each day, couldn't wait for the day to end so that we could just lie next to each other and fall asleep. Why did it have to end...?"

Marilyn was close to tears now. "I don't know Joe. Why does God allow things to happen in our lives, good and bad? If I had that answer I guess that I wouldn't be a cop, I'd be a spiritual leader or something. But I do know this...God has plans for all of us, and just like it says in Jeremiah, they are plans not to harm you but to prosper you, to give you hope and a future. You have to work on your future Joe, not your past."

A tear rolled down Joe's face. He sat wringing his hands as if he were trying to squeeze the guilt out from them. "I know that you're right Marilyn. I can honestly say that our marriage was a good one, a blessed one; we had so many gifts from above. My biggest problem is that I've been mad at Him, not wanting to accept that it's His will and not mine. I've been selfish."

"Think about Pat for a moment Joe. Do you think that she would want you to be moping around for two years, being mad at the Father, especially now that she is with Him?"

"Wow, when you put it that way... No, how could I be mad? And believe me; she's with Him for sure. She was such a spiritual person, always praying and reading her Bible. I wish that I could have been more of a prayerful person."

"Who's to say that you can't? No time like the present. Will you join me in a prayer?"

Joe moved to the chair next to Marilyn and they joined hands. Marilyn began...Father we thank you for this day and all of the blessings that you bring us. We thank you for this fellowship today, for allowing us to carry each other's burdens and share our concerns.   We pray that you will hear the prayers of your servants and show us the way to healing and comfort. We love you Father and know that you are a loving God. Light our paths as we wander through this life; show us the way. We know that there is no greater love than yours, and we wait patiently until that day when we can see your loving face. In Jesus' name we pray...Amen."

"Amen," said Joe. "Marilyn, do you think that I could take you to dinner? I mean... I don't want to be presumptuous here..."

"Presumptuous? I asked you out, remember? Joe I'd love to go out with you to dinner, if you don't mind me being a little picky about my food."

"Great," he replied. "You can be as picky as you want as long as we can talk some more. I actually feel good for the first time in a long time because of you. Can we exchange phone numbers; I'd like to be able to call you if I may?"

"Of course," she said as she wrote down her number and email on a sheet of paper. "The best time to call me is probably early morning after I get off shift. I usually try to get my workout in around then before I collapse for the day."

Joe handed his information over to her. "Okay I'll remember that. Here's my info; you can call me anytime."

They stayed a while longer, exchanging small talk and just enjoying each other's company. Marilyn was the first to get up and signal that she had to leave. "I hate to say goodbye Joe, but you know how it is when you work mids. I've got some things to do and I need another nap before I go in tonight. Give me a call when you want to go out, okay?"

"I will." As they left the coffee shop together and walked to her car, he said, "You know Marilyn, my wife was always very comfortable praying in public, whereas I was kind of shy about it. But praying with you today, I didn't feel ill at ease at all."

"That's good to hear," she said. "To tell you the truth, it's only been recently that I've prayed with other people. My friend Leslie taught me that prayer is the best medicine for the soul, and that you should never be ashamed to be seen praying, or to pray with and for others. I've found it to be very comforting."

"I agree. I need to change a lot of things about myself, that's one of them."

Marilyn opened her car door and gave him a hug before she got inside. "Goodbye Joe; I look forward to seeing you again."

"Thanks; I'll call you to set something up. Bye."

On the drive home Joe was still conflicted inside. He felt happy about having met with Marilyn, what a wonderful person she is he thought. But he still felt a twinge of guilt about allowing himself to be in the company of another woman. He remembered what Marilyn had said about Pat wanting him to be happy, and that she was with the Father as well. It made sense, and if he put himself in her place, if it was his death that had happened, he would surely want Pat to be happy here on earth. I need to move on, he said to himself. Maybe this is the time. Maybe Marilyn is the person to heal me. I need to give it a chance, for my sake and hers.

63
Domestic Problems

"Pete, the Captain wants to see you in his office," said Mac.

"What's up?" I asked.

"I don't know, he just told me to send you in when you reported for your shift tonight. I don't have a clue."

"Probably wants to give me a raise," I joked.

"I doubt it," Mac replied, "but see me when you're done in there...I'm curious."

"Will do." I knocked out the door and heard Steele's voice from inside, "Enter!"

I walked in and stood in front of the Watch Commander's desk. It's never a good idea to assume that your boss wants you to sit and relax. This is his domain, his platform for power and control. "Evnin' Capt...you wanted to see me?"

"Hi Shannon, yes I did. C'mon in and shut the door behind you."

I did as instructed.

"Have a seat. The reason that I wanted to talk with you is so that I can pass on some information that came from the States Attorney's office today. They spoke with the District Commander this afternoon, who then passed on the information to me so that you could be informed before you read it in the morning papers."

"Is it about The Hammer"" I asked.

"Yeah, apparently he pled out today rather than go to trial. I guess he thought his chances were better that way. He copped a plea to a reduced charge of attempted manslaughter, and the State agreed to drop the gun and drug counts against him. The judge gave him eighteen years in the joint. You okay with that Shannon?"

I thought about it for a moment. Rosato had tried to kill me and had taken time to plan it, to include buying a gun that he thought wouldn't be able to be traced. That alone made it attempted murder. But on the other hand, eighteen years is a long time. For a guy like Sal, being cooped up with people that he despised, and maybe even put a few of them in jail himself, the sentence was fair. "I'm good with it Captain."

"I'm glad to hear that," he said. "You know I've never discussed it with you, but I admire the way that you do your job. I've never heard a bad word about you from any of your colleagues or the public. I still can't understand what Rosato had against you, but I'm glad that he's gone and that you're not. You're a good man Shannon; an inspiration to a lot of your fellow officers. Keep up the good work!"

"Thank you sir."

"That's all I've got, hit the street Shannon."

"Yes sir."

I walked out of his office feeling pretty good about what was said in there. Steele threw around compliments like manhole covers—which meant rarely, if ever. To have him praise me was special. How could I feel bad now, especially when the good news involved justice being served? I was energized now—better let Mac know. I walked over to the Desk, "Hey Mac."

"How did it go in there Pete, any problems?"

"No. He was relating the news to me from the court today about Rosato."

"What happened, did they set a trial date?" Mac asked.

"No, he pled out to attempted manslaughter...judge gave him eighteen years."

"Man, that's going to kill him, he'll be a target in there for sure."

"I know—it's going to be rough on him. Strange thing though...I just feel compelled to pray for him; he's still a fellow human being. He just let Satan take over."

Mac got up to place a file on the review man's desk. "Pete you're a good man. And you're right; we do need to pray for him. One other thing while I've got you in here. Sgt. Castro on days told me that he got wind that DEA apparently made their case on that character that raped Marilyn. They may take him down very shortly."

"Should I tell her?" I asked.

"No, if she knows she may change her behavior in the event that he contacts her. We'll let her know when it's about to go down."

"Okay Mac."

"Better hit the street now Pete, your partner wandered in here a few minutes ago looking for you."

I walked out to the lot to our unmarked car. Marilyn was patiently waiting—reading the Bible. I opened the car door and sat down. She looked over at me and said, "Everything okay, seems like you were with the boss for a good while."

"It's all good, Captain said Rosato copped a plea today and got eighteen years. He just wanted me to know before I read it in the papers in the morning."

"Whew...I'm relieved. For some reason I was thinking that they wanted to split us up or something."

I laughed... "You're not getting rid of me that easy lady, you're stuck with me for a long time."

"Great!" she said. "I'm glad that there's not going to be a trial Pete. I just want that part of our history to fade away."

"Me too...I think this gives me some closure with him admitting his guilt."

"It was a double header." she said. "Didn't his girlfriend plead guilty on the DUI case?"

"Yep—The Hammer and his girlfriend are old news."

"Amen," Marilyn offered.

"Did you check everything…are we ready to roll?" I asked.

"Yep, let's hit it."

I put it in gear and rolled out onto 63rd Street. "Hey, I've never seen you reading the Bible before… Something new?"

Marilyn leaned over the back seat and tucked the book into her gear bag. "Yes, it is something new. The past few weeks I've felt such a strong urge to read the Bible… I'm ashamed to admit that other than the gospels of Matthew, Mark, Luke, and John, I haven't read it."

"Don't feel bad," I said, "lots of folks haven't even read the gospels."

"I know. But I'll tell you something Pete…I'm excited about reading everything about our faith. I've made a promise to myself to read it from cover to cover. In fact, that's why I've started to carry it around with me—any down time that I have is going to be spent reading."

I turned south on Pulaski while we continued to discuss the Bible. "Just so you know Marilyn… that cover to cover reading will only make you hungry for more. I've been there."

"That's fine with me," she said, "the more the better."

"Pete, check that out," said Marilyn as we approached 71st and Pulaski.

"What is it?'

She pointed over in the direction of the K-Mart parking lot. "It looks like we've got some kind of disturbance…a guy and a gal in some kind of argument."

I turned into the lot and hit them briefly with the spotlight just to give them a clue as to who we were. I parked our unit so that our headlights illuminated them as they stood next to an old beater. We got out of our car and approached them.

"Police Officers!" said Marilyn. "What seems to be the problem here?"

They were two people in their late 50's or early 60's. He was scraggily looking; thin with a beard and wearing a White Sox hat. She was plump and wearing a housecoat and slippers; she was probably six inches shorter than he was.

The woman spoke first. "Officers it's okay. I'm just trying to get my husband home before he gets in trouble."

"Whose car is that?" I asked.

"That ours sir," said the woman. "I've been driving around looking for him. He needs to come home with me before he spends all of his paycheck."

Marilyn turned to the man who had obviously been drinking. "Sir have you been drinking tonight?"

"Yeah, can't a man have a drink without everybody gettin' on his case about it?"

The wife spoke up, "Officer he does this all the time. He gets drunk on pay day and if I don't get him home in time he's spent almost all of it. I don't have enough money to pay the rent and buy groceries. I've got two grandkids livin' with me that my daughter left me with sose she could run off with some man. I can't have him spendin' all of that check on booze."

"Is she right sir?" asked Marilyn, "are you spending all of your money on booze?"

He looked like he was getting angry now. "It's my damn money and I'll spend it any way I want."

"It ain't his money Officers, it's all of ours. I can't work; I have to watch the kids every day."

I felt sorry for the woman; she was beholden to her husband for her welfare and that of the grandkids. "What would you like us to do ma'am?" I asked.

"Not much you can do sir, I realize that. Can you just make him go home with me?"

Marilyn went up to the guy and said, "Let me see some identification sir!"

"What for?" he asked.

"I'm telling you that I want to see some identification—now!"

Marilyn got right up in the guy's face. It was a risky tactic, standing directly in front of someone, but most times it causes them to recognize that you're in control and won't tolerate any nonsense.

"Okay, okay," he said. He reached into his pocket and pulled out his wallet. "I don't have no license anymore, you guys took it when I was driving drunk one night." He fumbled through it until he came up with a work ID and handed it over to Marilyn.

"Is that all you have for identification sir?"

"Pretty much..."

Marilyn took the wallet from him and did a cursory look through the contents and then handed it to the man's wife. She wrote down the man's name and address, and then took him by the arm over by our vehicle.

"Listen to me good...these are your choices. You can either go home peacefully with your wife right now, or I will lock you up for drunk and disorderly."

The man began to protest. "Hey...what...who am I bein' disorderly to?

"Quiet!" Marilyn commanded. "I'm not about to debate you on this—what's it going to be? Do you want to go home with your wife, or go to jail?"

"Man, that ain't much of a choice... I'll go home."

"Good," said Marilyn, "but let me tell you something. If your wife calls the police and tells us that you went back out here tonight, I'll be over to lock you up so fast that your head will spin. Do you understand me?"

He was beginning to get the message and lost some of his bravado.

"Yeah, hey I don't mean to hurt nobody. I just need to get a drink at the end of the week. I'm a hard worker Officer."

"I bet you are, but it's time to go home now. Go on and get in the car. Remember, no trouble."

The man walked over to the old car and got in the passenger side. I followed him and closed the door after him, glancing in the backseat as I did. I spotted two little blond haired kids asleep on the seat. They couldn't have been more than five years old. The wife got in behind the wheel.

"Thank you officers; God bless you both."

They pulled out of the lot headed toward home. "Nice job on that partner," I said to Marilyn.

"Thanks Pete. How sad of an existence is that? And those two little kids... I need to pray for that woman, her life must be unbearable at times."

"I agree; she's a saint to have to put up with him and a daughter on drugs who abandoned two innocent little babies."

We got back in our car and resumed patrol, neither one of us saying too much. Incidents like we just encountered have a tendency to snap you back in, to put lots of things in perspective—especially how blessed you are. The Teacher just took Marilyn and I to school...thank you Lord.

<u>64</u>
Gary's Last Stand

I was on my way home southbound on Pulaski, just crossing over the railroad yards at 71st Street when my cell phone rang. "Hello, this is Pete."

"Pete, Sanela Latarski here."

"Oh hi Sanela, how are you today?"

"Not good," she said. "Do you know where Marilyn is at right now?"

"She's probably on her way home, or on the way to the gym...we just got off shift a bit ago. Why, what's up?"

"Trouble...we need to find her—ASAP. DEA lost their tail on Walker last night, she could be in danger. We've decided to take him down as soon as we locate him; in the meantime we need to ensure that Marilyn is safe."

"Did you try her apartment?"

"Yes...she's not there, but we've got a unit standing by in case she shows."

"What about the gym?" I asked.

"That's Bally's, right?"

"10-4, she's been working out early mornings since the incident."

"Well she hasn't shown yet," Sanela replied.

"What about her workout partner?"

"I don't know anything about that," she said. "Can you call her?"

"No, I don't know her number. But I may know where she lives. Listen, I'm in my car now, I'll head over to where I'm pretty sure she lives and see if I can find her."

"Good. Call me back as soon as you find anything."

"Okay Sanela—keep me in the loop on this."

I didn't know much about Marilyn's workout partner, Kim. I first met her at our barbeque, but in driving Marilyn home once she pointed out an apartment building where she said that Kim lived. It was fairly close to her own apartment, and I was confident that if I saw the building again that I would recognize it. I headed in that direction and said a silent prayer that my partner would be okay.

Marilyn checked her cell phone for messages on her way to the gym. She saw that Kim had left a text message for her. *I hope that she's not bailing out of our workout this morning*, she thought. Only two weeks to go before the contest; I can't waste any time now, I need to stay focused.

Mar can u pik me up, car trub...the message read. She hit the reply key: *on the way.* Good, we're still on. She was right around the corner. She pulled in and hopped out, leaving all of her gear locked in her car. She bounded up the steps to the second floor and knocked on Kim's door. Down at the other end of the hall was a woman with a child, obviously headed down to the bus stop. The little girl had a book bag and the mom carried her cup of coffee, drinking it as they went.

All of a sudden the door flew open... Gary stood there angry as a bull that has just seen a red cape. He looked as if the top of his head was about to blow off—his eyes were bloodshot, his normally coiffed hair all askew. Before she knew what was happening, he reached out and grabbed her by the arm pulling her inside. He threw a punch at her, striking her on the side of the head near her temple. She went down hard, falling backwards onto the couch. She was seeing stars and felt woozy; she felt something odd underneath her... Kim! She sat up and saw that her friend was bound and gagged. She had a terrified look in her eyes, which were bruised and swollen. A sock had been stuffed in her mouth to muffle any sounds that she tried to make.

Marilyn turned around to see Gary standing there with a gun pointed at her. "You fuckin' bitch, you dimed me out...said that I raped you? You ruined my life you whore!"

This was bad she thought, he's desperate—irrational. I don't know that I can even reason with him but I have to try. Maybe I can get close enough to get the gun... Wish I had mine with me now; it's not doing me any good in the car. "Gary, what are you doing? Let's talk about this...you're getting way in over your head here. What do you want?

"What do I want? I wanted you, but you were too fuckin' good for me weren't you, with your holier than thou attitude. Too good to give it up after all the time and dough that I spent on you—like you're somethin' special? Well let me tell you somethin', you weren't all that good anyway."

Marilyn's cell began to ring.

"Who is that...who would be callin' you?"

She looked at the caller ID...it was Pete. "It's my partner; I'd better answer or he'll be looking for me."

"Go ahead, but remember I've got a gun on both of you."

She opened the phone—"Hi Pete."

"Marilyn, where are you? Sanela called me and said they're taking down Walker today; they had a tail on him but he slipped them last night."

"Oh. Well that's good to hear Pete. Is Beth feeling any better, because it could just be morning sickness?"

"Marilyn....what are you talking about? I said Walker is loose and you may be in danger."

"Okay, I'll see you tonight. Just tell her to say a prayer to St. Michael the Archangel. He'll make sure everything works out. See you later."

I heard her hang up. What just went on—it made no sense...? Why was she talking about Beth and St. Michael? Wait a minute...St. Michael...a prayer to St. Michael? *She's in trouble—he's there with her!* I pulled around the corner and spotted Marilyn's car in the lot. I looked at the building—this was it, the one that she had pointed out.

She said that Kim lived on the second floor, but which apartment?

I called Sanela back and gave my location. It didn't look good; Marilyn wouldn't have acted weird on the phone like that unless she was trying to send me a message. She needed me....now! I got out and went over to the staircase that led to the second floor. I saw a woman walking with a cup of coffee. "Excuse me ma'am." I showed her my ID..."Do you know a woman named Kim, she's a Chicago Firefighter and lives on the second floor?"

"Oh sure, I know her. Her apartment is the first one on the right at the top of the stairs. Is something going on?"

"I'm not sure ma'am...why?

"Well about ten minutes ago a woman was at her door, a good looking woman by the way, very fit if you know what I mean, and it kind of looked like she got yanked into the apartment."

"Thanks. I need you to stay clear right now. But listen...there are going to be some other police officers showing up any minute. A person's life may be in danger. Can you please let them know where I'm at?"

I bolted up the stairs, stopping to listen at the apartment the woman had described. Thankfully the doors in this building were cheap builders grade lumber—thin and easily compromised. My heart was pounding in my ears, but I took a deep cleansing breath and put my ear to the door....

"What did he want?

"Nothing," said Marilyn. "His wife is pregnant and she hasn't been feeling well. He was just telling me that she had morning sickness again—nothing to worry about."

"Good...you did good."

"Listen Gary, Kim looks like she's hurting. You knocked her around pretty good. I promise that she won't make any noise, but we have to get that sock out of her mouth, she's having trouble breathing."

"Screw her; she don't know how to listen—just like you."

"Gary I'm telling you, I'm taking that gag out of her mouth whether you like it or not—she's going to suffocate if I don't."

"You wanna get shot?"

Marilyn realized that she was taking a big chance here, but she had to help her friend. "You do what you think you have to do Gary, but I'm not going to sit by while she's suffering."

Marilyn thought to herself that this was an important juncture, a tenuous moment, if he allowed her to remove the sock she may be able to negotiate with him. She turned around and removed the sock...

"Aaaah... Kim let out a sigh of relief and took several deep breaths. "Thank you Marilyn; I was about to black out again. I'm sorry honey; he overpowered me before I knew what was going on."

"Yeah," said Gary, "she's a fighter. You got a tough workout partner there. For a minute I didn't know if I was going to be able to knock her out."

I was able to hear the conversation almost verbatim. Things were worse than I thought...he's got a gun and he's already beaten Kim. This guy is a loose cannon, I didn't know how much longer I could wait for backup to get here. I looked down where I had left the neighbor standing and signaled for her to come up. "I need your help; do you have anything that looks like a toolbox in your apartment?"

"Sure, my husband's got all kinds of stuff."

"I need to borrow it, quick—let's get it."

I went down the hall with her and grabbed a toolbox and hurried back to Kim's apartment. *I hope this works,* I thought as I knocked on the door... ***"Maintenance!"***

"What the... Gary looked at Kim, "What's that about?"

Without hesitation Kim answered, "The building's getting all new sprinklers; I'm next on the list."

"Send him away," Gary said.

"How am I going to do that I can't even get up off the couch?"

Gary went over and looked through the peep hole in the door. "Go away, we don't need you."

I had to think fast. "I've got to get this work done or I lose my job!"

"What's with this guy?"

I tried a different approach, just wanting to get that door opened. "If you don't want it done, just sign my form and I'll be on my way." I banged on the door again... "C'mon, I've got a lot of work to do today; you've already put this off twice."

"You stay put," Gary told Kim, "and keep your mouth shut! " He looked over at Marilyn, "You just open the door and sign whatever he's got and send him on his way. You try anything and you're dead."

Gary positioned himself behind the door when Marilyn opened it. He signaled with his gun for her to open it. Marilyn grabbed the door handle and opened the door.

"Oh, I thought that you were the woman that lives here," I said. "Is she around?"

Marilyn looked right at me as she answered, her eyes darting to her right, indicating behind the door—or at least I was praying that that was what she meant.

"She's out; I'm watching the apartment for her. Can I sign your sheet?"

"I guess so" I said. Again, Marilyn kept signaling toward the door with her eyes. It was now or never I thought. If I was going to make my move it had to be fast and violent, and it had to be now.

St. Michael the Warrior, be my shield...

I grabbed onto the doorknob and drove my shoulder into the door, following it around to the wall where Walker was standing. The force of my charge crushed him against the wall, causing him to discharge his weapon into the ceiling. In all of the confusion, and the accompanying noise from the gun being fired, Walker was quickly disoriented. That was my chance to seize the momentum. I flung the door shut and grabbed his gun hand at the same time in an attempt to disarm him. He was strong; his arm was like an anatomy chart with gnarled veins protruding from them, taut as a steel cable.

We struggled away from the wall, and I locked my hand on his revolver so that the cylinder would be unable to turn—the hammer continuing to rest on an empty chamber. Marilyn had been knocked to the ground from the force of my entry. She quickly got up and positioned herself behind Walker. As I struggled to control the gun, Marilyn hit him with a couple of hammer strikes to the side of his head, but they were seemingly ineffective. She finally positioned herself behind him and applied a carotid choke hold.

"Hang on Bens...hang on!" I shouted. "I was beginning to tire; I didn't know how much longer I could control this beast. Marilyn was hanging on to her choke hold like a woman possessed. We struggled around the room, Walker carrying us both like we were a couple of little kids being swung around by their father. A few seconds later, I felt him weakening and fighting for air. Marilyn's carotid control was working—he was fighting it but the lack of oxygen to his brain was too much. He went limp and was unconscious before he hit the floor.

"Bens, grab the gun!" I quickly took out a pair of cuffs and rolled this tree trunk of a man onto his stomach. "Give me a hand Bens!" It took two of us to bring his arms together to get the cuffs on. Once we had him secured we both collapsed on top of him.

"Thank you Lord, thank you Jesus!" I shouted.

"Amen!" shouted Marilyn.

"Oh my God Pete, I thought he was going to kill us both!"

I looked over at the couch where Kim was lying, still tied up. I got up to go over and undo her restraints when DEA burst into the room...

"Police! Everybody get down!"

We threw up our hands in compliance, not wanting to give them any reason to shoot. In situations like this where law enforcement officers' lives are on the line, emotions and testosterone kick into overdrive—anything can happen.

"We're cops!" I shouted. "Officers Shannon and Besnon—8th District!"

The agents eased up..."Everybody okay here?"

"Yeah, we're fine. That beautiful woman on the couch needs medical attention. She's a Chicago Firefighter, and she's a hero. Treat her as such."

We got Kim untied and had her sit up on the couch. Marilyn sat next to her and they hugged, rocking back and forth. "Kim, I'm so sorry. I never thought Gary could be like this, what happened?"

"It's a long story," Marilyn said. "He raped me several weeks ago, and I guess he's involved in drugs as well."

"Why didn't you say anything?"

"I couldn't Kim; he was under a sealed indictment. Only a handful of people knew what happened."

"Wow, you are one strong woman. You've been acting like nothing ever happened. I never would have suspected..."

"Believe me, it wasn't easy. I don't think that I could have made it without praying about it and asking Him to give me comfort."

The DEA scooped Walker up off the floor. He looked like he was in a daze, like he never knew what hit him. They marched him out of the apartment and down to the waiting Paddy Wagon. By this time half the District was showing up—all of the supervisors and the District Commander, as well as the news folks. They gave first aid to Kim, but were transporting her to the hospital for follow up. She really took a beating.

"Pete, I'm going to ride with her in the ambulance. She's gone through an awful lot—all because of me."

"Don't start that Bens, none if this is your fault. And besides, the good guys won didn't they?"

"Yeah, I guess you're right."

"And by the way, that was ingenious."

"What?"

"Inventing that story about Beth when I called and then talking about St. Michael... That's how I made the connection that Walker must have been there with you."

"That's all that I could come up with," she said. "He was standing right there, so I had to watch what I said."

"Well it was definitely the right thing. And incidentally, I'm positive that Michael went through that door with me."

"He must have," she said, "I went flying..."

"Like you had wings?" I added.

"Something like that."

"Hey, where did you learn to apply that carotid control hold so well? Man, you put him out in a heartbeat."

My defensive tactics instructor at the Academy was John Lanata. He made sure that we all knew how to apply it—said it might save our lives one day."

"Thank you Mr. Lanata," I said. "You must have been a star pupil."

"I learned all that I could; I didn't want to waste a minute."

"Shannon...Benson...are you two alright?" The District Commander was assuming control of the crime scene.

"Yes sir, we're fine. A little tired and beat up but we're fine."

"Good. I've got the Major Case Squad enroute to handle the scene. I'll see you two at the station later on. Benson, you get yourself over to the hospital and get that face checked out."

"Yes sir."

"Shannon, why is it that you always seem to wind up in the middle of every 'shit sandwich' that pops up around here?

"I don't know sir; I guess that I'm just blessed."

"Whatever," he said. "Nice job...both of you. I'm proud to have you both in my command."

We walked down the stairs to the waiting ambulance where Kim was being strapped down for the ride to the ER. Marilyn climbed inside.

"Pete...Marilyn?" said Kim. "Do you think that we could say a prayer of Thanksgiving together?"

"Of course, that's a great idea. Marilyn, do you care to lead us?"

We bowed our heads and Marilyn began... "Dear Father God, we honor you and praise your name. We give you thanks for blessing us today with the tools and strength to defeat The Evil One. Thank you for guidance, for comfort, and for love. We are humbled by it, and thank you for dispatching St. Michael to be our partner in battle, without him we would have surely failed. Strengthen and protect us always as we continue to put You first in all that we do. In Jesus' name we pray...Amen."

<u>65</u>
Being Grateful

The arrest was all over the noon and five o'clock news. Kim's injuries weren't severe enough to warrant an overnight stay, but they kept her anyway since she had suffered a slight concussion. Marilyn was treated and released, and after a very brief statement to investigators from all of us about what had happened, our Commander put us on admin leave for a week. Marilyn and I left the station together in my truck so that I could bring her back to where her car was parked at Kim's apartment complex.

"Pete thanks for rescuing me today. I really thought I was going to be killed, especially after I saw what he had done to Kim."

"You would have done the same thing Bens, if the roles were reversed. I'm just glad that Sanela called me and got me involved."

"You know...since I began working with you I've done more 'real' police work than I've ever done since I've been on the job." Marilyn shifted in her seat to look at me. "Pete, I think that He put me with you as a partner for a reason."

"Why do say that Marilyn?"

"Because I was adrift...I had lost my direction. The job was still important, but the significance of being a cop was being overshadowed by my bad choices in men and my risky behavior. I hadn't even been paying any attention to my spiritual life—hadn't gone to mass in years or prayed at all. It was all about me."

We were only a few minutes from the apartments now.

"I guess what I'm trying to say is, thanks not only for what you did today to save my life physically, but what you've done to save my soul."

I pulled into the space next to her car. "Wow Marilyn, that's some pretty powerful stuff. I don't know that I can take credit for all of that, but I will tell you this... You came into my life at exactly the right time. When Joe was killed I wasn't sure if I even wanted to be a cop anymore. And I hate to admit it, but I was disappointed in God...I felt like He had let me down. Imagine—I'm worried about myself, not Susan and the boys who had just lost the most important person in their lives. I was feeling sorry for myself."

"Pete..."

"Then Mac told me that you would be my new partner and I prayed about it—asked Him to let me know if I should continue down the same road. Should I remain a cop, or move on to something else?"

"And what happened?" She asked.

"You—you happened, you came along with your honesty, your morals and ethics, your love of God. That was my answer—He wanted us to work together...for good."

"I can't argue with that. I have never felt better about myself, nor felt so spiritually fulfilled as I have since we've been partners." She opened her car door to get out. "Not only that, but I've got two new partners rather than just one."

"Huh?"

"St. Michael Pete!"

"Oh yeah...you're right. I'll call you later; enjoy your time off partner."

"I will. You know how it says in the Bible that all things work together for good for those that believe? This mini-vacation will allow me to do my last minute prep for the Miss Illinois contest. God is good!

"Amen, see you later."

I was home in about ten minutes and was surprised to find Beth waiting for me. "Honey, is everything okay?"

She ran up and wrapped her arms around me, holding me like a child holds onto their security blanket when someone tries to take it away. "I know you called and said you were fine, but I couldn't concentrate at work so I came home early. Pete, I was just so worried...I needed...we needed to see your face and hold you," she said as she put one hand on her stomach. "Maybe it's the hormones, I don't know but I've never been this worried about you and your job before."

Her eyes filled with water as I held her and she turned her face up towards mine. I could almost feel her concern and the need to be reassured that I wouldn't leave her and the baby. "Beth...babe, listen. I'll be fine; we'll be fine. He is watching over us and He's given St. Michael the chore of watching my back. Nothing's going to happen."

"I just keep thinking about Susan and the boys losing Joe... I don't want that to happen to us."

"That's not up to us now is it? God has a plan for us; it's His will not ours."

"I know...I know. Pete I love you so much, and now that we're going to have a little baby, it's not just about us anymore—it's about our child."

"We'll be fine, and you'll be the best mommy in the world."

"Keep telling me that babe, because I have so many doubts about things."

"I'm here for you—always—and so is He."

<u>66</u>
Joe Finally Lets Go

Marilyn got home, put her gear in the front closet, and then collapsed on the couch. *What a day*, she thought! It was all just now sinking in...*I could be dead!* Gary was not unlike some of the psychos that she had studied in behavioral psychology classes. How could she have been so blind to who he really was? But one other thing became glaringly obvious to her...if she had died, if the Father had called her home, she was ready. That revelation, the fact that although she didn't want to die, but that if she did she wasn't afraid to, gave her more comfort than she could have ever imagined.

This past year had opened up a whole new chapter in her life; one in which she had finally found the real Marilyn—one that put God above all else. She had never really reflected on anything spiritual before, had never contemplated her blessings. Now it was all that she could think about. Her thirst for more of His love, to please Him in all that she did, to help others and to recognize that everyone was a child of God, had finally taken its rightful place in her life. Even the manner in which she prayed—not just Hail Marys and Our Fathers, but more prayers of gratitude—just talking with Him and thanking Him. Simple things like seeing a sunrise moved her to give thanks. She liked the new Marilyn much more than the woman that she had been before. She imagined that she had become the "Prodigal Daughter". She had squandered all her spiritual riches, and had finally returned home to find the loving, welcoming arms of a Father's love that has no end. It was good to be home.

She looked over on the coffee table—her Bible. She picked it up and read her favorite Psalm—Psalm 27:

The Lord is my light and my salvation—whom shall I fear? The Lord is the stronghold of my life—of whom shall I be afraid? When evil men advance against me to devour my flesh, when my enemies and my foes attack me, they will stumble and fall. Though an army besiege me, my heart will not fear; though war break out against me, even then will I will confident.

One thing I ask of the Lord, this is what I seek: that I may dwell in the house of the Lord all the days of my life, to gaze upon the beauty of the Lord and to seek him in his temple. For in the day of trouble he will keep me safe in his dwelling; he will hide me in the shelter of his tabernacle and set me high upon a rock. Then my head will be exalted above the enemies who surround me; at his tabernacle will I sacrifice with shouts of joy; I will sing and make music to the Lord.

Hear my voice when I call, O Lord; be merciful to me and answer me. My heart says of you, "Seek his face!" Your face, Lord, I will seek. Do not hide your face from me, do not turn your servant away in anger; you have been my helper. Do not reject me or forsake me, O God my Savior. Though my father and mother forsake me, the Lord will receive me. Teach me your way, O Lord; lead me in a straight path because of my oppressors. Do not turn me over to the desire of my foes, for false witnesses rise up against me, breathing out violence.

I am confident of this: I will see the goodness of the Lord in the land of the living. Wait for the Lord; be strong and take heart and wait for the Lord.

Finishing her reading and reflecting on her blessings, she got up to make some dinner for herself. She walked into the kitchen and saw the message light blinking on the phone on the counter. She hit the message button...*you have five new messages, first message:* "Marilyn, its Joe. I just saw the news about what happened today—are you okay? Please call." The next four messages were all from Joe as well. Her cell phone battery had been separated from her phone during the struggle causing the voicemails to be lost. *I guess that I should call Joe and let him know that I'm okay,* she thought.

She dialed his number; he answered on the first ring. "Marilyn, talk to me, are you alright? I saw the news and I've been worried about you all day."

"I'm fine Joe, mostly tired and a little sore but I'm okay. I'm sorry I didn't return your calls; I just got home."

"I was calling your cell too."

"I figured that you had. The battery became dislodged during the battle...sorry."

"No, it's okay, I understand. Listen...I don't know if I'm out of line saying this, but I figure that I've got nothing to lose if I do. I have been thinking about you a lot since we had coffee together you. I've wanted to call and set up a date, but I've been afraid."

"Of what?"

"About having my heart broken again...of caring about another person the way that I cared about my wife—I didn't want that pain again. But then when I heard about what happened today, it was like God was sending me a sign."

"What sign Joe; what do you mean?"

"A sign to let me know that it was okay for me to get on with my life...that Pat was with Him and she would want me to share myself with someone. I thought about you and began to pray that He would take care of you and heal you of any injuries you may have sustained. I asked Him to protect you and to please allow me to be a part of your life."

"Oh Joe...that makes me feel so good. And He answered your prayers by the way; they thought that I had a cracked cheek bone, but it turned out to be just a bad bruise."

"'Thank God for that. But that's another thing...since I met you last week I've had the urge...the **need** to pray. I've missed Him the past couple of years, but meeting you and seeing Pete and his family again has given me a wakeup call. I need Him in my life, every second of every day."

"Joe you are making inroads into my heart. I was just about to make myself some dinner, but if you haven't eaten already may I ask you to join me?"

Are you kidding? I've been chomping at the bit to see you all day...for that matter the moment that we left the coffee shop. Yes; what time?"

"Just give me an hour to clean up and get something started."

"No problem," he said. "I'll bring dessert."

"No way—I'm competing in a week. I'm still on my contest diet."

"Holy cow! You're still in the contest after what you went through today? You are an extraordinary woman Marilyn."

"I'm nothing special Joe, but I am a child of the most awesome God!"

"Yes you are...can't wait to see you."

"Me too. See you in a little while Joe...thanks for your prayers and concern."

"You're welcome Marilyn—bye."

She hung up the phone and reflected on the conversation. Joe was really concerned about her—about her!—her safety and well being, not just something physical. He wanted, no, he was anxious to see her...and truth be known, she was anxious to see him as well. In just one short week something had developed between them ... Things were coming together. Was it based in faith? Maybe, but for whatever reason they were heading down a path together and it felt good.

Marilyn got into the shower with a sense of comfort and satisfaction, knowing that her best days were still ahead of her. She was a victor...not a victim. God's promises were coming true in her life.

<u>67</u>
Miss Illinois

"Ladies and gentlemen...your new Miss Illinois—Marilyn Benson!" We stood and shouted, hugged each other, whistled, clapped our hands, and just went absolutely crazy. Marilyn stepped forward and accepted the trophy from last year's winner and proudly stood beside it. Photographers and admirers snapped photos from all angles, their flash units exploding like silent fireworks, lighting the stage like noon on a sunny day.

"Pete this is fantastic!" Beth said.

"It is, isn't it? But it's also so unbelievable to have her win after all she's gone through the past couple of months." I had to think that the Father had a hand in this. Marilyn needed to know that her new life was exactly what He wanted for her. This was the sign that she needed, that His way was **The Way**.

I saw Joe Murphy run up to the side of the stage and stand their waiting. After Marilyn had posed for what seemed like a million photos, she made her way over to him. She bent down and gave him a big hug and a kiss. Their new relationship seemed to be headed in the right direction. Joe was a changed man. I had not seen him happy like this since before he lost Pat. Whatever Marilyn had done to awaken him from his zombie-like trance was working.

Kim appeared from backstage where she had been with Marilyn, prepping her and giving her the motivation that she needed for the competition. "Marilyn, you did it, you finally did it!"

"I know...thank you Lord, thank you Jesus! I can't believe it Kim. That other gal was bigger, I was sure that she was going to win."

"I never had a doubt Marilyn. She lacked the one thing that no one else in the competition had but you."

"What's that?"

"Courage. After being raped and nearly killed by Gary, you didn't let it deter you from your goal. You are unbelievable girl..."

"Thanks Kim, but without all of your training and direction I would have fallen short. You're the best training partner ever."

The next half an hour saw dozens more photos and interviews from the local press and fitness magazines. Even ABC Channel 7 had a film crew there. They had a great success story to tell about a woman who overcame adversity to win not only a contest, but also her self-respect and confidence.

We all agreed to meet at Palermo's for a well deserved Italian dinner, complete with pizza. Marilyn rode with Joe to the restaurant, and on the way the floodgates opened for her. Through her tears she spoke to Joe. "These are tears of joy and relief Joe. I've been worried about so many things lately, and without prayer I don't think that I could have kept my sanity."

"What do you mean?"

"Trying to live up to Pete's expectations as a partner, trying to change my behavior from the poor choices that I used to make, going to school, preparing for the contest...Gary raping me and then the incident at Kim's place...I'm just mentally worn out."

Joe pulled over to the side of the road. "Marilyn you've been through a lot...more than anyone I know. But you've stood strong through it all. Why? Because you asked for His help. Remember in Matthew he tells us, '*If you believe, you will receive whatever you ask for in prayer.*' He heard you; He tested your faith—He loves you."

Still sobbing, she said, "Joe I asked Him for a lot of things, one of which was that He would heal your heart. I think that I got more than I asked for."

"Why?"

"Because not only does it look like He did that, but you're beginning to work your way into my heart as well. I want to keep seeing you Joe; I think that you are a special person and that you have so many things to offer to this world. I feel good around you, and although it's only been a few short weeks that we've known each other, I find myself wanting to spend more and more time with you."

"That's good to hear, because I've been praying about 'us' also. You have something that makes me want to be a part of your life. You have an inexplicable pull; I find myself being drawn to you and when I'm not around you, I can't wait until I am."

"I know. But promise me this Joe...we'll go slowly; we'll take our time and not do anything spur of the moment. I've made a commitment to God; I'm special in His eyes and I'm going to respect myself because He dwells within me."

"Agreed; I wouldn't have it any other way."

He gave her a kiss and pulled back onto the street, continuing on their way to the restaurant.

Pete and Beth were the first to arrive. They got a table large enough to accommodate everyone and sat down. "What a night it's been," said Beth.

"It's great isn't it," I said. "Things are going to be okay...for all of us."

"Pete..." She placed both of her hands on her stomach.

"What's the matter, are you okay?"

"Yes....." A big smile appeared on Beth's face. "I think that I just felt our baby move inside of me!"

I put my arm around her shoulders. "We are blessed Beth. I can't wait to see our little guy."

"How do you know that it's a boy?"

"I don't, I guess that I'm just dreaming that it will be a Pete junior."

"What if it's a little girl?"

I smiled and kissed her cheek, "Then I'll have the most beautiful daughter in the world."

Beth took a sip of water and thought out loud. "I never thought that I could be happy again after what we've been through the past couple of years babe. I felt like Satan had a hold of me and would never let go. Without your love and understanding, I don't know where I'd be right now."

"I can't imagine my life without you Beth. I never thought that I could love you any more than I have in the past, but since you've been carrying our child you've become radiant—there's a glow about you. You're the most beautiful woman in the world."

"Thank you babe; promise me one thing..."

"What's that?"

"You'll teach me the prayer to St. Michael. I need to know that he's going to continue to back you up. 'We' can't take any chances now."

"I promise. He's going to be a very busy guy working with his Midnight Warriors."

Epilogue

Pete and Beth eventually welcomed Pete, Jr. into the family. Both Pete and Marilyn finished their degrees and looked forward to ending their tour on midnights. But before they could act on their change of shift, the Chief of Patrol promoted them both to Detective rank and assigned them to the Violent Crimes Unit at Police Headquarters—as partners.

Joe Murphy and Marilyn became inseparable, a serious relationship emerging from what had previously been two people adrift without an anchor. Marilyn convinced Joe to return to the police department where he continues to rise in the ranks.

Matthew Roberts graduated from high school and was accepted at the St. Xavier University Business School. Andy Devine made him a full-time employee at the shirt shop with full benefits, and promised to adjust his schedule so that Matthew wouldn't miss any classes.

Susan O'Hara and the boys were flown to Washington, D.C. to attend a ceremony honoring her fallen husband Joe. His name was inscribed on the Law Enforcement Memorial, along with over 18,000 other officers slain in the line of duty.

Sal Rosato began serving his sentence in Joliet State Prison and was stabbed to death by another inmate just six months into his incarceration. His girlfriend Sally was re-arrested for DUI and was sentenced to one year in the Cook County Jail.

Sanela Latarski was promoted to the rank of Sergeant. Lt. Frank Borelli pulled some strings and had her immediately assigned to his unit.

Coming Soon
Chicago Warriors: Gripped In Fear

It had been a long day already for Maria, watching three of her neighbor's children as well as tending to her own five had worn her out. Now she was headed downtown to Chicago's Loop where she would spend the night vacuuming floors and emptying waste baskets in some of the tallest and most important buildings in the world. This had been her lot for the past two years; this is the plight of "illegals," as they were called. Unable to find traditional jobs, they worked at what they could to earn money to pay their rent and food bills. Her husband was a day laborer, getting up at dawn each day to stand en masse with others at the local convenience store in hopes that they would be given work by a landscaper or painter looking for extra help.

Walking from her apartment on Chicago's South Side to the bus stop on Pulaski Avenue at this time of night had always unnerved her, but she had gradually gotten used to it. So when she saw a man walking in her direction she didn't think much of it. She assumed that like her, he was probably a laborer and may have been returning home from a long day. As he drew near that all changed.

She sensed that she was in danger. "Hello..."

No answer from the stranger, but he passed. Relief washed over her. Then at that moment a vicious blow to the back of her head knocked her to the ground. Before she knew what was happening, she felt the stranger pick her up and carry her toward one of the houses. Still reeling from the attack, yet now becoming aware of even more danger, she tried to regain her senses.

It was dark...she saw the house was abandoned...now moving toward the back, to a garage.

"No!" She tried to yell but there was no strength in her voice, it came out as a whisper. The stranger dropped her onto the concrete floor.

Inside the garage she thought, have to get out!

9 781590 958414